BLOOD VENGEANCE

Book Three of the Blood Herring Trilogy

To my husband and our hobbit. You both give so much so I can pursue these stories, but I doubt you'll ever realize the inspiration you both give me everyday.
I love you dearly and I couldn't do this without you.

CHAPTER 1

GABE

It was strange. As a detective, my life had been absolute chaos, case after case. My one constant had been in fictional realms of writers like Koontz or Pratchett.

For the last month, my world had become still as stone and my focus was deteriorating. I'd been staring at the front of my book, the cover art growing fuzzy with my thoughts. An abrupt change in the protesters' typical, incessant chanting yanked me from that train of thought. It was an odd sort of relief, the outraged cry giving my mind something firm to grasp.

A comfortable dread settled in my gut and I tossed the novel on my nightstand, not worried when the bookmark fell out, and wandered from my childhood bedroom towards the living room. The worn carpet was rough on my bare feet. My parents' house had never been ornate. They'd made a simple home out of the single-level house, with a hodge-podge collage of family photos in mismatched frames adorning the hall.

The light was on in the kitchen, casting a pale orange glow across the large sectional and bookshelves that dominated the small living room. My roommate must be cooking. A pathetic part of me wanted to turn around; things were still awkward and I doubted anything had changed since I went to bed. I swallowed and marched down the hall, pausing to lean against the archway of the kitchen entrance. "What are you doing up?"

My companion's hair stood in every direction, like the long tendrils of an uprooted tree. The mass of tangles made her look even smaller than she was, her shoulders barely taller than the stove top she worked at.

"I want to see how paprika works this time." Olive said it as though she were adding spam to mac 'n' cheese instead of stirring a pot of steaming blood. "Using Ramen yesterday wasn't great, but at least it was different."

"You could always drink some cocoa." I pointed to one of the cupboards. Hopefully the tin I'd just offered wasn't expired.

She looked at me like something alien had sprouted from my skull. "No sustenance."

"No harm, either."

She just stared at me, those large hazel eyes blinking slowly.

I let out a breath and nodded towards the front windows. "Have you taken a look, yet?"

"It seemed disrespectful to go ahead of you." Olive turned the stove off, extinguishing the tiny flame before grabbing her pot with two over-sized oven mitts on her little hands.

"I could do that for you." I took a step forward but she waved me off, holding the pot steady with one hand.

"It's not heavy."

True, with her vampire strength, Olive's small frame could probably lift more than a perp on PCP. Hell, that was the main reason the court had decided she should stay with me during our shared trial. The judge hoped I might stop Olive if things went south. And yet, I felt useless letting the little girl handle that big pot on her own.

She poured the blood into a mug easily. Several spice jars sat at the ready and a spoon waited inside. She'd been at this for months; I guess we all handle cabin fever in our own way.

And it's not like we had lengthy conversations to fill our spare time.

Before stirring, Olive tapped a tiny amount of paprika and Kosher salt into the blood. The spoon made little tinks against the sides of the mug, like a dark fairy.

"Alright." Olive took a tentative sip and teetered her head in careful consideration. "Ready?"

"After you?" I stretched out an arm toward the front of the house.

The day had been moderate. Not as many flashing lights or inane questions shouted at the windows. We'd been hoping for a quiet night to match; cold evenings always seemed to subdue the crowd. There'd been some disgruntled mumbling, but now some voices stood out, their stress showing in a variety of tones.

"Okay everyone, you know the drill," Officer Stevens' voice was garbled through the megaphone. His tone was weary but intense. "You are trespassing. You all need to move off the lawn or I will be forced to arrest you."

"You can't suppress our right to free speech!" We'd heard this voice before, so I wasn't surprised when I peeked through two lattices of the shades. The woman had an obnoxious shade of neon hair, cut very short, and she always wore anti-vamp t-shirts and pants that revealed far more than they concealed. She'd been cuffed last week for smacking the patrol officers with her picket sign.

Her newest sign said *YOU RUINED OUR CITY* with a big, ugly cartoon vampire, *Xs* for eyes. My jaw clenched. The sign was obviously intended for all vampires, but the message seemed tailored for me. As though they knew.

The woman was facing down a good officer. Stevens had always taken the worst parts of this job with a dark joke and a lot of dignity. He and his wife had been expecting their first kid right before I was turned; she'd started getting wicked cravings for spicy foods and he'd only laughed.

Now, even his posture was run down.

"Ma'am—" Stevens' face had wilted over the last few months. The short beard he'd grown was greasy and his uniform was wrinkled. I tried to remember how far along his wife was. Was he dealing with this crumbling world and trying to figure out how to be a father at the same time? "we've been over this."

The woman pointed her nose into the air. "Yes, we have—"

"And—" He held up a hand. "I'm sure you'll remember how this ended the last few times."

He pulled out a pair of cuffs in his other hands, the moonlight bouncing off the unraveling chain. The woman pursed her lips, her body trembling as though her blood boiled beneath the thin surface of her skin. They stared at one another for a long moment, his body still and hers vibrating with agitation. Stevens jingled the cuffs for effect.

"Fine!" The woman stomped her foot and sauntered off, dragging her sign down the sidewalk with an ugly scraping sound.

Olive tsked. "It's kind of sad I'm more mature than that twat."

I dropped the lattice and scowled. "That's no way to talk."

She gave me a patient look over the top of her mug. Those hazel eyes didn't even quiver under my reprimand. "Is that what you would tell Lily?"

We stood in silence for another moment before I let out a sigh and peeked through the shades again.

Stevens had gone back to the perpetually stationed squad car. He talked to another officer in the passenger seat, a plump Spanish woman I recognized by sight but had never interacted with.

Harper probably knew her name; she was cute and he was a helpless flirt. Not that I could ask him. Even texting my old partner would put his job in further jeopardy.

And reveal the burner number to the police.

"Can you hear them?" I tried to focus on their speech, squinting as though that somehow helped. The audio came in patches like I was driving down the highway and kept losing the radio station.

"He says 'Some kids in Rockwood called in a vamp sighti ng.'" She tilted her head, her dark brows scrunching together. "She's asking if they're going and he says 'Nah, the kids are probably already gone.' She's..."

Olive paused and gave me a questioning look.

I sighed. "Just say it."

Olive nodded and continued, "'When will these fucking bureaucrats stop sending us to protect these freaking fang heads? I say, let the crowd take them, give them something for the front page and let's be done with these traitors.'"

My body turned cold, becoming rigid as ice. I knew that was a common thought among the force, but hearing it still cut something in me I couldn't name.

"The man says, 'The system is there for a reason.'" Olive nodded in approval. "Nice to know *someone's* on our side."

"Stevens isn't on our side." I let the blinds snap shut and shuffled back towards my room. "He's just doing his job."

CHAPTER 2

LILY

Our footprints stretched behind us, a long trail of tiny dark pools in the wet slush that passed for Oregon snow. The frost of early November bit the tip of my nose. Rubbing my hands together wasn't much use when my body was normally about room temp.

For the billionth time, I wished we could have driven. But the Swiss-cheese state of the roads and all the abandoned cars made it more than a little impractical.

Besides, then I would have been trapped in a tiny metal box with a very pissed-off vampire.

"And you know damn well the word Viking does not describe a person." Cyrus' indignation came out in quick plumes of steam.

I suppressed an eye roll. Sure, I knew that. I could even relate; it was impossible to count the number of times I'd considered chucking good whiskey at the TV while watching *Far and Away*. The only thing far or away in that flick had been Tom Cruise's debauched-leprechaun accent.

"*Half* the English language comes from Scandinavian roots but far be it from anyone to figure out the difference."

Cyrus' yapping was wearing my patience thinner than Kleenex. And the grim surroundings offered little in the way of distraction.

"Yeah, yeah." I searched my pockets for my smokes and Bic before shielding my light from the evening air. "And ya never pillaged, I'm sure."

"Most of us were farmers and fishermen."

A small spark crawled up the cigarette in red embers, the slow sizzle of relief creeping towards me as I drew in that first long breath. I held it in for a moment, my veins tightening in anticipation.

Booze was useless to vampires; our metabolism never let it near the brain. Luckily, the body's process for cigarettes was completely different. Everything tingled from my head to my toes, each nerve loosening one after the other. Smoke sat lazy on the breeze as I released the tension. In with the good, out with the bullshit...

"I didn't ask about your fellow villagers." The smoke curled around each word as I took another drag.

"That thing reeks." Cyrus fanned the cloud away, the plume dissipating under his big hand.

"Don't avoid the question." I made a point of ashing in his path. "We both know ya did your fair share as a *vikinger*."

Not to mention his later years as a pirate. Swashbuckling wasn't exactly missionary work.

He grimaced, setting his jaw so tight that the Norse dragons on his skull seemed to slither from under his dark Mohawk. "At least you used the right word."

I tweaked my eyebrows and plugged the cigarette between my lips, letting the smoke roll out through my nose like a sleepy dragon as we continued our macabre stroll.

The thin layer of snow only served to highlight all the shattered windows and busted doors. Battered cars, some missing their doors, were all over roads and yards in a variety of shapes and colors, like someone had smashed stained glass and left the pieces scattered every which way. The city had tried to consolidate the mess but the tow yards were full and parks were overflowing. So here they stayed. I nearly tripped over a moldy bag of clothes and Cyrus snapped at me to pay more attention. I bit back the snarky remark that came to mind.

If only they'd give me my bike back. I snorted at the very idea. It was a miracle I was allowed to go out, even with an escort. Not bloody likely the Court would tell me where they'd stashed my baby.

One house had siding riddled with bullet holes, the picket fence in ruins. The flower beds trampled and the plastic planters busted. One of those hideous flamingos stared at me through crushed and flattened eyes, old tire tracks splitting the hollow body. Many homes were a collage of different gang tags and unrefined images of dick. It was the world's ugliest art gallery.

People were pissed their homes were broken and ruined, so they destroyed someone else's. Misery always did love company.

"What are we even lookin' for? I get that Elias keeps comin' after these neighborhoods, but what does Ritti think we'll find?"

"We'll know when we see it." Cyrus kicked a deflated rubber ball out of his path. It flopped back into the street with a thick splat.

I scowled. "Bullshit."

Cyrus set his jaw again and I swore I could hear his teeth grinding.

Instantly, I regretted coming out. It would have been smart to question his motives earlier, but being locked up didn't exactly help me think clearly.

I moved to block his path. The wind grabbed my hair and I had to push the blonde ponytail out of my face before I spoke. "We both know she wouldn't have let me out on this field trip for some wild goose chase. How come I'm not locked up in my tower?"

"First of all, if you try to run we both know what I'll have to do." His gray eyes grew cold, like a sword in ice. "Second..."

Cyrus wasn't one to hesitate. The bastard would tease, backtalk, berate, and hassle. But unless he was torturing you, he seldom shut up.

"Oh come *on!*" I glared at him.

Cyrus crossed his arms and set his legs like he was expecting an attack. "You're the bait."

My jaw hung so low the cigarette nearly fell out. "What?"

"It's not like Elias has exactly lost interest in you. And then there's your shit-head brother."

I bunched the hem of my leather jacket in my fist, trying to keep myself from punching him. No doubt, Cillian deserved that title with a big trophy. And my psycho-ex certainly enjoyed taunting me. The logic was there but...

"I've already been their *guest*," I ground out, holding up two fingers. "Twice."

"I know."

"No, ya don't." I let my fist fall back to my side, curled and ready. "Don't even pretend ya do. And now, ya want me to prance around with a big ribbon on my ass?"

He grimaced but he didn't back down. Of course, he was tall with all his *vikinger*-muscle while I was short and scrawny from years of on-again-off-again famine, making me about as intimidating as one of those ankle-biters rich ladies shoved in their purse.

Cyrus lifted his chin, ever so slightly. "Technically, *you're* the enemy."

This time the cigarette did fall out, the slush extinguishing it while I gawked. My stomach tensed like someone had kicked me square in the gut.

It wasn't hard to see why Ritti felt that way, along with most of the Court. Hell, they'd only let me stay out of the dungeons because I'd proven useful.

But to hear it said out loud, and by Cyrus no less. Next thing, Ivan would be calling me a traitor. My past with Elias had fucking defiled me. But I didn't get much of a chance to consider how deep the rot ran.

Off in the distance was a noise so subtle, I might have imagined it. Except Cyrus' eyes ever so slowly scrolled in that same direction. His arms were still crossed and his back still stiff. He hadn't even bothered to turn his head. My face was still pointed at the broken asphalt, though I was looking directly up at my companion.

To any onlooker, we might still be standing in awkward silence. It wasn't much, but the ruse might give us a chance to decide what to do about the slowly fading sound of broken glass.

Rockwood wasn't exactly a ghost town. The homeless, both veterans and newbies alike, might try the free shelter when the community centers and malls became too crowded and the weather turned too cold. Or if they wanted a relatively private place to shoot up and forget what was happening. Granted, the number of needles rusting on the ground suggested privacy was becoming less of a concern these days.

On a wet winter night like this, a little breaking-and-entering was almost to be expected.

Cyrus flicked his gaze to mine and I gave a barely perceivable nod.

We turned and marched on, my hands shoved in my pockets with my shoulders hunched above my ears. Cyrus kept his chin high and his gate casual like he was strutting off some great battlefield. He scanned the right, I skimmed the left. Nothing of note, just more broken and battered homes.

At least our somewhat-act made further talking unnecessary. We could listen. Problem was, we didn't know what to focus on.

Vampire hearing is a bit like being the DJ to your life's audio, choosing what sounds get the most volume while the other racket becomes little more than white noise. Damn handy when some cabbage insists on crunching their popcorn in a theater, but harder to use when you don't know what to filter for.

Was I listening for more broken glass? The evil murmuring of a clandestine meeting? The footfalls of someone trying to follow us? The raspy moan of a dried husk?

All my questions came to an abrupt end with a single shout. Not a scared scream, more like an argument.

We halted, waiting for another one to resonate through the empty road.

Nothing.

"Great..." I murmured. What now? Search door to door?

We might just find some poor soul strung out of their ever-loving gourd. Whoever had made that sound wasn't thinking about who, or what, could hear them.

"Needle in a—" The sound of clattering metal halted Cyrus' thoughts. Bang. Followed by glass breaking. Crack. Then something kept being slammed shut. Thump.

Over and over, like a group of ratty teens rocking out for the very first time, unable to keep any semblance of rhythm.

Bang. Crack. Thump.

The lead singer came in the form of some chick screaming directions at her band-mates. Her backup was a male by the sound of it. "We don't *need* it."

"It would make life at home a lo—" A small smack cut her sentence short with a sharp cry of pain. "That hurt, you bastard!"

"Shhh." The second boy was far quieter than his friends. "You two want to wake the dead?"

"They're already awake." The girl muttered in a warbly tone like she might be crying.

We kept running, taking a sharp left onto Washington. We had to run about another block before we found the right place.

My heart turned to lead.

It was hard to remember the home's pre-war condition. After all, it had been dark and raining. And I'd been more than a little distracted at the time.

Now, the lawn was all weeds and dirt, but for one giant pine tree towering over the house. The wood shingle roof had clearly seen better days, with several wood tiles scattered about the front yard. And calling the remaining planks siding was a generous overstatement.

Aside from the ramshackle roof and sloppy siding, the door was splintered and busted to bits. Police tape still clung to it, tattered and limp, while the screen door hung on a single hinge, torn in several places. And yet, despite this easy access, almost every window was shattered inwards.

Maybe it had been the Starved but based on the crudely painted dead bats and third-grade-level images of vampires all over the front, I was willing to bet it was vandalism. At least wrecking this house made sense.

Cyrus and I nodded to each other and strolled up the walkway, crunching busted beer bottles and discarded food rappers underfoot; there was too much junk in the front yard to avoid. Besides, the band was still practicing.

We crouched outside the remnants of the door and looked through the opening.

Gabe's blood stained the carpet, dried to an almost black color. A separate trail of my own blood led to his deep puddle. The floral couch was gray and tattered. All the old bat's doilies were ripped and scattered, like discarded spider webs.

Through the opening for the kitchen, silhouettes walked back and forth, like crazy shadow puppets. One of them murmured under her breath, "You try cooking meat without a nonstick pan."

The girl flounced out of the kitchen, taking a sharp right down the hallway. Cyrus and I ducked behind the door frame, peering around the edge.

Her chin was high and her lip puffed as she stomped towards the bedrooms. She stormed like a toddler but she had to be at least thirteen. And she tried to look even older with enough makeup to cover a wedding cake. The girl's faded-blue hair bounced at the end of long dark roots with each dramatic step and her faux-fur boots squished on the soggy carpet.

Well, she certainly had her priorities straight.

"God, this bitch didn't have *any* food," a guy from the kitchen grumbled. "Just cleaning stuff"

"What do you expect, man? She was one of *them*." A second boy snorted. "I don't even know why we're here."

"Desperate times, dude." The first guy made a derisive sound right as the girl shrieked.

My muscles tightened and I rose a little. Cyrus placed a heavy hand on my shoulder just as the two boys ran down the hall, one with some kind of assault rifle strapped over his back and the other with a handgun, both shouting, "What?!"

"Look!" The girl whimpered, her tone suggesting a dead rat or something equally gross.

I strained my neck but there was just no way to see what she'd discovered from our vantage point. There was a long pause and some gagging before one of the boys chuffed. "It's just an overdose."

The girl whined through the dry heaves, "How can you be sure it's not one of her victims?"

"Nah, they wouldn't be crouched over the toilet." The second boy tsked. "Hey, maybe some of their stash is left. Go in and check."

"Screw you, Jimmy. You look."

"Would you two stop your bitching?" Heavy footsteps were followed by a wet splash. "Hey look what I found you."

"Ugh!" The girl gagged audibly, and it didn't sound dry this time. "I don't want it!"

"You were ready to cook in a vampire's pan not five minutes ago." Another wet flop. "Now you're getting squeamish about going through a stiff's pockets?"

My stomach rolled in on itself.

Portland had never been some cute little town where people left their doors unlocked. Not even in my long years. But still, to hear these youngsters talk so nonchalantly as they searched a corpse...

Cyrus removed his hand to tap me on the shoulder and bobbed his head, indicating we should go. I shook my head and pointed into the house. We should at least see what they found. Cyrus' lips tightened and he shook his head. Who knew why he didn't see my side, but I hardly cared.

I jumped through the doorway, barely avoiding Cyrus' grab for my ankle. "Hello, is someone here?"

Cyrus swore under his breath and a nasty flop sounded right before the three pairs of feet receded from us.

"Hello?" I repeated, adding a note of uncertainty to my voice. Yup, just a teeny-tiny girl, no threat here. Come out and chat.

They murmured behind a door, clearly disagreeing. Cyrus hissed my name from the open door but I ignored him. Lord knew what these kids had found. We could always black-eye them into forgetting they saw us, but I'd be damned before I let them leave with evidence.

The changes to the house were easier to see inside, and it wasn't just the dirt or the weather getting in. While the smells of mildew and rot weren't particularly charming, it was the wreckage that stood out. Her ugly floral sofas had been cut into ribbons, the stuffing all over the floor. The coffee table was in splinters and I didn't think we'd done that during the fight.

Oddly enough, the china cabinet was unmolested, all the teacups and plates neatly arranged behind glass that tried to gleam in the dingy light. There was even a lamp on the end table by the couch, though its shade was missing.

The carpet squished under my boots as I approached the first open door in the hall. Even chilled, the odor of vomit wafted right to me. The group continued to mutter amongst themselves from behind one of the closed doors, one of them *shhing* the others harshly. I tried to keep that door in the corner of my eye as I peered into the bathroom.

Even having heard the others, a choked gasp caught my throat and I covered my mouth with the tips of my fingers. "Shite."

A scrawny girl was hunched over the toilet, arms hanging loose, like a torn rag doll over the sides of the bowl. Bony shoulders peeked through the tatters of a gossamer blouse, a ribbon circling her waist like some hideous gift wrap. Beneath the short ruins of a jean skirt, her legs were thin and bony, one covered in dry blood from a wound I couldn't see.

Her hair was either filthy or dark, maybe both, clinging to her back and shoulders like a death shroud. Track marks speckled her skin. A syringe balanced loosely on the edge of her fingertips, the needle gleaming against the vinyl floor.

Her beloved vice didn't abandon her, not even in death.

"It ain't pretty." A small voice came from down the hall.

Instinct made me jump as I turned to find the girl sticking her head out with a curious glance.

I swallowed a thick lump and nodded. "Yeah, I'd have to agree."

She peered around the door frame, straining her neck to see past me. "Whaddya want?"

"Just heard ya in here." I shrugged. "It's awful lonely out there, been a while since I've seen a new face."

"Yeah, well this ain't no social club." A deep, rather forced baritone barked behind the door. "Beat it."

I rolled my eyes. "Lemme guess, he's gotta gun pointed at my head."

The girl's eyes widened to Bambi-sized orbs and she glanced to her left.

"He can pull the trigger." I held my hands up, nice and casual. "I can't stop him. But I doubt my friend outside would like that."

The gunman swore and the other boy shouted, "Thought you said you were alone."

"No, I said I hadn't seen a new face in a while. My buddy's handy in a pinch but he's not exactly fun at parties, if you know what I mean."

"Gee, thanks," Cyrus added grouchily.

Eh, he was already pissed I'd come in here. No reason to fret. This might be the most fun I'd get for a while.

One of the guys whispered behind the door but I didn't catch it all. Something about hair. The girl's eyes grew even larger and she gave the slightest of nods.

The gravity of that tiny gesture sank my heart. A hole blasted through the door. Pain burst across the left side of my face and I dropped to the ground. My hands became slick as I cradled my head. My ear felt like it had gone through a meat grinder.

Cyrus spat out a curse and stormed over, gun drawn. "Come out or I'll shoot."

"Like we'd listen to a couple of fucking vamps." The voice had a cold kind of anger behind it. Another blast sounded and the girl shrieked.

Cyrus crouched in front of me. "Great plan."

"How 'bout ya yell at me when I have both ears?" I snapped, crawling behind the opening of the living room and using the wall for shelter as another gunshot tore the air. "We're not here to hurt ya!"

"Yeah, 'cause we're gonna trust *you*," one of the boys shouted. "Did you really think we wouldn't recognize you, you ugly Irish leech!"

"Never a better insult than parasites," Cyrus grumbled. "They must've recognized you from that interview."

The fucking news wouldn't stop replaying clips of my infamous interview with Amber Wright, discussing the *relevance* with Gabe's ongoing case. People may not have cable anymore but bars were still in business and ID laws were out the window.

"Must've." I leaned against the wall. "Rush 'em?"

"You do realize that first bullet almost—"

"I'm aware, thank you!" I glared at the back of his head. "But we're already here, may as well make the best of it."

He muttered something unintelligible as another blast tore through the door and someone stormed towards us. It was like these kids learned their tactics from stampeding buffalo.

They were loud as rhinos and charged straight into the living room. I swept my leg to trip one. Cyrus took the other. They both fell in a mess of limbs and gunfire. The china cabinet's window shattered. And a nasty gurgling sound came from the back of the house.

I crawled over Cyrus to find the girl slumped over, blood trickling through her fingers as she clutched her throat.

"Oh shit!" I couldn't tell who said it. Maybe all of us.

I caught her as she fell onto the ugly carpet, flipping her to face me. Her small face drained of any color as red stained the faded blue hair.

The guys shouted something but I heard a grunt that told me Cyrus had them well underhand. And I had to focus. No way in hell I was letting this happen again. "Let me see."

She tried to keep her grip but I ripped her hand away like I was trashing a napkin. Something fell from her fingers, clinking on the floor. The guys shouted again but Cyrus growled at them and they shut up. The blood gushed down her neck rapidly as she shuddered and shook.

Getting that bloody bullet out would already be a challenge without her wiggling like a newborn.

I stared into her eyes, pouring authority into my tone. "You don't feel any pain and you are safe."

My eyes pulsed black with power. She stilled, though she was still making that awful choking sound. It was unsettling but at least I could work. I dug my finger into the hole, tearing her neck open as I fished for the bullet.

Her flesh was warm and squishy, making it easy to tell when my fingernail scraped the hot, solid surface of the bullet. She coughed blood on my face as I worked it out, flicked it to the side, and slashed my wrist with a fang. My blood pooled in the open wound before I shoved the gash to her mouth and willed power into my gaze again. "Drink."

She did so and the wound started to close, slowly stitching itself back together like I'd hit the rewind button on life.

"Ya can let 'em go now." I let her slide to the ground and she crab-walked away from me, clutching her throat and staring at me with huge eyes.

"We'll get a head start before they start shooting us." Cyrus crossed his arms. "Either that or I'm taking their guns since they obviously don't understand the basics."

I debated this and shook my head. "Nah, it's a nightmare out there."

I fucking hated guns but that didn't give us the right to disarm these kids.

The girl patted her throat several times, but she kept staring at me, unblinking. "What'd you do to me?"

"She saved you." Cyrus glowered. "After you tried to kill us."

One of the boys whimpered. "I wouldn't have fired if you hadn't come after us."

"We weren't here to hurt ya." Something shimmered and I bent to pick it up. The girl had dropped a necklace. I held it out to her. "And if your buddies can't be responsible with their guns, then they shouldn't be carryin' 'em in the first fuckin' place."

She scowled at the pendant still hanging from my hand. "I don't want that nasty thing. Jimmy took it off the dead girl."

I about dropped it but that felt wrong somehow. Like I was throwing away the last piece of that girl in the bathroom. But I certainly wasn't going to put it back on the corpse; I didn't have any desire to enter that tiled tomb. I settled on sticking it in my pocket.

The girl's scowl deepened but she kept her opinion to herself. Maybe realizing it would be hypocritical to give me shit for taking the necklace when her companion had snagged it in the first place.

"I wouldn't take any of the kitchenware. The lady who owned this place wasn't just a vampire." I walked towards the open door. "She was also bat-shit crazy."

Cyrus gave the boys a direction to wait five minutes before moving and learn some fucking gun etiquette before turning to follow me. "Have a nice night."

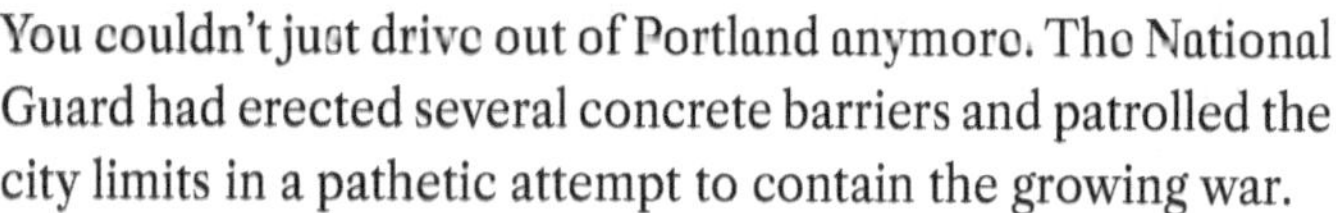

You couldn't just drive out of Portland anymore. The National Guard had erected several concrete barriers and patrolled the city limits in a pathetic attempt to contain the growing war.

We had to hop a couple fences and walk a few miles before Ivan could pick us up. Cyrus filled my adoptive sire in on our evening activities and I was promptly chewed out. Why hadn't I stayed with Cyrus? Why had I exposed us? Didn't I realize how easy I was to recognize? What if my actions made it back to the DA or hurt Gabe and Olive's case? Didn't I know what their case would mean to our kind?

"Guess it's a good thing we saved her, eh?" I crossed my arms.

Ivan stopped his lecture mid-sentence and the atmosphere of the delivery van became thick. Cyrus remained silent. When we stopped at the next red light, Ivan turned to look at me.

His face was a mismatched puzzle, with a nose and ears disproportionate to the chin and lips. I'd always taken a sort of comfort in his dusky face. Not now though.

That garish red light flowed over half the contours of his jowls with emphasized shadows. He looked like a demon.

"That—" he growled, "was a low blow."

I raised my chin. "So was tryin' to kill the kid."

Cyrus quietly cursed in the back. The light changed but Ivan's face wasn't suddenly angelic under the green glow. There was nobody behind us to honk or object to the extended wait. We had plenty of time to keep staring, maybe even wait for some tumbleweed to do its thing.

The wedge between us wasn't going away anytime soon. But, given the chance, I'd do it all again. And Ivan couldn't deny my point. If Gabe and I had followed protocol, Olive would have been *put down* under Court law and there would be no court date for Portland's tragic little orphan.

The pro-vamp media outlets loved that line. I doubted Olive cared for it.

"You don't like the system?" Ivan clenched the steering wheel so tight it squealed, finally pressing his big foot on the gas pedal. "Then you should *do* something about it."

The rest of the drive back to court was silent. Right up to the definitive click of being locked in my room.

CHAPTER 3

GABE

Our last preparations always consisted of Michelle fussing over our wardrobes and giving me far too much time to think. Being on the other side of the courtroom was like traveling through a looking glass.

Past cases wound through the tunnels of my mind. I'd always tried to be fair but these last few weeks made me question how well I'd done. Had my decisions really been based on evidence? Back then I'd only wanted to bring in vampires and most of my arrests were human knock-offs, men stabbing their wives with meat prongs. I'd always been disappointed when the medical examiner gave us their findings.

How had that bitterness and prejudice impacted my judgement?

Lady justice often peeked through her blindfold, prosecutors making deals or warrants being earned more by office politics than anything else. I wanted to believe in the system, but sitting around my home with nothing to do had me questioning everything.

"Gabe!" Michelle snapped, drawing me back to reality. Her cloud-gray eyes were cold and the twist of her painted lips told me she'd been holding out the offered bobby pin for quite some time.

"Huh?" was the best I could manage. After all, it wasn't like I was looking for a new accessory.

"For crying out loud." Michelle shoved the pin into my hand. "Put this in your pocket in case Olive needs it later."

Olive stifled a snicker as Michelle continued her investigation.

"Every day is a new first impression. You never know what they've watched."

Each day Michelle straightened my tie and added gel to any offending hairs that dared go astray. She'd tried shaving my scruff off the first morning. Apparently it didn't portray me as the clean-cut officer in my earlier photos. Just as I'd warned her, it had grown back within an hour, further exaggerating my lack of humanity.

Olive was always instructed to use *little girl words* and wear a dress. The more it flared, the better. Her hair was always down with a headband holding it behind her ears. The aforementioned pins kept the short hairs back from her face, so her eyes looked as large as possible. Her shoes were polished, the high sheen drawing attention to the ankle monitor.

Michelle had justified this choice by explaining, "It makes her look meek."

I'd asked Michelle if I should put mine on display.

Her reply showed she hadn't caught my sarcasm. "Absolutely not! You'll look like a criminal."

I didn't like the theatrics but I couldn't deny their value. So, instead of debating, I took the pin and pocketed it with a muttered apology. "I was thinking."

"Keep your mind here." She snapped as she covered Olive in a heavy miasma of hairspray. "You can't be wandering into one of your stories when we put you on the stand."

"This isn't my first rodeo," I droned.

"If you don't need me, just say so and I'll head out." She stood, smoothing the creases from her suit.

She had me there. We hardly agreed on anything and she resented me for some very good reasons. She'd been the first city prosecutor for the Vampire Police Bureau. She'd dealt with many of the VPB's growing pains, waded through the worst cases, learned from many hard-fought losses, and taken far more wins. And, despite her worst flaws, she did so with a moral compass. I couldn't deny that.

She was vain, petty, and high-strung. But all of that made her an extreme hassle for the other side, even if her runway tactics just made me question right and wrong all over again.

"There." She turned to the heavy door, her auburn curls bouncing with each click of her heels. "Let's go."

Our entrance had silenced the courtroom the first few days. Everyone except the bailiff quietly gawked at the vampires who dared to stand trial.

People no longer hushed or stared as we entered. Their murmured conversations continued, their glances only briefly darting in our direction. Some even pointed with accusing fingers and jerking thumbs.

Judge Taffet entered and the bailiff bellowed for all to rise. Everyone obeyed, the judge took her place behind the bench, we were allowed to be seated, and Michelle stayed standing. "The defense calls Detective Gabriel Collins to the stand."

The courtroom murmured and Judge Taffet hammered her gavel immediately. All the eyes on me carried a weight that slowed my steps.

Despite what we see in crime dramas, defendants were rarely called to the stand. Only the defense could call their client and it eliminated any ability to plead the fifth once prosecution took over. Michelle didn't even want to call me, but if she didn't, calling Olive later wouldn't hold the same weight. We'd all agreed it was worth the risk.

Walking to the stand was still like walking to the gallows. My steps grew heavier as I went and I struggled to keep my gaze straight ahead, avoiding a direct look at the jury. I raised my hand, swore my oath, and sat, trying to keep my posture straight. It wasn't difficult with the back of the chair digging into my spine.

Michelle only covered the basics, verifying how long I'd been on the force. Five years total, one-and-a-half with the VPB. And why had I joined the force? I gave simple answers, how I'd dreamed of protecting people since I was a kid.

"And why did you join the VPB?"

I swallowed. "Because I lost my father in the original massacre."

The courtroom murmured but it was short lived. This wasn't really news. Michelle nodded. "That must have been very hard."

"Yes." I closed my eyes but that only made things worse. Images swam to the surface. "I saw two vampires pull him apart by the arms. Like two dogs with a rope-bone."

"And how did you feel about vampires from that point, while joining the VPB?"

"I hated every one of them." I gritted my teeth, resenting myself with every word.

Michelle nodded and paced past me, her hands clasped before her. "Can you walk us through what happened the night Captain Murphy died?"

I nodded solemnly, glad to switch topics. I went over the basics, careful to avoid outright lying. I had entered the house alone (technically true as Harper had gone around back.) I had found Ms. Stafford beating a restrained Lily to a pulp. While confronting Stafford, Captain Murphy had threatened our lives, offering to spare me if I conspired with him against the human population.

I'd shot Miss Stafford and Captain Murphy had returned the favor. When I died, Lily had brought me back. Just not the same as before.

"Thank you, Detective. Nothing further." Michelle nodded and walked back to our table. The District Attorney stood and snapped his collar.

Adam Gordon was a charismatic and engaging prosecutor, making his speeches all the more fascinating. He walked with confidence, the stride a perfect fit to his square frame. And when he spoke, he used his large hands subtly, orchestrating each point. I might have liked him in other circumstances. Maybe we could have swapped stories over a couple of cold ones.

In our current roles, he was too effective for my taste.

"*Mister* Collins—" he smoothly picked an evidence bag off the table with two large fingers, letting the pistol inside swing for just a moment, "do you recognize this?"

"It's a gun." I tried not to sound snide, but really, it was a standard Glock. Black and simple. Nothing distinguishable about it. Though, I had a good idea which one it was.

"That's a start." Mr. Gordon chuckled, his slightly crooked teeth lining up in a grin. He tweaked a single brow at the jury before turning back to me. He stood close to the witness stand, forcing me to look up at him. "Though I'm surprised you don't recognize your own service weapon."

"Do you remember every pen you've ever signed with?" I managed to keep the tone level but a snicker from the jury told me that the sarcasm hadn't been lost.

Michelle had to be glaring a hole through my skull. "Objection, Your Honor! Leading the witness."

Judge Taffet shook her head, her tight gray bun bobbing side to side. "Overruled. Continue."

Gordon nodded deferentially before he turned back to his table, dropping the gun off and tapping on the evidence bag a few times before he spoke. "You testified that you went to the residence of Miss Angela Stafford because you were worried about this–," he snapped his fingers a couple times, as though he was thinking, before looking up, "Lily Edwards, is that correct?"

My throat turned tight. "Yes."

"Can you remind us all who Lily Edwards is?" He turned towards the jury, his hands open in invitation.

"She's a witness and private investigator in the last case I was working on." Everyone already knew about Lily. Our interview with Amber Wright was being replayed over and over the news. I certainly wasn't going to help him vilify her.

"And *what* is she?" The venom he sunk into the single word left little doubt what he was driving at.

I debated avoiding his question for a moment, maybe making him work for it, but that wouldn't look good.

"The first vampire I'd met since my father's death." I tried to punctuate that last part.

Mr. Gordon clapped his hands once, like he was giving himself a high five. "Right, and how did you know she was at Miss Stafford's place?"

"I followed a lead from an informant." I left out that the informant had been some kid who stole Lily's phone. Michelle and I agreed that explaining how I'd reached these conclusions would be convoluted and make the jury feel stupid.

"Did you know that Miss Stafford was also a vampire?"

"I had suspicions but no proof."

"But you knew Miss Edwards was a vampire?"

"Yes." Skirting the truth about Harper was one thing, but I wouldn't outright purger myself. Debatable ethics? Maybe, but I was only a man.

"And yet you testified that you went in, alone, to save her."

"She was helping me solve a case."

The DA smiled. It was brief but chilling. He leaned back against the table, lifting the evidence bag with the gun slowly. "So you went in, armed with your service pistol, ready to save a known vampire that was helping you?"

"Objection, Your Honor!" Michelle snapped up. "Asked and answered."

"Sustained." Judge Taffet looked over her glasses at the DA. "We've heard all this before. Move it along, Counselor."

"Of course, Your Honor." Another bow of the head. "Trying to provide context, my apologies."

He managed to make it sound remorseful. God, he was aggravating.

"Mr. Collins—" he walked quickly and loomed over the witness stand in four easy strides, "you'd gone there, conspiring with a vampire, and armed. There, you shot your previous Captain of the VPB and rescued your vampire conspirator before she was killed. Is this correct?"

"Objection, Your Honor!" Michelle stood. "Asked and answered, *again*."

"Sustained." Judge Taffet let the warning seep into her tone. "*Counselor*."

"Apologies, Your Honor. Allow me to get to the point." Gordon smiled reproachfully with another bow of his head. "Mr. Collins, in the end, we only have your word that Captain Murphy was colluding against humanity. How can we be sure you didn't conspire to become one of the undead?"

The courtroom fell silent and I chewed on the tip of my tongue to keep from lashing out. Someone sneezed. Michelle's nails tapped on her table in a soft rhythm.

"Objection, Your Honor," Mr. Gordon said so quietly, you might have leaned in just to hear it. "Witness is Non-responsive."

"Sustained. Answer the question, Mr. Collins."

I took a breath just to buy myself an extra second but I still hadn't come up with a better response.

CHAPTER 4

LILY

G abe's face turned resolute from the defendant's stand, like he'd decided to face some great monster. *"If I was going to lie about how I became a vampire, don't you think I would come up with a better story?"*

I about spat my nuke-warm blood all over the TV. Some of it went down the wrong pipe and I coughed, blood dribbling from the corner of my mouth. Vampire or no, that still fucking hurts.

"Elegant," Alex snorted from the corner couch, his lanky arm draped over Darren as he rolled his dark eyes.

"What's Gabe thinking?" Maria grabbed a tissue off the nightstand. The multi-colored beads in her hair clicked when she handed it to me, sitting cross-legged beside me at the edge of the bed. "He's supposed to make the public like him."

"Well, he managed to get Lils." Darren took a sip from his Mountain Dew and adjusted his beanie with one broad hand before leaning against my best friend. "How hard could a jury be?"

I glared at Darren, unsure what to say to that. Maria had a point about toning it down, winning over the people. But secretly, I'd have been disappointed if he had.

Still...

"Well, nothing's better for romance than going on the lam," Alex said it like he was trying to be funny, but the comment held a bitter note. Maria and Darren both looked between us, but no one said anything. Alex's dark eyes locked with mine for a moment before we both looked away.

Back in the courtroom, the DA responded, *"If I thought you could lie better, I would have started there."*

I bristled as Michelle objected, the DA withdrew, and let her take over. The redirect didn't go very well; Michelle kept it short. Probably for the best.

The jury had all heard some version of this, speculation was all over the news. They looked ready to doze off, but when Michelle called Olive, even the judge sat up straighter. All eyes locked on the small girl. She looked like a cupcake on the march, her frilly dress twirling and shiny shoes snapping on the floor as she climbed into the witness stand. Her head and shoulders were barely visible once she sat.

Maria adjusted like she was having trouble getting comfortable again. "I still can't believe Michelle took Olive's case."

"The people like her better than Gabe." I craned my head like I might be able to see over the top of the stand and get a better view of Olive.

My guts still twisted whenever I saw her. Sometimes I was grateful for her role in my rescue. Other times, anger simmered just beneath the surface, every awful thing I'd suffered in captivity battling for attention in my skull. All our hopes were wrapped up in one tiny, duplicitous package. And I couldn't decide how I felt about that.

Michelle eased Olive into it, talking about the basics first. What kind of life did she have before she was turned? She'd been newly orphaned, only having lost her parents and sister about a year ago in an accident. She'd just fought with another kid in her group home. Someone had stolen her suitcase and the administrator had done nothing but hand her a rubbish bag for her effects. She'd spent the whole day searching and found the thief on her own.

"Bet that makes you proud, 'ey Lils?" Alex chuckled, his manner more mild. "A little PI in the making."

My only answer was a loud gulp. I didn't like where this was headed.

"It was one of the older boys, Ryan. I found it under his bunk. When I tried to take the suitcase back, he said little babies don't need to carry anything important." Olive blew out an angry breath. *"I punched him. I know I shouldn't have but my mom gave me the case for vacations. I wanted it back. When they separated us, I got punished for starting the fight and he still didn't return it."*

"Objection, Your Honor." The DA braced himself on the table as he stood slowly, like he was tired. *"Relevance?"*

"Every story needs context, Your Honor." Michelle smiled indulgently. *"And at least I'm asking new questions."*

A couple of people in the court chuckled before the judge banged her gavel again.

"Alright, let's drop the cute commentary." The judge rolled her eyes. *"Overruled, but I recommend you get to the point, Counselor."*

"Of course, Your Honor. Now Olive—" Michelle leaned on the stand, like it was the closest thing she could do to putting her hand on Olive's shoulders. Before, her tone had been simple, pleasant, and direct. Now it was soft, inviting, and patient. *"Please take your time with this next part."*

Olive nodded gravely.

"What happened the day after your suitcase was stolen?"

"Yes ma'am." Olive flinched at her military tone, then sat up a little straighter. Somehow, it only made her look smaller. *"I went to school and I was still angry. By the time I was walking back, I was thinking of running away. I mean, who would miss me anyway?"*

Her voice caught on that last part. My throat tightened. I didn't want to hear this. But Olive persevered and I couldn't bring myself to turn the TV off just to be a chicken shit.

"Then this van drove slowly along the sidewalk. I wasn't foo—" she stopped herself, her lips twitching as she reworked her sentence. *"I wasn't dumb, I'd never get in some guy's van for candy. But he didn't do that."*

She paused again, her shoulders hunched and I swore she squirmed for a moment. Was she fidgeting? That girl had faced down men three times her size and made a pithy remark about tag. But there, on the witness stand, was Olive out of her depth?

"What happened next?" Michelle asked it softly, her tone consolatory. I leaned in instinctively, though I could hear her just fine.

"He... he asked for directions." Olive stuck her chin up as her eyes took a faraway look. *"He had a map out and he was asking about Alberta Avenue; even I knew where that was."*

Despite the proud remark, her tone was bitter.

"So you helped him with the road?"

"Objection, Your Honor!" The DA looked ready to roll his eyes. *"Leading the witness."*

"I'm sorry, I'll rephrase," Michelle tucked one of her red curls behind one ear and averted her gaze from the judge. *"Olive, what did you do next?"*

Darren sat forward. "Oh, that was slick!"

"What are you talking about?" Maria asked. "She had to rephrase."

"That wasn't the point." Darren smashed a button on the remote and the DA paused with a rather unflattering look wrinkling his face. I always forgot you could do that these days. Darren rewound the live feed and paused on a shot of the jury. "See? Right there, they look annoyed."

He was right. Some of them scrunched their eyebrows or twisted their lips.

"Yeah..." I drew out. "They're listenin' to Little Orphan Olive talk about her kidnappin'. I'm pretty pissed too."

"No, that's not it. Olive's story is interesting. I know that's hard to hear Lils—" He held up a broad hand to silence my protest and I snapped my mouth shut, "but it is. Michelle wanted the DA to interrupt her."

I considered it for a second. It made a twisted kind of sense. Michelle was trying to tell a story that the audience wanted to hear. If the prosecutor interrupted her, it would irritate them. It was silly and manipulative, but do it enough times and those little things would add up, maybe even buy the defense some brownie points.

"Leave it to you to notice something so obscure." Alex shook his head, the blond spikes swaying with the motion.

"That's why you need me." Darren grinned and his cheeks flushed under that burly beard.

"It's part of it. Now, hit play, would you?"

Darren obliged and we picked back up with Olive's answer. *"I started to point toward the road, told him he could go down two streets and take a right. But it didn't matter."*

"Why was that?"

"Because right when he said 'thank you,' the side door of the van opened and two guys jumped out." Olive closed her eyes, her small face flinching at the memory. *"They grabbed me."*

"Did you try to get away?" Michelle's tone was more solid this time, but not indigent.

"Of course I did!" Olive's eyes snapped open and her small voice became fierce. *"I tried to pull away and one of them broke my arm. I screamed, but the other one's eyes turned black and he told me to keep quiet and go with them."*

"I'm sorry Olive." Michelle placed a hand back on the witness stand, tilting her head to one side. *"And did you?"*

"Yes, but I didn't want to." Olive sniffed but she was sitting up straighter. Being defiant was more natural to her than being a victim. Michelle's straightforward question had given her a

small bit of bravado and she was grasping it for all she was worth. *"I couldn't control it. It was like someone tied strings to my legs."*

"And what happened next?"

"I got in the van, and there were three other girls. They told me to sit with my new sisters. I still couldn't control myself, so I did. We drove for a long time, I watched the clock on the van's radio tick by for over three hours as they picked up more kids."

"Did anyone say or do anything while they were driving?"

"Yes. They kept saying things like 'Little brat should be around here somewhere,' or 'There she is.'"

"Oh, dear god." Maria put her painted fingertips to her lips like she could hold in the horror. "They weren't hunting at random, they were looking for specific kids."

I was balling the forgotten tissue in one fist while my now-empty coffee mug shook in the other.

"What happened next, Olive?"

"They took us back to this warehouse, lined us all up in rows. Some of the kids wet themselves while they were told to just stand there, wait for orders." Olive wrinkled her nose and sneered like she could still smell it. *"I never counted, but we filled most of the warehouse."*

Michelle swallowed before she pressed on. *"What next?"*

"They started insulting the kids who'd wet themselves, telling them they better grow out of those diapers. They jeered and teased us, even though we couldn't talk back. They kept poking fun until everyone was crying."

"Bastards," Alex growled.

My hands itched. Part of me wanted to leap through the TV and give Olive a huge hug. The other part wanted to find these asshats and thrash them. Especially my brother.

"They kept going, it seemed like for hours, all the while more kids peed themselves." Olive sniffed, swiping the heel of her hands across her eyes. I barely cough the red tint of a tear on

her palm. *"One girl had just started her period, she bled right through the back of her jeans. When they noticed, they..."*

Olive's face turned a mixed shade of green and purple, her small shoulders quaked. Michelle didn't prompt her, just looked on encouragingly. Finally Olive closed her eyes, tucking her jaw into her body.

"They threatened to drain her and make everyone watch."

Darren spit his last swig of Mountain Dew back into the can and set it aside. Even the DA had the decency to look horrified.

"What happened next, Olive?"

"We all just had to stand there and watch each other be ridiculed. My legs were sore and some of us shook from the strain. If we closed our eyes, they ordered them open. There wasn't a clock on the wall, so I couldn't be sure how long we'd been there. But these other men came in and told them to stop. When the first group finished and stepped away, the new group came through and told us all to stop crying, stick our chins up. They went through one by one, making us stand in perfect, quiet attention."

Maria shook her head, strands of beads snapping against each other. "After all that, they couldn't even leave them with a little dignity?"

"Then the new men stood at the front and yelled at the group. They mocked us for how helpless we were. How they could just walk through and drink each and everyone of us and we would just have to watch. We had no power."'

CHAPTER 5

GABE

S lamming my front door barely muffled the reporters or their myriad of questions. The thick wood hummed with their energy as I leaned against the door, raking my fingers through my hair. "Why didn't you keep going?"

"You know we don't want to overload the jury." Michelle double-checked all the blinds were closed.

"Overload?" Olive kicked off her shoes and carried them off to the back bedroom.

"Too much emotion at one time can wear someone out." Michelle flicked the metal of one blind, nodding with the sharp snap, as though she'd accomplished something. "They need time to decompress. Maybe watch a sitcom."

"But now they don't know the whole story." I checked the sliding glass door and backyard. So far, we'd only had one reporter brazen enough to stake-out there. The department was more vigilant these days, but you never knew. "She'll have to go back on the stand."

Hearing Olive testify had been rough. Just imagining the next part made me wish for something I could break with my bare hands.

"Exactly." Michelle twisted her lips in a self-satisfied smirk. "Now they're going to spend the whole weekend wondering what happened."

"That's incredibly manipulative." Olive's tone held a note of esteem as she padded into the living room in her pajamas.

"That's half the job." Michelle gave Olive a little wink as she dug through her briefcase.

Olive cocked her head, like a curious bird. "What's the other half?"

I held up my right hand.

"Telling the truth, the whole truth and nothing but the truth." I cast a sidelong glance at Michelle's amused expression. "So help you, God."

"Aww, you remembered." Our lawyer snorted and for a moment, I think she forgot to hate me. Then her eyes flicked back to the suitcase and the smile vanished. "Okay, that's just weird."

"What is?" I dropped my hand back to my side.

"I thought for sure I had some notes in here."

"Notes?" Olive tilted her head.

"Yeah, you know." Michelle buckled the case, her lips twisting as she idly scratched her scalp. "Things I noticed you doing in court today. Things to stop."

At this last one, she glared at me.

My hackles rose against my better judgment. "What else should I have said?"

"Anything," she quipped as she fished through a back pocket on the case. "Anything would have been an improvement over acknowledging that he was accusing you of lying. Damn, I must have left them back in court."

"So you leave notes for your clients behind, yet you criticize us for how we communicate under questioning?" Olive crossed her arms.

"Hey, you want to win this?" She zipped the back pocket closed and rubbed her eyes with her free hand. "Man, I can't believe I did that. I'll go back and grab them."

When her hand fell away, she'd smudged some of her make-up. Only then could I see the tired rings she'd so expertly covered before. My righteous indignation melted.

Asking about the failing health of Michelle's sister, widow of my former Captain, would probably only yield a curt, barely polite reply.

If there were any other way to legalize vampire blood, to save her sister, besides representing me, I doubt she would have been here. She probably spent every hour she wasn't with us crashed next to Barbara, hunched over her laptop like a crazed programmer.

Olive opened her mouth to say something.

"That's fine," I gave Olive a pleading look, hoping she would drop it. "We'll see you Sunday for prep."

At this, Michelle looked mildly surprised but nodded and made her way towards the door. "Get out of sight until I close it. I don't want to see those PJs on tomorrow's front page."

Olive did as Michelle asked, hiding in the hallway. Michelle opened the door, the muffled questions instantly rose in volume and intensity. The latch of the doorknob clicked into place and I rushed to engage the deadbolt. The media probably wouldn't come into the house but a protestor might try.

Or did I have that backwards?

Either way, the lock was one more barrier between them and us, pathetic though it may be.

Olive glanced down, examining the flannel pattern on her pants. "What's wrong with my pajamas?"

"Nothing." I scoffed and leaned back against the door as though I might fortify it. "But Michelle knows how quickly an image can change a jury's mind. You already talk like Spock in a college course, and she wants the jury to see you as a child."

"Ah." Olive nodded. "Flannel bottoms aren't sufficiently whimsical."

"Probably not."

She considered this a moment before looking at me. "Dinner?

I pushed a hand through my hair and nearly grimaced at the hard feeling of gel. "Sure."

We fished through the bags of blood until we found two that matched. She was debating between seasoning it with cayenne pepper or garlic powder as the pot warmed on the stove.

We decided to eat it like soup, using bowls instead of the typical coffee mugs. Mostly, I think we just wanted a reason to sit at the table and pretend things were normal. The awkward silence only grew with every slurp.

"Gabe?"

"Hmmm?" I said around a spoonful.

"Have you forgiven me?"

I stopped mid-slurp, along with my thoughts. She stirred her blood slowly, in a variety of patterns, swallowing a hard lump of nothing. My parents' old clock tick-tick-ticked away, emphasizing every second I failed to reply.

I considered lying. Without Olive, we'd never have gotten Lily back. And hearing her story in court had given me much needed context. Then again, hadn't she had enough people manipulate her in this world?

"It's not about if I can forgive you." I downed my entire bowl in a quick gulp. "I'm not the one you'll confront in the mirror."

I rinsed my bowl quickly and left. Olive didn't even look up from the table.

Hours passed and I lay on my bed, staring at the ceiling. Our little exchange swirled in the empty vacuum of my skull. Sometimes distant, like seeing a vaguely familiar face across a crowded room. Other times closer, dancing in stunning patterns that were impossible to ignore, with a parade of questions straight behind.

What should I have said? What could I even expect from her? Olive had become an orphan in both worlds. She would forever be a traumatized soldier trapped in the body of a ten-year-old. How could she retain any hope in this state?

But she had. That hope had driven her to rescue Lily. And forced me into an impossible choice. Was I blaming Olive for her betrayal or my own failings?

A noise like dull thunder broke through the ceaseless chain of questions. The low, steady rumble rose outside my bedroom. Almost like a march but with every step out of sync from the next, without any rhythm or timing. The noise grew closer and closer as I went to my window.

As I grasped the cord for the blinds, a scream reverberated over the inconsistent drumming. I couldn't tell if it was male or female, all I could hear was the abstract terror, as though fear itself had created this sound. I yanked the cord, the blinds lifted, and my guts rolled over themselves.

The protestors and press intermingled as they ran, tripping over audio equipment, cameras, broken picket signs, and each other. Some of the people on my lawn tried to crawl away, clawing up great clumps of earth but making absolutely no progress. Screams echoed, amplifying the pain as people trampled each other; one fell silent, three more rose to take their place until all my senses were awash in panic.

"What's going on?" Olive's steady tone broke my trance and I instinctively lashed out, punching through the window and shattering the glass.

"Dammit!" I tore my arm back, blood running from knuckle to elbow. Agony scored my flesh, deeper than the new lacerations.

Olive rushed into my room and grabbed my arm to examine. "What did you do that for?"

"It'll heal." I ripped a piece from my curtains and wrapped it around the arm. The pain dulled, adrenaline flooding my system and helping me focus. "We need to go."

Olive nodded and yanked the remaining curtain down, using the cloth as a shield while she cleared the rest of the glass from the frame. The city's civil defense siren rose to fill the tiniest of gaps between screams.

CHAPTER 6

LILY

Everything burned. Every cell in my body boiled and bubbled below the surface, the meat melting right off my bones. And then the sweetest nectar coated my tongue, covering the foul taste of ash. Wherever it flowed, the pain cooled.

As the pain receded, my eyes focused. With each draw of blood, the form in my arms sharpened and the cool relief chilled my very marrow. I dropped her to the ground.

I'd never learned her name. For all I knew, she had none. She'd been cattle, fed only to be fed upon.

They hadn't even bothered to dress her. Her hair was slick with grime, thick and plastered to her head. There was so much dirt on her face and body, I couldn't be sure of her ethnicity. The skin appeared gray, but even under all that muck, I could still make out thick patterns of bruises and bite marks, especially on her legs and hips. Her arm was broken and I still couldn't remember when or if I had done that.

Then she moved. She clawed her way up my body, her mouth gaping, ready to take every drop back. With every heave of her body, I sagged under her weight, our faces inching closer. And closer.

Just when I thought it couldn't get any worse, her face morphed to that of the overdose. She reached for me, grabbing my neck and pulling me closer. Her breath was foul and I could see the back of her throat as her jaws opened wide...

I gasped, shooting straight up. Hair was glued over my mouth and eyes. Salt smothered my lips. I breathed in, deep and fast, breathing the words in and out in rapid succession as I shoved my head between my palms. "Just another fuckin' dream."

The mantra didn't stop my shaking limbs. They still quivered as I realized what had drawn me out of the nightmare.

The siren slowly filled my senses, a low wail of agony. The whole damn city was crying out in pain. The boots of every soldier in Court pounded through the halls, as they readied to battle another swarm.

I clutched my blankets and gritted my teeth, forcing myself to stay still. The last time I'd tried to help, I'd been pinned to the wall with my hands behind my back while Ivan lectured me on how much time I was wasting. My little outings were one thing but letting me join in the battle was out of the question.

A new sound interrupted my thoughts, like a boulder tossed in a pond, the large ripples distorting everything. My phone's ringer rose higher and higher.

No cheery tune. No funky ringtone. Just an old-fashioned ring that sent dread deep in my body. I closed my eyes and tried to will it away. It was no good.

The mayhem enveloped me. The siren. The boots. The ring.

All repetitive. All chaotic. All consuming.

Especially that fucking ring.

"Son of a bitch," I snatched the phone off my nightstand and stood. "What?!"

"Now, now, darling..." Elias crooned. "That's hardly necessary."

"Eat shit and rot." I hung up and waited.

He held out longer than before, maybe a full two minutes before ringing back from a different number. "Are you quite done with the melodrama?"

"Are ya gonna get to the point?"

"Can't a man just call his wife for a simple conversation anymore? Must everything be rushed?"

No point arguing about the *wife* bit. I'd tried several times and it did no good.

"Ya didn't just *happen* to think of me at the same time you're releasin' another horde on the city." I clenched my jaw and tapped my foot. "What's your bloody message this time?"

I just wanted to be off this phone and done with it.

We'd tried to trace the call a few times but Darren and the techno-wizards hadn't had any luck. Something about towers and signals that I didn't understand.

We'd tried to track the phones to accounts, but they were always burners or the phones of missing persons. He used a different number each time.

Granted, these little chats were the only reason I was even allowed to keep the phone. Not that it did me much good.

"You always were impatient." Elias chuckled. I set my teeth, willing myself not to take the bait. "You remember our wedding night?"

I snorted. "I remember it didn't last too long."

Okay, not the most original insult, but at least it might derail him.

"Should I have taken my time?" Elias recovered smoothly, without even a hint of irritation. "I was planning to spend all eternity getting to know you."

I scratched my arms and tried very hard not to remember any of the times he was implying. Memories I'd once looked back upon with bitter-sweet love. The simple moments lying in bed, talking before our day started. Our time together had shaped everything in me. In a way, I guess the same was true of Elias.

"If you're lookin' for phone sex, call a nine-hundred number," I retorted. "Some of 'em will give you a good whippin' for an extra twenty-five cents. So if we're done here—"

"I guess you wouldn't like to know about the girl and your detective, then."

My words became a thick lump in my throat.

"Pity, I thought you liked them." The too-quick click was a bucket of cold water.

"Wait!"

It was too late. He'd already hung up. I dialed back and the phone didn't even ring. Didn't bother going to voicemail. Just gave me that wretched, high pitch, three-tone trill before announcing the number I'd dialed wasn't in service. The phone slipped from my hands, slamming against my foot and landing on the carpet just as the electronic operator asked me to please check the number and dial again.

"Fuck!" I rushed to the closet, grabbing the first pair of jeans I found and yanking them on, under my nightshirt. I didn't bother with underwear or socks, I barely even thought to grab my coat. I snatched my boots, hopping into one at a time as I beat on the door wildly. "He called! He called!"

It was the only reason I had the phone, the only reason they'd ever open my door for me. The guard unlocked it, a look of confusion melting into shock as I bolted under his arm and into the hall.

"Wait!" The century called after me, "Ma'am, stop!"

I ignored him, bounding down the hall and into the crowd of bustling vampires. I elbowed and slinked my way through, the guard still shouting and several vampires snapping behind me. A large hand wrapped around my arm, yanking me to a complete halt. "Stop!"

My infamous snark had just sentenced my friends to their death. No way I was going to leave them unprotected. I spun, punching my guard in the gut. The thick mass of vampires and my sudden move made it hard for him to react. He bunched up in pain, bending over. I brought my knee up into his face and he finally let go of my arm. I dove back into the group, assaulted by bellows of rage as people processed what I had just done.

I'd finally made it down the hall, I could see the grand staircase that would lead to the exit.

"Stop her." It wasn't the voice of my guard this time. This voice was feminine and unfamiliar. Guess people had decided to act.

But I was almost there.

If I just kept moving, kept ahead of the crowd, I could get out. I could get to him.

My feet pounded the stairs, the space between steps giving me gaps to squeeze through the people faster. Everyone stopping to look back at the shouting behind me wasn't exactly helping. Still, I'd made it about half the way down before people started to understand.

They reached for me, becoming a sea of hands. I couldn't fight them all, so I ducked and squirmed. A few managed to nab my shoulders or wrists for a moment before I twisted away.

Someone managed to get a decent hold of my elbow before I threw it back in their throat. They let go to cradle their larynx as I hit the floor at the bottom of the steps.

The giant double doors of the mansion beckoned. Each door was framed by twin windows, lighting my path to freedom through the forest of legs and feet on the floor.

I crawled, slowly trying to make my way, unseen from my would-be captors. Some fancy high heel drove painfully into the back of my hand and someone else kicked my side.

I instinctively rolled away from the kick just as the owner of that foot tumbled on top of me. Their body weight crushed all the air from my lungs; I let it out in a pained gasp. The person was too heavy to push off and I had no leverage in my current position. The crowd caught up and the person on top of me lifted their head.

"Lily?" Cyrus' face contorted from shock to anger. "What the hell are you doing?"

"Let me go!" I tried to claw away.

The warden stood, snatching my wrists and pinning them to the small of my back. Without any support, my head slammed against the floor and my ears rang as Cyrus hauled me to my feet.

I couldn't make out what people were saying, only the myriad of shouts and that awful ring.

Finally, one voice broke through, and dread settled deep in my bones.

"What is the meaning of this?" Her voice was cool and quiet but it rang with authority. All the anarchy settled in an instant.

Nobody spoke. Everyone made room, squishing together so the Queen could take the situation in.

She wasn't very tall but her posture held a regal power, ramrod straight with her head high and her chin pointed out. Her dark pantsuit complimented the bronze tone of her skin and her charcoal hair drifted in tight finger waves to her shoulders. She looked like she was about to take over a fortune-five hundred company and still be back in time for tea.

Ritti's copper eyes were cold and calculating as she surveyed the situation.

"Lieutenant Krog, explain why the traitor is out of her room?"

"Not sure, Majesty." Cyrus straightened, making sure to lift me to an upright position. "I just... stumbled upon her."

"Did we not lock her room and station a guard outside at all hours?"

"Yes, Majesty." The guard made his way down the steps, the crowd parting for him. "I'm sorry, she pushed past me and into the crowd before I could stop her."

"I do not accept excuses." Ritti pointed one long manicured finger at me. "Even this one will tell you that. If you cannot keep your charge behind a locked door, then what good are you to this Court?"

The guard swallowed and bowed his head. "None, Majesty."

"I suggest you correct that." She turned that cold gaze on me. "Lilé, I shall give you one chance to explain this outburst."

Cyrus' grip tightened, pinning my arms tighter and stretching my muscles painfully. I winced and bit my tongue to avoid crying out. Showing weakness now wouldn't help a damn thing.

"Well?" Her single word resonated throughout the entrance, demanding an answer several times over as I struggled to control my thoughts.

"I was tryin' to get out, Majesty."

Some people gasped, and a few murmured before Ritti let out a humorless chuckle. "Obviously. What I want to know is why?"

I swallowed as the guilt settled in my gut.

"Elias called—" More murmurs and I had to speak up, "he threatened Gabe and Olive. I just wanted to help."

"Do you not see everyone around you?" Ritti waved her hand slowly to the crowd. "All these people, many of which would already be on their way if not for your disturbance, and you thought that *you* would make the difference?"

Ritti stepped forward and lowered her voice so only Cyrus and I could hear her. "Do you really not realize that kind of thinking is precisely why you are in this mess, to begin with?"

All my hope sank like a stone in water. I let my head drop with it.

"Consider your message delivered." Ritti turned about and with that the crowds rushed back to their tasks, their masses swallowing the Queen as Cyrus handed me back to my guard and he ushered me away.

CHAPTER 7

GABE

You always heard the Starved before you saw them. The sound of sneakers pounding across the ground couldn't compete with their flesh slapping rapidly on the blacktop. Their dry-husk moans echoed in the small spaces between screams.

Some crawled, their elbows in high peeks over their shoulders, like a deranged insect. Others dragged a useless limb, oblivious to the asphalt grinding their flesh. Their skin was loose and gray, decaying as their bodies had self-cannibalized in the search of nutrition. Many were already hunched over victims, their faces buried deep into whatever body part they came across first.

The massive horde only thinned as individual Starved branched from the main road into homes; cries of pain rising from each residence in a morbid chorus. The crowd didn't help. Less than an hour ago, these people bickered and debated from opposite ends of my lawn. Now they all ran with a single purpose.

Running into the danger was like swimming against the heavy current of a river. For every inch I might have gained, someone's shoulder or backpack would smack me back two.

Olive had an easier time; she was short enough to slip through the crowd. It was impossible to keep track of her.

The Starved rose and fell over her, like a tsunami crashing on a pebble. And just like that, she was swallowed whole.

I yelled for her but it was useless. I tried to remind myself that Olive wasn't a typical girl. Her training and her experience would see her through. Besides, the meager life left in Olive's veins wouldn't be enough to entice the monsters. And I didn't have time to think about it.

The city may not want me anymore but I swore an oath.

I grabbed the first Starved by its head with two hands. The decaying skin was soggy and slimy, like a rotting sponge. The thing barely had time to rasp as I squeezed. The skull was brittle, crunching beneath my grip. Dry bone sliced the back of my knuckles as brain squished through my fingers.

My next target had their fangs buried into an indecent part of their victim, the man screaming and pummeling it with his fists while his buddy tried to pull it off. The gesture was noble but useless.

I was on my way when a man with a mohawk stepped in front of me, pulled the friend back, grabbed the creature's neck, and yanked. The victim howled in pain as Cyrus broke the creature's back over his knee. "Run!"

His buddy grabbed the victim's arm and hauled, urging his friend to go as the man cried and stared at the pool of blood coming from his groin. Cyrus turned and we locked eyes.

"Where's Lily?" If the Court was here, no way Lily would be far behind.

"Still under lock and key." Cyrus turned and shot a nearby Starved. "But she'll be glad to know you're okay."

A rock fell in my gut but I didn't have time to process the disappointment.

"Shall we tackle these beasties together?" Cyrus fired again, over my shoulder this time. His grin was wicked, sending a small chill up my spine. He looked like a mad child playing whack-a-mole.

"Can't." I kicked one nearby, sending it flying with a dry hiss. "I can't be seen with you once this is over. It'll jeopardize everything"

Cyrus nodded sharply. "I'll give her your regards."

A Starved clawed my leg as he left. I grabbed its neck and threw it to the ground, stomping on the skull before moving on.

And so it went. I couldn't tell how long it lasted or even begin to guess how many I put down. It might have been ten or it may have been fifty. I just kept going, one at a time. Some of the victims I saved. Too many I reached too late. But still, I kept going, crushing, punching, kicking, and beating. If I didn't catch them off guard, the Starved would defend themselves, biting whatever skin they could sink their teeth into.

Long strands of blood dried over each of my arms, marking where I had healed. There was a huge hole in my shirt from one that had snapped at my side. Not to mention the thick layer of ash all over me, broken only by thin trails of sweat and blood.

Only the familiar strobe of red and blue could break my violent trance.

The lightbar flickered back and forth, back and forth, highlighting shadows of violence around me. The creatures swarmed over the parked cruiser, their bodies slapping loudly on the metal. Muzzle flashes brightened the front of the vehicle in uneven pops as everyone surged past it, encasing the shell in their panic. One emphatic beast was crawling through the busted windshield, oblivious to the glass shredding its internal organs.

I pushed through the crowd, bowling through the mass of bodies for several seconds before I realized I was somehow back in front of my own home; this must be the cruiser that was stationed to guard Olive and me.

Hope flooded me as I shoved through the mass of people. Was that Officer Stevens in the vehicle, still holding his own? Could I help him?

I had to toss several Starved out of my way, smashing their skulls before I could finally grab the cruiser door and force it open. My stomach sank inwards.

Stevens would never see his child grow up. He would never learn if they had their mother's insane penchant for spicy food. He wouldn't even see their first day of kindergarten.

His body was slumped against the driver's seat, like a worn-down man too tired from a long day of work. His eyes were wide open and vacant, a gaping gash in his neck matching the expression on his face.

I barely had time to register this as his partner turned her gun on me, screaming obscenities. Pain tore through my shoulder and throat before I could choke out a response. Thank god for her ignorance of vampires and the Starved still clawing at her from the windshield.

She had two targets and she'd been aiming for my heart. Just a little higher and...

I tried to tell her to calm down but my throat was in pieces. I clutched at the wet tissue out of instinct, blood trickling through my fingers. She started to scream something else until I yanked the Starved away from her with my free hand.

It writhed wildly, the windshield carving away chunks of flesh as I pulled it past Stevens' body. Long teeth snapped at my arm as I slammed its skull against the doorframe. It didn't stop and I had to repeat the action several times more before the creature disintegrated.

The officer gaped as I held out a hand, still unable to talk. She pulled away, flinching but she didn't aim the gun at me again. People and Starved continued to pelt the outside of the vehicle with heavy thumps as they crawled over the top or ran past it. Several pushed past the open door, slamming the door on me and bumping me against the frame over and over.

Another monster landed on the hood, crawling fast towards the broken glass.

Her mind was made up for her. She grabbed my hand and I dragged her past Stevens, slamming the door on the Starved's face and drawing her into the crowd. A wild idea formed in my mind as we ran against the current of chaos.

"Where are we going?" She didn't pull away, maybe some sense of duty or self-preservation reminding her about the enemy of her enemy.

I stopped on the sidewalk, just outside the human-stampede, and pointed at the oncoming horde.

"Oh *hell* no!" She shook her head vehemently

"Protect and serve," I rasped, worried she wouldn't hear me over the surrounding chaos. Her stout face scrunched in indignation.

"That's all well and good for you Vampboy, but I can't just bash things in while they try to eat me!"

I pointed at her gun and the center of my forehead.

Her frown deepened for a moment. I made the gesture again. Finally, the frown slackened as she looked at her gun than me, understanding dawning. Something heavy weighed in her mind.

I just gave her precise directions on how to kill me. She could shoot now and no one would ever know what had become of me. But I had also just saved her.

"We—" I coughed to clear the blood from my throat. "We can do this."

Her scowl returned. "Did you say that to Captain Murphy?"

"People are dying," I growled, though still raspy.

I turned my back and walked away, forcing myself not to look over my shoulder. Either she would shoot me or she wouldn't. At least jostling in the crowd would make it harder to aim her service pistol.

As I wove back into the panic, a handful of Starved launched on a mother, pinning her body over her son. "Mommy!"

I rushed forward grabbing a Starved in each fist and smashing them together before tossing them aside, not bothering to watch them burn. A third and fourth charged, defending their food as they grabbed my legs and sank their fangs deep. I tried to kick them off, when another lunged off the pile, teeth bared.

Its head exploded and the dry body slapped against me just before it crumbled.

"Okay, Vampboy." The officer shot the one gnawing my right leg. "I got your six, don't make me plug a hole in it."

My spirits rose to her challenge. She blew another's head off while I crushed the last one's skull. The mother surged to her feet, sobbing and hauling her son into her arms.

We took off in silence. It didn't take me long to realize the people and Starved were both depleting. Even still, screams echoed down every street and corner. We couldn't save everyone. But I hated myself with every door we ran past. I'm not sure why the officer followed me.

Finally, a door down the street slammed open. Olive backed out, dragging a Starved by both ankles. The creatures clawed and spat, grasping the door frame with their feeble fingers. Olive raised her arms and, with a quick snap, as though she were shaking out a towel, she dislodged the creature and smashed it against the front porch.

It still flailed, now clawing at her. It scratched and tore her pajama bottoms. She calmly pulled it to the sidewalk before whipping it around like a jump rope. The creature's skull made wet squishy noises while she swung it back and forth several times. The body started to disintegrate and she dropped it, turning cooly and striding back into the house in a quick march.

I hadn't realized we'd stopped running until reality kicked back in.

My companion gulped. "What did those psychos do to her?"

I finally found my voice and called out, "Olive!"

She turned and looked at me, still several houses away. Her hair was everywhere, she was filthy, and her pajamas were tattered ruins. But her expression was serene, filled with a subtle purpose. My whole body chilled even as I walked towards her.

A sudden roar filled the empty echoes between screams, a deep rumbling that disturbed the air. A motorcycle flew down the street, around parked cars and dead bodies, towards us. My spirits rose again.

Somehow, Lily had made it to us. I couldn't imagine what she'd said to get out of Court but she was here. We would figure this out, together.

Then all my hopes plummeted.

I'd only seen him twice, but I recognized the way he moved instantly. As though Loki, god of mischief, wound through every gesture. The bike slid to a halt in front of the house and the rider ripped off his helmet. Cillian's scarred face twisted into a horrible grimace as Olive turned to him and ran without hesitation.

"Olive!"

The officer and I bolted forward, but we were both too far away, still a few houses down.

"Freeze!" My companion raised her firearm.

Cillian condescended to sneer at her before running up the sidewalk. The officer wasn't a bad shot, but vampires are fast and she couldn't make up for that speed. A few bullets may have caught his shoulder or torso, the easiest target, but not one took his skull.

Cillian was on Olive in a heartbeat. She flattened and slid under his legs, punching straight upwards.

Cillian keeled over, holding his groin and growling, "Cheap shot!"

"No such thing." Olive turned on him. "You taught me that."

She leaped and twirled, aiming her heel for his cheek. He caught the kick. "Good girl."

He spun her by the leg and slammed her on the ground. Her body snapped against the concrete like a whip, bouncing back upright as Cillian lunged and snatched her head.

My feet finally found the lawn in front of the house, but it was too late. I saw his lips move but the words were lost in my scream.

Cillian wrenched Olive's head around and ran off, leaving his bike abandoned. I lunged forward trying to catch her. She grew weightless, her ashes sifting and slowly falling through my arms. Her hazel eyes turned gray and then those burned too.

CHAPTER 8

LILY

Banging at the reinforced steel door would only bust my hands up, wasting precious energy to heal. Pacing the hard dungeon floors made my calves ache. They wouldn't give me an ashtray, so the sink was now filled with cigarette butts. Even with the lingering smoke, the dungeon air wasn't terribly different.

All I could do was wait for bad news or torture. I wasn't sure which would be worse.

It finally occurred to me that I might want to reserve the last of my cigarettes. I'd need more than a smoke after they were done with me.

As I shoved the half-empty pack in my pocket, my fingers tangled in the drug addict's pendant. I'd completely forgotten about it, but now it was an odd solace in my isolation.

I lay on the bench-bed, letting it dangle overhead. The long chain wound in and out, like an exotic braid. The metal seemed pretty sound, maybe not gold but something pricey and hard to break. The teardrop pendant probably wasn't a precious stone, but it wasn't cheap glass.

The only way I could describe the design was hypnotic, like something I might have seen on a hippie in the eighties. There were sapphire and amethyst swirls with a tiny fleck of green and gold, just off-center. It kept staring at me, like it was daring me to discover some hidden secret.

Or was I just overthinking, trying to avoid my other thoughts?

Still, it seemed like an odd choice for a girl who died of an overdose, but maybe it had belonged to her family. Hell, maybe she'd only been recently addicted after the city's downfall. Anything was possible.

Something about the piece nagged at me in a way that I didn't understand, reminding me of that strange turn in my nightmare. Why had my brain substituted my victim's face for the overdose girl's? I'd seen a lot of violence in my time, but I'd never changed the details of a dream like that.

My thoughts were shattered as the door creaked open, the heavy metal scraping over the concrete. I shoved the necklace back in my pocket and sat up, waiting for the worst. Someone from Cyrus' squad was probably coming to take my feet to the fire.

I curled my toes and flinched instinctively when a large silhouette filled the door. Ivan looked like he was about to be tortured himself. His face was twisted in anguish, his big shoulders hunched, and he wouldn't meet my eyes.

"What?" I stayed seated, leaning on my palms, bracing for impact.

He started by telling me Gabe was fine and I knew exactly where this was headed. I should have expected Cillian would do it; he was Elias' lapdog. Somehow, that made it worse.

I didn't have the energy to cry. It must have shown, Ivan didn't ask any idiotic questions about my well-being. Just sat next to me on the metal bench and waited.

I gulped four times before I could finally say, "At least you and Ritti got what ya wanted."

Ivan sighed, his wide shoulders deflating with the gesture. "Sometimes, I forget how young you are."

I snorted in response, mostly because I had no idea where that had come from.

Ivan dragged a hand down his face, the wrinkles and jowls looking even longer for it. "Vampire age is so irrelevant after a while. But you and Alex haven't even seen five hundred years. You don't know who you are yet."

"Don't talk to me like some stupid kid." I gave him a sideways glare.

"Your sensibilities are still so human," he said like he hadn't heard me.

"And what are Ritti's? Or yours?" I thrust my chin up. "What exactly justifies murdering a girl for how she came into our world?"

"Experience," was his immediate answer. "Watch empires crumble over and over, see how the smallest decision can lead a whole country astray."

"Yeah, we've all got history," I bit out. "What of it?"

"You have your *own* history." Ivan's face still sagged. "Watching a nation starve is no laughing matter, but that's different than seeing history lapse in cycles. I saw Vladimir Sviatoslavich assemble his armies. I watched him convert from paganism to Christianity with the mind of a scholar only to defile pagan statues."

He let that last sentence fill the dungeon and echo back to me.

"Well, la-de-fuckin'-dah." I glared. "And what did ya learn from all that?"

"Nothing at first." He laughed but it was dark. "It wasn't until I saw Alexander II's mangled body that I realized how a leader's bias infects their nation. And that was nearly nine hundred years later. That's my point."

"What? That vampires still think it's cool to be vague and mysterious?"

He glared. "Good lessons need time to brew."

"Humans seem to do just fine with their limited life spans."

"Do they?" Ivan stood and looked down at me before turning to go. "How often have they tried to correct the mistakes of the past by disciplining the heirs of those choices?"

"If we're so fuckin' wise, then how come Ritti didn't come into the light?" I lifted my chin. "Seems to me a lot of fuckin' trouble would have been solved if we'd have stopped hidin' a long time ago. Maybe Olive wouldn't have even been turned in the first place!"

He stopped with his palm on the scanner, his voice low. "You really are young."

And with that, he left.

I tried to be indignant, but without someone to argue with I only felt hollow. There was an empty pit in my soul where the guilt and what-ifs ran amok.

If I'd made it out the door that morning. If I hadn't tried to go out the door and delayed everyone from getting on the scene. If I hadn't gotten snippy with Elias.

If I hadn't betrayed Elias in the first place...

It was all selfish, assuming that I could make the slightest difference. That I could have changed a single thing. I was just finding an excuse to mentally flog myself. But the misery provided the illusion of control, and in this tiny cell, it was my only cold comfort.

I barely bothered to look up when my door screeched open again. Cyrus snorted but it lacked energy. "You just had to run."

"I couldn't have left 'em."

"I told your cop something like that. He looked disappointed." Cyrus pushed the door closed with his boot and took out a large knife, flipping it in the air and catching it by the metal tip. "You know I take no joy in this."

I swallowed and nodded. "Ya don't want anyone else to have to dirty their soul."

Cyrus grimaced.

"So what now?"

He blew out a breath, juggled the knife again, and nodded decisively. "We find out if you really are the traitor."

He walked towards me with steady purpose. Only now did I review his attire. Basic black t-shirt and sweatpants, breathed better since the room didn't have ventilation. And he'd be working hard.

Then there was the tactical belt, covered in silver knives and spikes of varying size and shape, from tiny needles to a thick cleaver that would sever my arm with one swing. He'd even brought a small kitchen torch.

I gave the drain in the center of the floor a quick glance and my guts clenched. Even in Elias' dungeon, I'd never been tortured. Oh, I'd been hurt, my bones had been broken. My arms wrenched from their sockets. Hell, my throat had been slashed so deep I'd nearly died.

None of that would compare.

I'd heard the screams of Cyrus' victims before. Even in passing, I'd pitied every one of them.

This would be prolonged. It would be endless. My blood and ash would swirl around that drain but the stench of my pain would still linger in the room, thickening every day. Any relief would only serve as a reminder that more was coming.

"Let's get this over with." He grabbed my shaking arm and hauled me to my feet. I shot the heel of my hand into his nose.

I hadn't planned it, I just reacted. And that was exactly the problem. I was too terrified to think straight.

Luckily for me, Cyrus hadn't expected it either. He'd pulled back on instinct but not before I'd crushed his nose upwards. His backward momentum saved his brain. Still, getting your nose busted hurts like hell and the pain is overwhelming. It gave me a split second.

I grabbed his wrist and bit hard. It's not an ideal place for feeding, too many ligaments and tendons. But nutrition wasn't my goal.

My teeth jarred against bone but Cyrus still screamed, smacking the back of my head in blind fury even as he dropped the knife. It clattered to the ground with several rings, echoing as a chaotic bell in the concrete hole.

I threw my elbow back, not sure what I hit. Maybe his groin or his gut, it didn't matter. It pushed him back and I lunged for the knife.

My fingers graced the handle of the blade just as my head snapped back and I slammed onto my back. Cyrus held the tip of my ponytail in his hand as he stepped over my body. "Good try."

I swept my leg, trying to trip him but he skipped right over it. I swept it back on the second footfall and he toppled across me.

He moved fast, crawling towards the knife. I grabbed wildly, my hand stung as I sliced the palm on one of his tools.

I'd been so focused on the immediate threat that I'd completely forgotten about his little kit.

Just as Cyrus grabbed the knife hilt, I snatched a needle from his belt. He turned but I was faster, plunging the spike deep into his spine. It resisted for a moment as I drove between bones and into the spinal cord.

Cyrus grunted as his body became heavy, like a sack of potatoes across my body. It took several seconds of squirming to get out from under him, all the while keeping an eye to be certain the needle didn't fall out. I finally wiggled free and sat in the middle of the cell.

Well... now what?

I was already in deep shit for trying to escape. And I couldn't sit here forever.

Eventually, someone would come and they wouldn't be thrilled with what they found. It'd be even more damning. Best thing would be to just yank the needle from Cyrus's spine and apologize but... that wasn't exactly appealing.

"Fuck…" I punched the floor and swore again as several bones snapped. When they finished healing, I cradled my face and screamed my rage into my palms.

If only I'd made it out earlier…

Oh, that was a terrible idea.

I peeked between my fingers, only to find Cyrus glaring at me. The needle was deep in his spine, cutting his brain's signal to the body. Until he healed, he was about as mobile as a lump on a log. And because the blade was silver, his body couldn't push it out. That was my only saving grace here and the only reason I had time to come up with this stupid idea.

Still, I didn't see an alternative.

"I'm sorry." I crouched over him, unloading his belt.

I left the cleaver, it was too bulky for me to carry with any level of stealth. The blow torch was small and I checked it five times to verify it was turned off before zipping it into my pocket with the necklace.

His knives fit into the sleeves of my boots, though not snugly. Still, I knew how to handle them. Finally, I pocketed the needles, using two of the larger ones to spin my hair into a bun.

Grab my hair once, shame on you and what not. I also looked a bit conspicuous wearing a long nightshirt over jeans with a leather jacket.

I debated snagging Cyrus' shirt, but I'd swim in it and getting it off without dislodging the knife was a risk I didn't care to take. I didn't have a bra so I turned my back to Cyrus as I stripped my jacket just long enough to pull the nightshirt over my head and zipped the coat back up.

Finally, I crouched in front of Cyrus, tilting my head to look him in the eye. "I'll leave the door open so they find ya sooner." I tried to think of some compelling argument, but all I had was, "It's not me."

And with that, I grabbed him by the arms and dragged him to the doors. I winced as concrete grated the skin from his face but it wasn't like I could carry him.

It took a little finagling and I had to give up watching for the needle, but I finally got his palm onto the scanner. The first scan came back wrong because I had it at a funky angle. A couple of awkward attempts later, the panel lit green behind his hand and the door popped open. I set his body back on the ground and checked his spine.

Needle still in place. I blew out a breath of relief and pulled the door open, that heavy scrape announcing my escape.

CHAPTER 9

GABE

The painted bricks of the interrogation room loomed as they never had before, the old office chair felt foreign under me. The two-way mirror had become a force field, shielding me from an unknown realm I used to consider home.

I'd barely heard the officer apologizing when she took me into custody. We'd just argued at dinner. Now Olive was no more than soot on my skin. The arresting officer had offered to help me clean my hands but I'd pulled away, like she was offering acid.

I'd seen death before. After the first massacre, the remains of my father hadn't been enough to fill his coffin. Now there wasn't even anything to bury. I couldn't just wash her away.

Two detectives I'd once joked with sat me down and tried to ask questions. I couldn't respond. They took this as reserving my right to remain silent and I was grateful for the lack of proper protocol. Michelle arrived, demanding they remove my cuffs as she pulled me out of the chair. She held my elbow stiffly, moving me fast and barking orders in a tone fit for a military sergeant.

Not even the monotonous muttering of the paparazzi pen-etrated the void of my mind. Not until someone shouted, "That little bitch deserved it!"

My head snapped up and my body became stone. Michelle urged me forward, yanking my elbow with all the success of budging a brick wall. I didn't have to hunt long to find my perpetrator.

A broad man with a red face continued to scream obscen-ities. Tension built in my shoulders and neck, the weight of several hours under grief being lifted bit by bit.

The man's venom came out in spittle as he called Olive several more names in such rapid succession I couldn't follow. Probably for the best, my fists were already shaking.

Michelle hissed in my ear, reminding me not to make a scene, gripping my elbow tighter and tighter.

The man finally stopped, grinning like the host of a late night comedy show. "Whatcha gonna do about it, you over-sized mosquito?"

Something about how he said it reminded me of several conversations Lily and I had in the beginning, before we un-derstood each other. I'd been a complete prick to her, even stooping to call her a *suck head* once.

She hadn't exactly been patient with me, she'd called me on my shit and given it right back. And it had only riled me further

"Nothing." I forced my hands to slowly relax at my sides. "I don't bother with cabbages."

The borrowed insult felt awkward on my tongue and the guy's grin fell into a confused mass of wrinkles. I let Michelle guide me to the car, scolding me low in my ear.

She continued to reprimand me all the way home, the words slowly sinking through my gloom. She wasn't wrong but I didn't care.

"Does it matter? Olive is gone, we're going to lose."

At this quiet grumble, Michelle stopped her tirade. She didn't bother to argue the point and silence accompanied us for the rest of the drive.

We pulled up to my home and she ushered me through the throng on my front lawn. They tried to antagonize, question, or console me, depending where they stood on the sidewalk. It all gave me a raging headache. I was so tired; I just wanted to collapse in my misery.

But all that exhaustion vanished when we stepped into the house. I opened the door and gaped for a moment. Michelle, who hadn't expected a sudden stop, barreled into my back, swore, and then peered around me before hissing, "Get in before they see her!"

That cleared my paralysis and I rushed in, pulling Lily into my arms and burying my face in her wild hair.

Her skin was soiled but smooth against my own. The blonde curls were covered in soot and grime, and she smelled heavily of cigarettes.

But she was here.

I clung to her even as she kept whispering, "I'm sorry," against my chest

"You'd better be!" Michelle slammed the door and double-checked the windows. "Do you have *any* idea what kind of danger you're putting him in?"

Right as I started to tell Michelle to back off, Lily said, "I know, I know. Shit, I'm so sorry. I didn't know where else to go."

That single statement was cold water on the brief flame of hope. I swallowed and gently pushed myself away, holding her by the shoulders at arm's length. "What do you mean?"

I'd just assumed she'd come because of Olive, that she'd come back when things got bad. When it mattered most.

But she was the Court's captive. They didn't even let her out to fight.

The dingy scent of ash on her skin became ominous. And the way she worried her bottom lip made me want to squirm.

"Lily?" I tried to ask it gently, willing it to be something else. "How did you get here?"

She sighed, held up her hand like she was planning to stroke my cheek but changed her mind last second and snatched it back. "I broke out. They were about to..." She eyed Michelle, chewing her cheek before saying, "They were about to interrogate me. I didn't know what else to do."

"So what, you ran off from some simple questions?" Michelle didn't understand Lily's statement but I did.

The Court had warned me from the minute I found Lily that she was a prisoner of war. She may be done with Elias, but her brother was his henchman and Elias still publicly claimed her as his wife. No matter how you spun it, it looked suspicious.

They'd planned on beating the truth out of her.

Lily wiggled in my grip. "You're kind of hurtin' me."

I snapped out of it, realizing I'd been squeezing her shoulders, reassuring myself she was standing here.

"Sorry." I loosened my grip, sliding my palms down the worn leather of her jacket. Even as I processed it all, I couldn't bring myself to drop my hands.

She'd been in the Court for months now. They'd given her a bedroom as a cell and never thought to torture her before today. She'd never thought to run away before. Now, she'd not only fled, she'd taken refuge in my home. The one place they wouldn't dare follow her.

"Michelle, leave."

"I'm not leaving my client with a fug—"

"I said—" I had to keep myself from looking at Michelle as I growled. I could feel the power pulsing in my eyes, "leave."

Lily's gaze wavered. Michelle was silent for several seconds before her heels clipped across the tile entry. The door cracked open, the crowds outside shouted for only a moment before she slammed it shut. Knowing how Michelle planned, she'd left herself just enough room to slither out without showing the press my guest.

I waited until I heard the latch click before asking, "What happened?"

She looked at the kitchen floor intently. I waited.

She gulped, looked at me, then looked back down. "Elias baited me and I tried to escape."

"Well, yeah. And you succeeded." I didn't get why she was starting there.

"No." She shook her head. "Earlier today."

She pulled away and paced the kitchen, laying it all out. Waking up to the siren, Elias' call. It took everything I had not to pull her back to me as she explained his taunts, but she was an animated thinker. She needed to move.

Finally, she got to her first failed attempt and the snap decision to escape as Cyrus had threatened her.

"Wait, Cyrus was going to interrogate you himself?" It didn't track. Cyrus cared for Lily and he had subordinates. He hadn't sounded bitter about her earlier. He hadn't even hinted at the idea of what was to come. Then again, we'd been in the middle of a battle.

She shrugged, looking helpless in the simple gesture. "I don't think he could bring himself to shirk the responsibility."

"Maybe." Cyrus certainly did have a highly developed sense of duty. "But how did you get out of the Court? Those cells are locked into a hallway with yet another lock."

"Dumb luck." She rolled her eyes and collapsed into a dining room chair, slumped over the table with all the grace of a deflated balloon. "Someone left the dungeon door ajar. The rest of Court was still a mess from the earlier chaos, so I slipped into the crowd and out through the garage. Trucks were still going in and out, so I caught a ride in the bed of one. I hopped a few of your neighbors' fences, had to black eye one to forget me. Then I busted the lock on your sliding glass door to get in. I'll pay for it, I promise."

"It's fine," I snickered despite my best effort. The first time I'd met her, Lily had broken a window fleeing from the VPB. Here she was again, worrying about the most inconsequential damage she'd caused.

I went to sit beside her, scooching the chair closer and stroking her back.

"I'm sorry," she repeated after several minutes. "I've gone and made everythin' worse and now I dragged ya in with me."

"We'll deal with it." I continued to rub a slow circle over the growing knot between her shoulders.

She crossed her arms and flopped her face down, groaning into the table. "I'll try to get out of your hair as soon as I can."

At this I stopped moving. "No, you won't."

"Gabe..." She looked up slowly and shook her head again. "Michelle is *right*. If the cops find me here, you're a dead man. Your whole case hinges on ya *not* havin' conspired to become a vampire."

"And I didn't." I held her face in my hands, making sure she couldn't look at the floor to avoid me again. "Look, you were outside the law for a long time but I was in it—"

"So was Captain Murphy," she deadpanned.

"Yeah, lately, it's occurred to me just how screwed up it is. But you either believe in the system or you don't."

She searched my face for a long moment. "I'm not sure I can trust that."

"Then trust me." I laid my forehead against hers, more to reassure myself than anything else.

She took in a long breath and let it out. "We can discuss this in the mornin'. I'm too tired to argue."

I chuckled. "You must be exhausted then."

"Shove it." She slugged my shoulder but it lacked any enthusiasm. We sat quietly together for several minutes before she said, "Gabe, I'm sor—"

"Don't start again."

"No, I'm sorry I wasn't here for you and Olive."

"You have nothing to be sorry for." I sat back and ran my thumb over her cheek and chin. "Not unless you're mad I didn't come by after they slapped this ankle monitor on me."

"Of course not," she snorted. "Ya couldn't risk your case or revealin' where the Court is. Besides, I wasn't the friendliest last time we talked."

She was right; I'd called trying to help and she'd scolded me for it. I'd been too frustrated to understand she was pushing me away. She was still trying to, even now. And I wasn't sure how much longer I wanted to keep pulling her back in.

Our relationship was complex; it had potential. I just wasn't sure what kind.

Lily slowly stood and rubbed her face. "I think I need a shower."

I swallowed my reluctance to let her go and nodded. "First door on the right."

"I remember." She rose and started towards the bathroom, stopping with a hand on the doorway of the kitchen. She opened her mouth, closed it, then tried again. "I don't even have a shirt."

"I'll leave pajamas on the counter." I drew my hands through my hair. "But that's not what you hesitated to say."

She ducked her head down, but at least she didn't deny it. She just leaned against the wall and softly asked, "Did she suffer?"

It was my turn to look away. "No, it was quick. But she went down swinging."

Lily smiled over her shoulder, a single dimple showing up on the corner of her mouth even as red tears welled in her eyes. "That's our girl."

CHAPTER 10

LILY

Blood and grime swirled around the drain in a semi-translucent vortex. It was almost calming, watching the water and dirt intertwine. Eventually, it ran clear and I still didn't know what I was doing.

Everything leading me to Gabe's had been sheer instinct, even as I yanked the glass door open and kicked my boots off. The reality hadn't settled in until I sat at his kitchen table. I stood and sat several times over the course of an hour, wanting to leave, but where else could I even go?

What the hell could I say to him? What could I offer besides more trouble? I'd been on the verge of leaving when he'd come home. And all my resolve had crumbled in his arms.

I sighed and leaned my forehead against the shower wall, letting the water run down my back. The tile was warm from the water, yet it didn't feel nearly as warm as my head had been in Gabe's hands. Or my cheek pressed against his body when he'd held me.

"Fuck," I groaned.

"Did you say something?" Gabe asked quietly.

Like a complete idiot, I yelped and jumped to cover my body. There was a thick shower curtain between us and Gabe would never peek. My cheeks still stung from the desire to blush as I tried, and failed, to calmly say, "No, nothin'."

"Sorry, I was just dropping off the pajamas." A sardonic chuckle met my ears. "Do you want me to wash your clothes?"

"Um, yeah. Sure. Thanks." I was still gawking at the curtain like it might sprout the alternate universe I so desperately wanted to fall into. It wasn't until I heard the door close that I realized what had just happened.

Had Gabe seriously just offered to do my dirty laundry? In the midst of this nightmare, that simple offer seemed entirely too... domestic. And it made me feel even shittier for imposing on him. I sank to the floor of the tub and hugged my knees, trying to think.

Whenever I tried to solve one problem, one of the other million on my plate would overwhelm me. If I wasn't debating where to go, I was debating what to do next. When I realized I had no real resources, I then wondered if Gabe and I could make whatever this was work. When I realized now wasn't the time to worry about romance, I remembered everything I'd contributed to this whole mess.

Only one thing was certain; I couldn't hide in the now cold shower.

Being here put Gabe at risk and made me just as useless as sitting in the dungeon back at Court. But I was so tired, and I wasn't going to find a solution right now.

I started to shiver and my teeth chattered when I finally turned off the water and peeked around the curtain. Of course, Gabe wasn't there waiting.

He wouldn't do that, but there was something remarkably vulnerable about climbing naked from his tub to put on his clothes. As I pulled on the large shirt and yanked the pants up, I had a bit of sympathy for the night Gabe first realized I was a vampire.

He'd been drunk on my blood and needed a serious scrub. I'd had to loan him Darren's sweatpants and shirt. Much like

I did now, Gabe swam in the borrowed clothes. It hadn't occurred to me how exposed he must have felt.

Our roles were reversed for very different reasons, but I started to realize how much trust he'd put in me even in those early days. When he didn't know me and had even threatened to stake me. I wasn't sure what to think of that.

I tried to brush my hair with my fingers but it was too thick and the only thing I found was a comb that would've snapped on the first try. So I tossed the wet mass into a messy bun, further tangling it but getting it out of my way. Then I triple-checked the drawstring on my borrowed pants before rolling up the hem several times so I wouldn't trip.

Finally out of excuses and stall tactics, I exited the bathroom. The warm scent of blood made my mouth water. I'd been intending to go straight to bed; get some rest and think straight again. But my stomach growled in protest and my feet drew me directly to the kitchen sure as a cartoon mouse after cheese.

Gabe was stirring a pot at the stove, still wearing his filthy slacks and button-down. The contents of my pockets were laid out neatly on the table, the cigarettes next to the pendant and Cyrus' stolen tools. Again, that feeling of domesticity felt like an alien invader in my life.

"Smells good." I grabbed my trinkets and stacked them with my jacket and boots by the door for safekeeping. The table felt like the wrong place for them, not sure why.

"Olive has..." He took a deep breath then pressed on. "She'd been toying with different flavor combinations."

"I see." My heart seized in my chest. I wasn't ready to talk about her in the past tense. But to do anything else would be a lie and she deserved better.

"Yeah." He gave me an expression that was probably meant to be a smile but it didn't pass. He turned the stove off and filled two mugs before passing one to me.

"Thank you." I sipped tentatively. Paprika. Interesting.

"I figured escaping didn't include stopping for dinner."

We moved to the table and I tensed at the sight of Gabe's hand on the back of the chair next to me. He let out a shallow sigh before taking the seat across from me instead. Even as the rest of my body relaxed, guilt pinched the inside of my stomach.

Why did the idea of him sitting next to me again make me nervous? Was I worried that Gabe would try something ghastly, like holding my hand? It was insane, I had just been debating the idea of making this work and yet I was still pushing him away.

We didn't talk for the rest of dinner. Just sat there in a semi-awkward silence, letting everything about us, Olive, and this screwed-up world fill the gap.

When we were done with dinner, Gabe washed the two mugs and the pot. I dried the dishes and put them where he pointed. When I turned back from putting the mugs in place, Gabe gently wrapped his fingers around my forearm. I stopped, expecting a question or comment but he pulled me into his arms again.

"Can you just stay here for a second?"

The proximity made me both uncomfortable and secure at the same time. I didn't know if leaning in would lead him on, but I didn't want to pull away.

After a second, I wound my arms about him and tucked my head under his chin. "Okay."

At some point, we ended up sitting on the couch, still curled around each other.

You'd think after months of smoking, the smell wouldn't bug me anymore. But there is something very different about the scent of cigarettes and the stench of burning upholstery.

My eyes stung and watered as they popped open. I couldn't see anything through the thick red and black waves that coiled around every surface.

"Oh shit!" I wasn't sure which of us said it but we both leapt off the couch.

The fire lurched from every corner of the room, climbing up the old bookshelves and lapping greedily at the pages. It crept across the carpet, coming for us like a swarm of locusts. Long tongues of flame licked the air before us, ready for a taste. The smoke surrounded us in tendrils, wrapping around our bodies.

Gabe grabbed my arm and dove to the ground on the other side of the couch, where we'd find the only fresh air. I wasn't sure if this was leftover instinct from his human days or just trying to find a practical way to see. It didn't matter.

In this tiny rambler, the fire consumed everything and smoke billowed from every crevice as we squirmed across the rug on our elbows and knees.

Smoke and flames curled and coiled from the hallway, into the kitchen. How had it gotten so far before we'd noticed? An electric fire would have taken its time, the smoke would have woken us earlier. And why hadn't the smoke alarms gone off?

Something cracked in front of us and Gabe yelled. He rolled away from a book shelf that had crumbled to the floor, smacking blindly as fire raced up his leg. He kicked, spat, and cursed as he tried to douse it. But it wasn't doing anything.

I threw my body over his leg, hugging the flame.

"No!" He shoved at me but I held fast. My skin melted with my borrowed shirt and I screamed something inhuman.

You'll heal, you'll heal, you'll heal.

Not that this was any kind of comfort as my skin popped and blistered under the heat. When I finally let go, my flesh was raw and tender, the front of the shirt was gone, but I'd doused the flames.

"Come on!" I grabbed Gabe's collar and crawled for the door. Everything hurt and we didn't have time to move gingerly, so I was putting all my weight on the blistered skin of each palm. Just moving my arms made me wish I'd stayed in the dungeon, stretching the fresh wounds with each gesture, ripping them open over and over.

Finally, the glass door reflected a warped version of this reality. Phantom flames and ghostly wisps of smoke danced across the double-paned glass. I crawled over my stuff and reached for the handle. I was ready for it to scald my skin, but it was surprisingly cool to the touch. I yanked the door open and fell onto the patio, grateful for the cold slab of concrete. Gabe crawled over my body, dropping something with a soft thump before falling next to me.

It took several blinks before the sting left my eyes and my vision went from a mess of blurs to the vague form of Gabe. It was only then that I took in the surrounding racket.

Screams from folks out front. And sirens.

"Fuck!" I moved to stand but Gabe caught my wrist, only letting go when I yelped as he accidentally grabbed the burned skin.

He released me instantly with an apology. "What are you doing?"

"They can't find me here."

He looked at me coldly then nodded. "Fine."

Then he reached for his ankle, wrenching the monitor off with a loud beeping sound before lobbing it back into the burning house and slamming the door shut.

"What do ya think you're doin'?!"

"Let's go." He picked up something off the ground and pushed it into my arms. "Put your shoes on."

Sure enough, he'd grabbed my boots and jacket. I held them with my mouth agape. "You're not comin'."

"I'm not asking." He took off running and hopped the first fence.

CHAPTER II

GABE

We hopped the same fences Lily had used earlier, sticking to the shadows. Most people would be gawking at the sirens and fire trucks out front, but we couldn't risk being seen. The ankle monitor would be damaged in the fire and it was now a well-established fact that vampires turned to ash when they died.

I'd bought us time. For what, I had no clue.

My defense of not being in league with vampires had actually gone up in smoke. I tried not to dwell on that, focusing on hopping over the next fence. Then the next. Finally the sirens were too distant to hear as we stopped in an alleyway. The brick was rough against my back as I leaned against the wall, letting the adrenaline drain so I could finally think.

"You asshole!" Lily punched my shoulder with far more zeal than earlier. "What'd ya do that for?!"

I slowly looked at my shoulder then at her. "I think I should ask the same."

"Someone ought to smack some sense into ya! Ya just threw your court case through a blender!"

"Violence is never the answer." I pushed a hand through my hair. "You do realize the minute that house caught fire, my case was screwed?"

"What do ya mean?"

"That place will be picked over by crime scene techs and investigators. Your fingerprints were everywhere. The back lock was busted. They won't have a hard time identifying a recorded PI's prints. That alone would intrigue a rookie. Not to mention your clothes are still in my washing machine."

All the rage fell from her face and she looked at the ground. "Shite."

"It's fine."

"No, it's not!" She tossed her hands up and stomped down the alley, her boots squishing in the slush. "I should have just stayed away."

"And if you hadn't been there tonight? If I hadn't fallen asleep in the living room?"

This stopped her pacing.

"If I'd been in my room, I might not have made it out."

Even as we'd fled, it'd been hard to ignore the billowing smoke from the back bedrooms. I didn't know if it was one of the protestors or someone from Elias' side. I wouldn't put it past either one. But that fire wasn't an accident.

Lily bit her lip and her shoulders stayed hunched.

"Hey." I stepped forward and gripped her shoulders, waiting until she looked me in the eye. "I'm probably alive because we passed out on the couch."

She squirmed in my arms and I forced myself not to pull her closer. She surprised me, leaning her forehead against my chest, and sighed, "We have to move. We'll attract attention, lookin' like this."

She had a point. I looked like I was wearing a bad John McClane costume, shoeless and covered in soot. With the pajama pants and ruined shirt under her jacket, she looked like a grimy rag doll. Granted the layer of soot probably helped both our pale skins blend better with the shadows but we were not inconspicuous.

"Got any ideas?"

"Only one, though it's probably not the brightest." She backed out of my grasp slowly and walked away, apparently leading the way.

***

"That rat bastard changed my lock," she huffed. "I was paid up through January!"

"What's it matter? It's not like you have your keys."

"It's the principle," she grumbled as she crouched on the floor, investigating the shiny new doorknob of her old business. "I don't suppose ya have a paper clip?"

"Doubt it." I fished in my pockets, surprised when the tip of my finger grazed something. I pulled it out and a small chill ran through me.

"What?" Lily's face scrunched into a small mass of wrinkles.

I couldn't answer at first. I just stared.

"Gabe?" Lily stood, scrutinizing the tiny bobby pin in my palm. "What is it?"

"Nothing." I swallowed and offered it. "Will this do?"

"Not-uh." She crossed her arms. "Not 'til ya tell me what that was about."

"Just take it." I held it out a little further.

She arched a brow and tapped her foot. The small drum of her boot sounded like the hands of a clock, ticking away.

"It's ridiculous."

She gave me a look that told me I was only wasting more time.

"It was Olive's. Michelle gave it to me for safekeeping and I forgot I had it. That's it."

Lily's shoulders sagged and she stopped keeping time with her foot, staring at the pin as though it had thorns. "Oh."

"Oh," I repeated numbly. We stood there in awkward silence for several seconds before I held it closer to her. "It's just a hairpin. I'm not even sure she used it."

Lily nodded but didn't move. The last few hours had been spent ducking around street lamps and fleeing from a fire. There had been so much to occupy us. And in one second, this unexpected reminder brought Olive back to the front.

"We need to get inside." I edged the pin even closer, praying she'd take it.

Lily sighed and gingerly took it before crouching in front of the door.

It took her a couple of times, clicking through each tumbler one by one. She cringed every time she bent or manipulated the pin into a new shape. But finally, she pulled the mangled pin out and twisted the knob.

As the door creaked open, stale air wafted around us. There was barely any light coming through the window, turning furniture into silhouettes. It seemed like our feet made tracks in the dust, despite the office only having been closed a few weeks. Made me wonder if dust would plume from the futon.

Lily must have thought the same, as she ran a finger over the wood desk and sighed. "I need a drink."

She stormed around the heavy desk and yanked the bottom drawer open. Something clinked before she popped up and placed two stacked glasses on the surface. Next came a plus-size bottle of Powers whiskey.

I let out a low scoff. "A PI to the bitter end, huh?"

"The job had its perks." She unscrewed the cap and filled both glasses generously with the amber liquid. It sloshed out rapidly as she nearly upended the bottle before gently sliding one across the desk. "We can't stay here long, but one night should be alright."

"Any reason to think they didn't bug it?"

"No scratches on the new lock. Well, none before now anyway. And we're the only one's disturbin' this dust."

Made sense. At least it gave us a place to think.

Lily filled her glass twice as full as mine before coming to stand next to me, leaning on the desk and staring at the wall.

We were silent for a long time, her taking long gulps as I sipped slowly. The whiskey tasted worse than it smelled but at least it was something to do. Something other than tossing the tumbler at the offending blank wall in front of me.

"Why bother drinking if you can't numb the pain?"

"Because ya can never numb it." She swirled her glass in tiny circles before taking another full swig and wiping her mouth with her sleeve. "Being drunk was always an illusion. Like going to a movie and coming out ready to battle a dragon. You should understand that better than anyone."

I scrunched my brows when I turned to find her looking up at me.

"You've always got your nose in a book, tryin' to walk in the steps of your favorite characters. Didn't ya feel the ache of loss every time you closed the cover?"

I couldn't respond. I wanted to say my love of literature was more than just a futile attempt at escapism, to say it had all been about expanding the boundaries of my mind, into the impossible. And maybe that was true. But at the end of each chapter, when I went to bed at night...

"Is that why you started smoking?"

Her laugh was short and sad. "The nicotine just takes the edge off."

"But booze can't." I looked into the glass before me.

She sighed but it wasn't frustrated, just a slow exhale as she tried to think. "Drinking and breathing have different access points to the blood brain barrier. I've even seen a few vamps try pot over the years, but that's never really interested me."

"So, what does interest you?" After all, she had to have some kind of distraction.

"That's obvious," she snorted. "I try to be useful. I'd like to pretend I'm makin' the world a better place."

There was a bitter bite to her tone that I didn't understand. I only knew she needed some kind of reassurance. Another two sips of whiskey bit my cheek and nothing new came to mind. "You succeed."

"Huh?"

I took another swallow, coughed at the sting, and spoke up. "You do make the world a better place."

She looked at me for a few seconds before shaking her head. "If there's a cosmic balance sheet, I'm definitely in the red."

No point in arguing she'd made mistakes, everyone did and some of hers carried grave consequences. "I think you're forgetting a lot of payments."

"Like what? What could possibly balance out the shit I've done? Just look at *your* life since I stormed in." Lily downed her glass before ticking off each account on a long finger. "I've derailed your career, put you in life-or-death situations multiple times. I've made ya a fugitive, twice. And.. what the hell are ya laughin' at?"

It started as a low rumbling, just a snicker. But with every sin she'd added, it was just too ridiculous. I'd finally put my glass back on the desk to avoid spilling.

"Would ya take this seriously?" She slammed her empty tumbler on the table and crossed her arms.

"Don't break your glass," I said between belly laughs. I kept going and she kept looking like she smelled a rotten bowl of fruit. She even went so far as to arch a pale brow.

It was all too much.

My abdomen ached more with each laugh; I had to support myself with a palm on the corner of her desk.

Between red tears, I could barely make out Lily's scrunched-up face. Or the twitch of her mouth at the corner. That single dimple popping in and out of existence.

Finally, she gave in, laughing and scrunching her eyebrows in confusion as her shoulders quaked. We laughed for several more minutes before the laughter ebbed and I was able to say, "You still think you run the world."

My comment tempered her chortling. "What do ya mean?"

I wiped the final tear away and stood to look at her. "I was a cop before I met you. I have bullet scars. And being in the VPB, I was bound to come across a vampire at some point."

"But—"

"*And* who's to say I wouldn't have met one of Elias' goons? Especially with Murphy under their wing."

Her mouth hung open like she was waiting for a response to tumble out.

"Do you think any of them would have taken my insults so lightly?"

I let the question hang between us, dancing with the dust motes in the moonlight. We stared across that pale beam, examining each other before she finally said, "What about Elias?"

"He's a megalomaniac and a narcissist. What about him?"

"If I hadn't betrayed him, he might never have gone on this crusade. How many people would still be alive if not for me? How many kids like Olive would still have their innocence?"

"So your betrayal is the whole reason Elias went bad? He had no plans to do this before you married?"

She looked at her feet. "You don't understand. He was always so gentle—"

I scoffed. "And his reaction has been completely rational."

That stopped her.

"Even if he was pure as the driven snow before you met, his reaction was still a choice. He could have chosen forgiveness. He could have become the boogeyman in some cave. Hell, he could have become a monk in some mystical monastery and kept working the stock market on the sly." I pushed a hand through my hair. "But no, he's taking all those bad memories and punishing the whole of humanity."

She was still staring, though her mouth had moved several times like she was trying to come up with something to say.

"The sins of the father are the sins of the son." I looked at my feet. "I've always struggled with that passage of Christianity. I just don't see how anyone can hold the sins of previous generations. And that's exactly what Elias is doing. And you're taking all the weight of his choices while he's content to slaughter and enslave."

I let my monologue hang between us, taking great interest in the grunge between my toes.

"Have ya forgiven yourself for what you did to save me?"

The question caught me off guard and I snapped my head up to find her blue eyes wavering in the moonlight.

I hadn't told anyone about releasing the van of Starved. Even Michelle, with our attorney client privilege, had no idea. But one look in those sky eyes and it was obvious she knew. "How?"

"When I came to, you had to get a chain off my leg. Then, while we were waiting for the Court to come pick me up, you winced at every single sound the Starved made." She shrugged but it was somehow sad. "I didn't know what it meant at the time. But I've had a lot of time to think lately."

Of course she'd pieced it together.

"So, have ya?" The question wasn't harsh or accusing; I think that took me by surprise. That earnest tone held so much hope. And I couldn't deliver. If her actions, a mere lack of forethought weren't forgivable, how could mine be? I'd intentionally sacrificed countless people to save her. And I would do it again. I would burn the world just to have this dreary conversation.

I picked up the bottle and filled my glass to the brim. She sighed and downed the last droplets in her tumbler. "Where the fuck do we go from here?"

CHAPTER 12

LILY

Waking up curled against Gabe on the lumpy old futon, watching his eyes flutter open felt... wholesome. And unnerving.

We slowly untangled from one another and silently stood, stretching in the gray morning light. I yawned and Gabe ran a hand down his face before rubbing the sleep from his eyes.

Whatever this was, sharing a toothbrush was apparently still awkward. Which was just stupid.

"Seriously, we've swapped spit and you're worried about this?" I rolled my eyes when Gabe still hesitated. I nudged it closer. "I only have one."

"All this junk and no spare." Gabe shook his head and got to brushing, then tried to rinse the ash from his shirt in the tiny sink of the hallway bath.

I'd snagged fresh pants from the bottom drawer of my filing cabinet, along with some underwear. Too bad I hadn't kept an extra bra in there. The fucking things were pricey and I'd never put aside money for a spare. It felt weird without it. Guess I should have been grateful to find any of my stuff. The landlord probably hadn't even bothered with an eviction notice after I was outed online as a vampire. "Never saw the need for an extra toothbrush, but nobody likes that fuzzy feelin' on their fangs after a stake-out."

"But you kept moist towelettes and hand sanitizer?"

"Do ya know how many rubbish bins I've rummaged through?" I arched a brow as I kept watch over the hallway. It was early Saturday, so with any luck, none of the other tenants would show up.

Unless it was our usual luck.

"Metaphorically?" Gabe stopped rubbing at the gray smudge that clearly wasn't leaving his collar. His pants, burned and holy, were a lost cause so he took the pajama bottoms back now that my ass was covered.

I snorted, "We don't all have a CSI team to do the dirty work."

"Hey, I've done my share of dumpster diving. I just never needed enough disinfectant to fill a tub."

I snorted. "That stash would last a couple of weeks if I was lucky."

That feeling of domesticity settled in again and I wasn't sure what I thought of it. We still had way too much going on to settle this. Besides, you can't give what you don't have, and I wasn't even sure I liked myself.

God, Freud would have a fucking field day in my skull.

But we didn't have time for that now. We needed to get cleaned up and head out.

"Ready?" Gabe interrupted my musing as he wrung the last bits of gray water from his shirt.

I shook my head, hardly able to remember what we'd just been talking about. "Let's check the supplies while that dries. It's cold out."

His brows rose a fraction but he didn't question the sudden shift in my tone. We walked back into my old office and sat down to review the available tools. With only pockets for storage, we had to be selective about what we carried.

The knives were easy, fitting into the loops in my boots.

Gabe smiled appreciatively as he held up the two tiny flashlights. "Who still keeps these in the age of smartphones."

"Old habits. Besides, there have been many times I needed my hands free while holding a flashlight. Smartphones aren't as easy to grip with your teeth. "

"That's sanitary." Gabe grimaced as he pocketed one and handed me the other.

Thank god the landlord hadn't snatched my cashbox. I had to strong-arm it open, busting the latch to pull out the unsorted stack of bills.

I flipped through the cash quickly before laying it on the table. "A little over a hundred."

"That's it?" Gabe eyed it skeptically.

"I was expecting to be out of the office, I'd recently deposited most of it." We split it as evenly as possible. There wasn't much use for cash in the city, but you never knew. There was only about two dollars in change. We almost dismissed taking it, but Gabe pointed out it wouldn't make any noise in my tighter pockets.

The kitchen torch was small and easy enough to carry. And we might want the extra warmth. This all made sense until Gabe forbade me from using it to light my cigarettes.

"Ya really want to stress test this, don't ya?"

"Huh?"

I crossed my arms. "Just imagine an irritable vampire withdrawing from nicotine."

He scoffed and pocketed the torch. Whatever, we could debate this later. I only had half a pack left anyway. We proceeded through our limited resources until everything was either in our pockets or the rubbish. Gabe suggested I just wear the dead girl's pendant under my shirt so it wouldn't attract attention.

My skin scuttled as I held up my hair and he fastened it about my neck. Maybe I should have just left it behind, but neither of us even brought the idea up.

I let my hair fall back down and Gabe smoothed it before standing. "Okay, let's go."

I swallowed and nodded, looking around the office one final time.

It had taken years to build *Strictly Confidential Investigations* on my own, finding clients and interning with local PIs. Working around Ritti's endless and vindictive schemes to undermine me. It had been my little piece of normalcy. My independence.

My anonymity was shot. The Court's resources wouldn't back me. I'd never be able to fake all the paperwork or build anything like this again.

I'd been tired of hiding, but I wasn't sure what else to do with myself. It had been a monotonous, comfortable existence. But, I'd drop-kicked my life out a third-story window with every choice lately. While I couldn't regret a single decision, I still wasn't ready for the unknown.

I only bothered to lock the door in order to avoid the cops being called.

"Ready or not..."

We had to duck out of sight when the ground rumbled, watching as the National Guard turned a corner in their usual patrol.

We waited until the quiver of the ground subsided before nodding to each other.

"This is stupid," I grumbled, though I kept walking without hesitation.

"Neither of us are the type to sit around twiddling our thumbs." Gabe shrugged. "We might as well try to find answers."

We didn't know what we were looking for, but we both knew where we were headed. Gabe was meant to be dead and

I was on the lam. This might be our only chance. So we were going back to where everything started.

Risky, especially with Court scouting the area but there had to be a reason why the hordes started there over and over. Elias had to be protecting something. This was where my hunch came in.

"Do you think the lair is in her house?"

"It has to be close. I mean, where the hell else do the Starved keep comin' from? Those trucks aren't rolling out of Elias' ass."

I'd read every report on the first wave he'd released, forcing poor Darren to print everything and run it past security before handing it over. It must have cost him hours but I couldn't help myself. I'd been one of those creatures, ready to kill in my blind need for blood. If not for Gabe and Olive...

It was the darkest version of the most basic question. Where did we come from?

And I needed an answer.

"Alright, but you said this place was huge." Gabe pushed a hand through his hair and scanned the road with his eyes, reading his innermost thoughts in the air. "So we need a hidden building that's very tall, very ornate, and has storage for several trucks in the middle of a low-income neighborhood."

"Ya see why I didn't tell Ritti?"

Gabe's eyes kept scanning, but he nodded.

Rockwood couldn't hide the grandeur I'd glimpsed, every wall covered in art and tapestries that would make museum curators drool with balconies to make the whole living area feel open.

Sticking a building like that in this neighborhood would be like tossing the Mona Lisa in a stack of children's finger paintings. Both might be charming but there would be a noticeable difference.

We turned mechanically, following each other into the dark. Our shoes squished as we passed several dingy and busted bars, and one of those self-storage places that seemed to be thriving in the broken city. Made sense.

People scrounged every penny they could, even if it only gave them a place to stash their stuff, away from the elements. Plus this one still had moving trucks behind their big gate. That was a luxury very few could afford and everyone dreamed of these days.

Especially near Rockwood.

We finally came back to the residential area, passing a few more cheap apartments, then several houses, until we stood on the disheveled lawn. Gabe gulped audibly. I stayed quiet.

Seeing this place had jostled me, but I certainly hadn't died here.

CHAPTER 13

GABE

The dilapidated details were more crisp in the daylight. Miss Stafford's house was so flush with the ground it looked like a tumor, growing directly from the earth. I slowly scanned, trying to take in everything at least twice before squaring my shoulders and marching forward, Lily directly behind me.

The inside was even worse. The foul scent of decomposition covered everything, intensifying the gruesome nature of the place. My gaze naturally fell on the deep brown stain near the couch. I knew it was mine but that didn't feel right. It took several moments before my sight drifted the extra few inches, to a spot clearly soaked with new blood.

I gave Lily a weary look. "Something you want to tell me?"

She let out a heavy sigh.

"Just a little friendly fire." She rubbed absently at her temple but put her hand down when she caught me looking.

"That close?" I scrutinized the spot, like I might find a wound.

Lily glanced away. "I wasn't tryin' to hide things."

"I know." There'd been a lot going on. We'd hardly had time to catch up. But still...

"Cyrus was just escorting me around Rockwood." Lily shrugged. "Tryin' to lure Elias out."

I balled my fists as she quietly explained what had happened. Yes, I understood the logic. With Elias taunting Lily, he was showing his weakness. The Court was smart to exploit that. And it made me want to go find a fight. We stood in silence while Lily shuffled on her feet. "Do ya want to know more?"

I blew out a breath and shook my head. "Just wondering how much carnage one house can take."

Lily snorted. "Some places just feed on violence."

I nodded numbly and stepped forward, taking stock of the damages, old and new. It was a strange sensation, walking into a murder scene where I was one of the victims.

Lily followed slowly, analyzing my face. "Do ya miss bein' a cop?"

She closed her mouth hard, like she was trying to eat the question.

"Not really."

The answer surprised me and it took a moment to gather my thoughts. She didn't push.

"I haven't really had a chance to miss it, with everything else going on. But..." I walked into the kitchen and closed a swinging cabinet door. "I think I miss the certainty."

Who was I if not an investigator? What purpose did I serve in this world? I looked up and was startled to see my feelings reflected in her eyes. The same look I'd seen as we'd left her office.

We both stood silently, letting it sink in. Even if we got through this, what would we do on the other side? Who would we be? And that was excluding the fact that we were both fugitives in every sense of the word.

Maybe that's why we'd come here. One last case to solve.

"One day at a time," I muttered and started to look around again. "Alright, you know vampire architecture better than me. If you were trying to hide a three-story secret lair...."

She shook her head and twisted her lips in thought. "I would have said one of the rundown apartments we passed..."

"But?"

"Someone would have walked in the front door and spotted everythin'. Sure ya could disguise the lobby but someone would eventually look through a window and they couldn't control every small kid that wandered by to get a lost ball."

"They would have been discovered."

She nodded.

"What about the dungeons?"

"What about 'em?"

"Well—" I opened the pantry and started pushing boxes aside, "court keeps dungeons underground. Even Alex's rehab center had a hidden entrance to an enclosed basement."

"But this place wasn't a dungeon. I mean, okay the bottom level was, but everythin' else was extravagant."

"Were there any windows?"

Her face scrunched in thought.

"Now that you mention it, no... I didn't see a lot of the place, but he didn't even have 'em in his library. I thought it was weird but..." She paused as I rummaged. "What're ya doin'?"

"Looking for a secret entrance." Most of the containers I moved were cleaning supplies. Lots of Clorox wipes and bleach, almost exclusively floral scents. I suppose it made sense I wasn't moving coffee cans or soup, considering where I was. It was just strange she took so little effort to camouflage herself. Guess she'd never expected company. Then again, humans would have presented little more than fresh take-out. Which all made her bulk-size tin foil a little confusing.

I leaned back out of the pantry, scanning the now visible crevices. "There's no visible foundation or window wells from the outside, so you'd think there isn't even much as a crawl space."

"Therefore, any second level would have to be hidden."

"Yeah, and I doubt she'd want to take her meals on the main level." I motioned to the front window then drew a hand through my hair and tried to think. Lily's basement had been hidden with a palm scanner, but I didn't see any such screen.

"Everyone needs their cable repaired or a dishwasher replaced." Lily squeezed past me, into the pantry, her back pressed against my chest as she ran her hands along the interior walls. "Even a morally corrupt vampire can only black-eye so many before people would notice everyone who came in went missin'."

And service people might see the open pantry.

"Ah." Lily smirked her single dimpled grin and pulled on something low with a thick click.

Something in the walls groaned, like an engine trying to start in the bitter cold. Lower, something else rattled like a chain rotating over a mechanism, and a dark hole opened to our right.

"Talk about old school." She snorted, pulled out her flashlight, snapped it on, and walked down the newly revealed stairs. "We haven't used this method since the bootleg era."

I walked behind her, a little unnerved by the growing scent of bleach.

CHAPTER 14

LILY

The light switch at the top of the steps clicked uselessly three times before I gave up. Not surprising, there wasn't anyone left to pay utilities and I doubted preserving the crime scene was top priority with the city going to hell. We were just lucky the door was built with some kind of touch-latch or we might never have gotten in.

Each step creaked under my boots as I scanned everything with my flashlight. The air grew stale and sanitized, the scent familiar and ominous. Alex's rehab smelled just like this; cleaning products with the undercurrent of rot. But given the residence, I rather doubted anything so charitable was behind the stench.

Gabe took more time behind me, his beam floating around me in a far more methodical way. I fought every urge to turn around or warn him. He was an experienced investigator, whether he knew it or not. And he'd seen his fair share of crime scenes. I still braced myself as I made it to the bottom.

Everything was a wash of rust and death.

Red soaked every bit of concrete in long trails and huge splatters, all in various shades of decay. She hadn't bothered to have a drain installed in the floor. Instead, Miss Stafford had opted for a glass-top dining table and metal chair, both shining like new. On the back wall was an old chest freezer, with a curved structure and teal color that belonged to the fifties.

A hand landed on my shoulder and I jumped before remembering I had a partner this time around. My misery was grateful for the company.

Gabe urged me forward gently and I stepped to the side, letting him take everything in. He absorbed it in a different pattern, first highlighting the chest, the walls, and lingering on the table.

"Feeds on violence." The tiny room held his words and gave them back in faint echoes, like the soft voices of the dead. "How did your people miss this?"

"Police and media were camped out front for months, keeping the vandalists and Renfields out." I walked around the table and shoved my free hand into my pocket. "We can only black eye so many people at a time."

Miss Stafford had meticulously cleaned every inch of the table; streaks shone in the glass top and there wasn't so much as a spot on the legs. My reflection stared back at me from the table, disturbed by the ghostly beams from our lights. Blood can be removed from concrete, it only requires some elbow grease and hydrogen peroxide, every vampire knows this. She'd kept her dining area neat and still left her victim's blood to paint the walls.

In the short time I'd met the old bat, it was like Jeffrey Dahmer was trying to hide in Betty Crocker's skin. This house was just like her soul, all gaudy floral patterns and ugly old-lady taste up top, hiding the macabre butcher.

There was a thick suction sound and then a reek that made my stomach roll inwards.

"Dear God." Gabe's body was tight as he looked into the freezer. One arm held the chest top open, shaking with all the weight of a car. His jaw popped several times as it moved back and forth. He just stared, not even bothering to cover his nose with a sleeve.

I closed my eyes and tried to prepare myself before walking over. What a useless activity.

Miss Stafford had closed Kimberly Ashland's eyes, but the girl's expression was not peaceful. Even in this rotted state, the green and gray skin swollen and bloated, she managed a grimace. Her hair looked even bigger without a neck or shoulder to measure against. I only recognized her because she still wore those big-bug glasses. Of course, I doubt I'd be happy if my head was one rotting part of a foil wrapped pile. Gabe scanned the contents, his light bouncing off the remaining foil to reveal at least a dozen more parcels. Some smaller, maybe hands. Others large enough to be a torso or legs.

I had to look away. "Why would she keep this?"

"She loved Kimberly." Gabe let the lid fall shut with a thick slam. "In the voicemail they left for us, the girl was mesmerized to hold still while she died and Stafford still apologized."

Gabe's scowl deepened and he closed his eyes. Was he trying to block out Kimberly's screams?

The odor lingered and we decided not to, exiting the basement far quicker than we'd come into it. I found the catch in the pantry and pressed it back in place. The chains groaned and the cavern closed. The dim light of day felt cold.

Kimberly had been a nutty little twit with a serious blind spot for the company she kept. Hell, the last time I'd seen her, she'd been cheering for my death. But nobody deserved that.

It was a long time before Gabe spoke. "Show me the girl."

"Haven't ya seen enough for one day?"

"If you don't want to see her, then point the way."

I sighed and rubbed my eyes. She'd be even worse than before, we could smell the rot coming in. Still, I couldn't bring myself to back out and let Gabe see that by himself.

"Follow me." I walked past him and went through the kitchen doorway, down the hall, past the hallway bath, and leaned against the bathroom doorframe. There wasn't enough room for both of us. That's what I told myself, anyway.

Gabe screwed his face into tight containment, kneeling at the edge of the soggy carpet, tilting his head this way and that in slow, methodical patterns. "Did you check out the body?"

I shut my eyelids tight. "We didn't have time."

He made a *hmmm* sound that was neither confirmation or disagreement before he leaned in closer. "She has track marks."

My eyes popped open and I peered in. "Yeah... the syringe is right there."

"No." Gabe plucked a wash cloth off the sink and gently held her arm to the side. "I mean, bite tracks."

I squinted into the dark and spat out a curse. He was right, up and down her arm were clear bite marks, the distinct four-puncture pattern of fangs.

"What the hell?" I kneeled lower and tried to get a better look. There were tons. The image reminded me of that shift in my nightmare. Was this what my subconscious had been hinting at?

"I don't know. Maybe she's one of Elias'..." Gabe let the sentence stop. Neither of us wanted to use his livestock terms.

"But then, what's she doing here? And how'd she get hold of the drugs?"

"Not sure." Gabe slowly lowered the girl's arm. "Did you look through the rest of the house after you were shot?"

I shook my head. "Didn't think it'd be good manners to stick around."

"Let's see what else we can find. Those kids and this body are too big a coincidence to ignore."

CHAPTER 15

GABE

A couple hours turned up a whole lot of nothing. We even pulled out several drawers, only finding Stafford's billowy dresses and expensive perfumes. Despite her *little old lady disguise* and tacky floral furniture, it was all high-end quality, like she wanted to stand out from the repetitive background.

The kitchen only revealed a surprising number of plates, knives, and other kitchenware. Based on her basement, I didn't understand her keeping such a collection.

"Might have been for her Renfields." Lily slammed the cabinet hard enough that it bounced back open. "We still have to figure out where we're goin' to stay."

I nodded and leaned against the wall. "We can't go to Harper's. It'll compromise him."

"Too bad, I could really use his laugh about now." She leaned against the counter. "What about Michelle?"

My eyebrows merged.

"What?" She squirmed. "You've got attorney-client privilege there."

"Yeah, and the news is camped outside her house." I shook my head. "Trying to get quotes and updates on the case. Probably even worse with me gone."

"Fine." She tossed her hands up. "Where do you fancy we crash?"

As though on cue, a heavy *wallop* echoed down the street as vibrations hummed up through our feet. A low rumble, like a dragon rousing from his slumber.

We stared at each other, waiting. True, Portland experienced earthquakes, maybe twelve a year. But this wasn't the same sensation. Not unruly enough. And we were in a supposedly abandoned part of town, the roads too full of trash for even the National Guard to patrol.

The rumbling grew and we went to the windows.

My stomach instinctively sank. I could never forget the deep blue of these trucks. They were featured prominently in one of my worst memories.

"Lilé..."

Lily's body clenched as her human name crackled through a loud speaker, the truck coming ever closer.

"Lilé..." Her brother drew the old name out again, letting it drift along the December air. "I know you're in there."

Lily spat a curse and started to march towards the front door. I grabbed her elbow. "You know it's a trap."

"We both know he's not alone." She nodded towards the back door. "You can escape, while he's still pulling up."

"We are not doing this again." I held her arm tighter. For all I knew, I was bruising her but right that moment I was fine with it. Just so long as she stayed.

"Did ya want me to come find you, sister dear?" Cillian chuckled darkly as the high pitched squeal of brakes tore the air. "I was always partial to hide-n-seek."

"Do ya really see an alternative?" She hopped on her feet, ready to run.

"Yeah." I pulled her further into the house. "We make them work for it."

Just as I finished my sentence a heavy, metal thud echoed around us accompanied by the dry-husk rasping of the Starved. My insides ran icy and Lily tensed in my grip.

"I'm not so certain my teammates will have any luck findin' *you* though." Cillian *tsked*. "Be an awful shame if they got distracted."

"Gabe..." Lily whined, tugging but not pulling away. My mind raced.

"Why is he putting so many resources into recovering you?"

At this, Lily stopped, her mouth agape.

"I don't know how he found you here but that took effort." I forced my mind to work, doing what I could to ignore the greedy noises of the Starved, growing more persistent with each passing moment.

"He considers me his." Lily pulled again, pleading. "He's not the man I married anymore."

"So he sends a whole truck of Starved just to coerce you? It doesn't make sense." I yanked her back and headed towards the door. "Not unless he's scared of you."

That halted her protests.

"Stubborn as ever." Cillian's tone was less playful now. "I'm goin' to count from three."

As the countdown started, I placed my hands on her face and stared into her blue eyes. "You have something. I don't know what, but it's something that threatens him. You can't give up."

She shook her head. "'I can't take any more lives on my conscience."

"Two..." Cillian drew the word out in a weary tone.

I swallowed and kissed the top of Lily's head. "I'm sorry."

I shoved her into the kitchen and booked it.

I barely heard her hiss, "Gabe, no!"

But it was too late. I was on the front lawn, hands up, and praying Lily wouldn't come after me.

CHAPTER 16

LILY

All I could do was watch in horrified fascination, crouched behind a curtain covered in mold and stinking of old piss. What the hell was Gabe up to?

Cillian wasn't going to stop just because he had a hostage. Though my brother looked rather entertained. "What are ya playin' at?"

"No game." Gabe had his hands up.

"Then can I assume she'll pop out of your pocket?" Cillian peered around Gabe, as though he was waiting for a magic trick. The vamps behind my brother might have snickered, but it was hard to tell with the Starved's hungry groans.

"It's just me." Gabe sounded so much calmer than I felt. Every muscle ached with the urge to run but if I went out there, Cillian might just kill Gabe. He was here for me and Gabe's legal case posed a rather large threat to Elias.

"Please." Cillian shook the idea away, and snorted. "Ya were together during the house fire; no way you'd let Lilé wander off on her own."

"Maybe, if you hadn't turned her to ash." Gabe managed to make a choked sound around the words.

Cillian paused, squinting, then stepped forward, letting his rifle hang loosely from its strap and digging into Gabe's pockets without any notice.

Gabe pulled back but the other vamps behind Cillian all trained their weapons on his head. My brother's grin was so wicked, his scars curled with it. "I'm not gettin' fresh with ya, big boy."

I could only imagine the irritation in Gabe's face as Cillian emptied his pockets, tossing our meager supplies to the ground.

"Liar," Cillian snorted before shouting, "Spread out, she's somewhere in the house."

"Shite." I looked around wildly. I was in enemy territory. Even if I hid in the secret basement, Elias would have installed it. They would know about it. I didn't have long to think as people approached the house and something creaked at the back door. "Double shite."

I sprinted to the pantry, my body slamming into the frame when I skidded across the floor in my haste. I bit my tongue to hold in a cry of pain just as something shattered in the front. I'd barely scrambled under the lowest shelf, next to the Lysol cans and a giant mop bucket, when boots thumped throughout the house.

Fuck, fuck, fuck. Adrenaline was rushing through every nerve and sense, making it impossible to think. I was one woman against armed men. What was I going to do in this pantry, wash their mouths out with soap?

A black boot fell into view. Smaller than I'd been expecting.

Great, Cillian had brought his little kiddy soldiers. I'd been so focused on Gabe, I hadn't even noticed. I wasn't sure if I was relieved or enraged.

While they were smaller than me, I'd faced these little brats before. They were well trained and could still overwhelm me. The tiny boots marched into the kitchen announcing that the cabinets were clear. Another voice joined the first but I couldn't figure out what they were saying. It was like they were talking past a mouthful of cotton.

"What?" The first voice chided. "I couldn't make that out."

An annoyed grunt from the second voice.

"Oh, are you trying to say something?" I was pretty sure the first voice belonged to a girl. Girls have a particular tone when they are taunting someone.

Another annoyed grunt followed by stomping that came closer and closer. In the doorway to the pantry, a scrawny silhouette turned around and pointed directly into my hiding place.

"What?" The bitchy little girl flounced past the grunting boy, her ponytail swinging wildly. "Sure, the boss's wife is hiding with the canned goods."

The boy sighed heavily and rubbed at his face, before turning around and clicking the button of a flashlight. It skimmed over everything in my surroundings. My muscles tensed and I slowly curled my fingers over a can of Lysol. It wasn't exactly mace, but it was all I had. Maybe I could surprise the kid and b-line it out the back.

If they caught me, Gabe was doomed. I had to get out of here and find help.

The light blinded me and I pointed the can in the kid's direction. In my haste, my finger slipped from the spray nozzle. I started to scream just as a tiny hand slammed over my mouth. My eyes widened as the kid held a finger over his lips. "Shhhh."

It was the only thing Ronald had ever said to me. Not exactly shocking, seeing as he didn't have a tongue. But I was too stunned to reply.

I hadn't seen Ronald since Olive had double-crossed us, handing me over to Elias. I'd just kind of assumed she had killed him or he was back in their ranks. But here he was, his scrawny face etched with worry. He looked over his shoulder as his comrades tore the house apart.

It was an awful ruckus, drawers being thrown to the floor and furniture being tossed about. Ronald looked back at me, removing his palm slowly and backing up. He held out a hand, as though begging me to wait before he started pulling the pantry apart.

Cleaning supplies and foil quickly littered the floor, some of it slamming on top of me. It took a minute for me to get it. He was covering for me, literally. His team was ransacking the house, he had to make a good show of it.

God knew why he was helping; I hardly knew him. But I wasn't going to argue about it either. Finally, I was covered in crap, barely able to see the blurry silhouette of Ronald through a tub of wipe and a slowly leaking container of Swiffer wipes with some sickly floral scent.

Ronald hunted in the closet for only a moment before the secret door opened and he ran into the hall, loudly grunting and pointing towards his find.

His team ran to us and then followed him down the steps. At the bottom, I could hear them giving him a hard time for finding nothing but rotted meat.

Every muscle in my body coiled, and I had to restrain myself with each set of boots that marched past me.

Cillian started swearing and shouting outside. "Alright, pretty boy. You're coming with us."

I set my forehead against the ground, letting the still-leaking cleaning fluid flow over my neck and hair, diluting my tears as the engines roared to life and rolled away.

I didn't know how long I waited in the pile of cleaning supplies, but eventually, I had to get up. The pool of Swiffer juice had started to sting my eyes.

It slowly occurred to me how lazy Cillian had been. He should have come into the house, checked everything for himself. It was like he'd just given up, taken the consolation prize.

Now I was skulking through Rockwood, sneaking around, and following their trail.

That nasty muck Oregon had to accept for snow made it easy, even from a distance. Was this Cillian's plan? Was he using Gabe as bait?

Maybe. He'd found me. He'd been certain I was at the house, so driving off like this seemed too easy.

Still... Gabe wouldn't even let me go into their custody. No way I could just leave him.

CHAPTER 17

GABE

C illian cuffed me and secured a bag over my head before tossing me in the back of the truck. Habit made me worry about air for the first few miles. When I realized my lunacy, there was only a cold comfort.

What now, genius?

It wasn't like I could call for backup. My only company was clawing at the walls, falling over each other with each turn or bump in the road. Guess I should have just been grateful these things didn't crave undead blood. None of them so much as tried to chew on me, but listening to their hungry noises in the dark was still unnerving.

I squirmed and flipped, trying to get off my stomach without hitting any of them. All the while, the creatures hissed and spat, like angry jackals. I kept waiting for something, the anticipation winding me tighter as I blindly flopped in the dark.

I finally made it to my knees, only to be tossed backwards by a sudden brake, slamming into one of my undead companions before hitting the side of the truck with a metal thud. I slowly slid down the wall with a pained, "Oof."

Those things still crawled over my legs but at least they weren't sitting on my neck.

The drive wasn't long, maybe fifteen minutes. It was impossible to track the turns; the Starved kept jostling me, making me lose any sense of direction. One of them crammed a knee or elbow into my neck. Pain slammed through my spine as I bucked wildly to get it off me. Not an easy task with my hands bound behind my back in a rocking vehicle.

The only thing breaking this undead tedium was the occasional pothole or a shout from the cabin, but I couldn't make out anything through the noise around me.

I tried to think of my next play but I could plan about as well as I could see. There was no way to track our location and even if I could, who would I relay it to? Cillian had kept me alive to lure Lily, but Elias might not agree with the assessment. He might just plug a hole in my head and be done with it.

It would certainly be an explosive end to my court case. Not that it held much hope without Olive. Michelle had been right to focus on the wayward orphan.

My brash actions had only expedited my execution.

Finally, the truck lurched to a halt and the vibration stopped.

Guess we were here.

The hollow thump-thump must have been the truck doors opening and closing. Voices rose slowly, fading in and out under the hungry hissing next to my ear. I tried to listen for anything useful but I only caught partial words. Neck. Track her. Movers.

Great, I'm sure I'd save everyone with that explosive bit of intel. Something clinked and snapped at my back. Too late I realized it must be the lock and latch for the truck, which meant I was leaning against the–

I tumbled backwards, the top of my skull cracking on the ground. The laughs of my captors bounced off the surroundings, echoing in my skull and compounding the pain. Were we in a parking garage?

If only I'd said something clever to wipe the presumably smug grins from their faces. But all I could do was groan, unable to even cradle my aching head.

"Of course, he has a hard head." Cillian was still chuckling as he lifted me by one arm. "Explains how he put up with my sister."

I slammed my head backwards, connecting with something sharp, and Cillian threw me into the side of the van, swearing and spitting. "Fucker hit me in the mouth!"

His voice sounded strange. Maybe he'd bitten through his tongue. The idea made me grin despite the blistering headache pounding through my skull. Something slammed into my ribs and gasped.

"Think you're smart?" He grabbed my hair through the bag and lifted my head at an unnatural angle. "Just wait until you've run out of your usefulness."

CHAPTER 18

LILY

They'd have seen me if I didn't maintain my distance. The roads were covered in this nasty mush, and the truck's tires were huge. So I followed the tracks, making sure to slow down any time I could hear the engine ahead of me. When I came to a large intersection, everything became muddled.

The whole place was filled with tire tracks in various sizes. Worse yet, the newest treads came from the wrong direction.

"What the..." I looked up the road and immediately saw the problem. The moving company and self-storage center we'd passed on our way in.

My trail was muddled by the suddenly booming moving business.

I spun wildly like I might summon a new clue with some mystic dance. All I did was mishmash the tracks with boot prints. "Fuck!"

All the while, Gabe was going through lord knows what. Only I knew he'd survived the fire, let alone that he'd been taken hostage. And I'd lost the fucking truck.

Cillian had all but outright admitted he'd started the fire, which made this the second time he'd tracked me down in just as many days. But I couldn't even follow this big ass truck in the snow.

"Where are ya, you giant asshole!?" I screamed down the street. "Come and get me!"

My own voice echoed and faded, leaving me completely alone. I sank to the ground and hugged my knees, trying to ignore the cold slowly seeping into my jeans.

Shrieking like a banshee wouldn't help anyone. It was stupid and would only serve to get me captured. But what could I do alone?

Nobody had found Elias' hidey hole and it hadn't been for lack of trying. All I had to follow were some slowly melting, and then abruptly vanishing, tire tracks. Plus the knowledge Cillian was somehow tracking me.

Something nagged the back of my mind, like an obnoxious kid yanking on the tip of my ponytail. Cillian couldn't be tracking me by phone, I'd left all electronics back at Court. But somehow, he'd known where I was.

What could I do with that? What could I do with any of it?

I couldn't stay in the road forever but where was I supposed to go? There was no office to camp out in and no friends to heckle me at home. No home at all. It almost made me miss my luxury prison cell.

None of my friends were comfortable at Court. That was the biggest reason Alex was pissed.

He was tired of being relegated to the background, wringing his hands every time I decided to throw caution to the wind. Maria and Darren were more forgiving but Alex had dealt with my shit a lot longer. How long before they all jumped ship? Could I really blame them?

All of this just compounded the loneliness writhing in my gut.

I couldn't save Gabe alone. Going back to Court was the obvious choice but also the worst. They'd toss my ass back in the dungeons. Probably assign someone I didn't share a history with to interrogate me. And none of that guaranteed they would search for Gabe.

Human authorities were also out of the question. They'd shoot to kill and never even bother asking questions. Plus, even if they did believe me, and magically decided to suddenly help Gabe, they'd be slaughtered.

The only option made my teeth clench until my jaw ached. Going there would put him in harm's way and jeopardize his job. I couldn't.

But there wasn't an alternative.

I sighed, stood, and started down the street. Hopefully, Gabe would forgive me later.

CHAPTER 19

GABE

Covering my head in the truck might have been overkill, but it was an understandable precaution. Leaving the bag on my head in the cell? That reeked of petty vengeance.

No light filtered through the flimsy plastic, so the room must have been dark. At least they'd secured my hands in front of me, allowing my shoulders to relax a little, even though they were chained to the floor. The awkward angle only let me stoop or sit. The forced posture left a nagging ache in both my legs. Laying down was useless, it only made my sides hurt too.

It was impossible to even mentally escape. Whether I was trying to imagine the ending of my book or remembering my last night with Lily, the growing aches throughout my body kept drawing me back to the present, forcing me to slowly steep in the unknown.

There was no way of telling time; I might have been here hours or a whole day. The occasional clatter or clang outside my cell would heighten my senses, every muscle clenching at the possibilities.

Once in a while, there was a specific rattle, as though someone was rolling up an old garage door by hand. One of the

Starved would hiss and spit while the guards would laugh, debating what part of the creature they should poke.

One was dumb enough to shoot for entertainment. The bullet snapped off the concrete and ricocheted off something metal before the shooter's companion started shouting. "You idiot, Captain is going to see the hole!"

"So what?" The shooter snorted. "Not like he plays gently with the crypt keepers."

Their voices were small. Must be a couple of the child-soldiers. A sharp slap resounded through the hall.

"Youch! What'd you do that for?"

"Captain's gonna know we wasted ammo, you big idiot." The first kid's voice grew fainter, like he was muttering while walking away.

"Hey, wait up!" That rattly-door noise came back before the second kid started to run down the halls. Their receding footfalls echoed over and over, bouncing off the concrete into oblivion.

Something in my surroundings felt familiar but I was too groggy to figure out how.

The sluggish train of my thoughts was completely derailed when my own cell rattled open, light weekly filtering through the sheer plastic over my head.

"You're more interestin' than I gave ya credit for." Cillian's tone was laced with something unfamiliar. I didn't have time to identify it before he pulled at my chains, apparently unlocking them, and yanked me to my feet. "Boss wants a word."

He pulled me along, jerking my restraints left or right to guide me, only speaking when there was a step or he needed me to pause. There was a pensive nature to his silence. As though a single word might shatter everything. Others snickered and commented along the way but Cillian barely offered a sarcastic response to his comrades.

We stopped and he wrenched the bag off my head. I had to blink several times before my eyes could adjust. His gaze was stone, the mismatched eyes emitting something that made my guts clench. He leaned in close as he unlocked my manacles, hissing. "Watch what ya say."

I hardly had time to absorb the comment as he jerked an elaborate wood door open and shoved me inside. My mind raced and my eyes still stung. It was easy to recognize the library from Lily's description. Two stories of tightly packed shelves. Covers ranging from worn leather to modern print, becoming obscure as the shelves rose higher and higher.

"I'd apologize for your accommodations, but I rather doubt you'd believe it." The speaker waved a long, imperious hand as he stood, flipping through a book on his large desk. "Being at odds doesn't mean we can't be civil."

"I'm your hostage," I scoffed. "Isn't it a little late for that?"

He chuckled as he turned, leaning casually against the desk with a wine glass, filled to the brim. "I see you share my wife's propensity for blunt honesty."

The note of approval in his tone made my stomach convulse. "Pretty sure she's asked you to stop calling her that. Repeatedly."

"Old habits." Elias shrugged, the simple gesture at odds with the rest of his waistcoat-and-pocket-watch ensemble. "Please have a seat, Detective Collins."

I debated my chances of killing him. The heavy boots thumping up and down the halls reminded me of his back up. My hands clenched, the knuckles turning white. He was here, right in front of me. A couple steps and I could ring his throat. But Cillian was closer and there was an army just outside the door. It wouldn't be a sacrifice, but suicide.

It might still be worth it.

I crossed my arms. "I'd rather keep this short."

He studied me over the glass of wine, dark brown eyes weighing something in me without comment.

I'm not sure what I'd expected Elias to look like. The dapper gentleman routine and English accent closely aligned with

Lily's description, but somehow, it didn't fit with all the chaos and destruction he'd wrought on this city.

"I'll get to the point then." Elias put the glass down and steepled his long fingers before him. "I'm curious. And I doubt very much I'll have the chance to sate this curiosity again."

"Because I'll be dead?" What was it with me poking the bear? Especially when the bear always seemed to be an angry vampire ruler.

Elias cracked a big grin. "Not by my hand. You're far too useful."

I felt my brows creep towards each other but managed to keep my mouth shut.

"Simply put Detective, Lily has changed quite drastically. I'm not sure what I expected but the woman I married is no longer in existence. I'd like to understand the new values she has so readily embraced."

Seriously, this guy wanted to gossip about our common... *connection* with Lily? That made no sense. The city was in ruins thanks to him and he was hyper-focused on his lost love?

"Why would I tell you anything?"

"Oh, I'm sure you'll cooperate." Elias motioned to the plush chair across from him. "In the meantime, I'd rather you be comfortable."

My eyes rolled before I could stop them. "Is that a poorly veiled threat of torture?"

"Not at all." He waved the notion away. "I can't risk harming my greatest asset, after all."

Asset. Huh?

I eyed him for another moment before walking forward and collapsing in the chair. "You do realize that even without me, she'd still refuse you."

Maybe I should try to kill him after all, since I was going to get myself beheaded anyway.

Elias' mouth ticked up at the corner. "I don't fancy this to be some ridiculous love triangle."

I'd interviewed Reinfields and serial killers. This was the strangest conversation I had ever walked into. "Fine, I'll play along. You can ask and if it doesn't put her in danger, I'll answer."

"I sense an addendum to this offer."

I nodded, "I get one question."

Elias shook his head but his eyes stayed pinned on me, intrigued. "I can't risk my mission or people to indulge selfish curiosity."

His answer surprised me. I'd expected a quick agreement, assuring he'd only lie to me in the end. Instead, he was outlining his boundaries. Did Elias actually think he was right?

It would explain his odd respect throughout this conversation and even his safety caveat. I'd always assumed Elias thought his cause was righteous, but more in a rationalized sense. The way people justify theft when they're struggling at home or eating an extra cheeseburger on a bad day.

But this felt like someone who genuinely considered his actions necessary to improve the state of the world.

I shook the thought away for now. "My question is simple; how am I your asset?"

CHAPTER 20

LILY

P art of being a liaison is being able to reach your contact in an emergency, keeping their information locked in your skull at all times. So I wasn't surprised the address led me to an apartment building, just annoyed by the sheer size of the damn thing.

It wasn't like I could casually trot down the bloody hallway until I found the right unit. And that was assuming my contact was still home. I knew from the news he hadn't made it out of the city before marshal law was enforced. But a lot of folks had fled to the sanctuaries in schools and community centers, taking refuge in the high numbers.

Then again, those same people might blame the big guy. The news hadn't been kind to him.

I approached from the back on my way in, watching the windows. The building might have been nice once, but now a good chunk of it was boarded up or barricaded, especially on the second level. The first level was mostly shattered glass and ragged curtains fluttering in the wind.

They hadn't even bothered cleaning the blood off the walls or sidewalk. A moldy old rabbit toy was half-buried in the slush, an ear ripped off one side, the exposed stuffing covered in decaying blood.

I sighed and closed my eyes, listening intently. There were a couple families left, most chatting about the next horde or the news. Gabe's sudden disappearance was a big conspiracy. One family insisted it was all a cover-up so the police could take him out, just to avoid the trial. Another said Gabe was out of the country by now, living it up. I guess when you're trapped inside, any entertainment will do.

Finally, I heard a distinct bark of a laugh and the deep voice I was looking for. "Go fish!"

A wide smile broke my face. Hearing his warm tones almost made me cry. The fact that he was talking with someone, however, made me squirm.

"Ah come on!" An unfamiliar lady teased. "There's no way!"

"Go..." Harper exaggerated the word playfully, "fish."

The woman snorted before I heard a light slap, maybe her palm smacking the table as she retrieved a card from the stack. "I guess that'll work."

Another smack, probably adding a set to the table.

Dammit. I hadn't counted on him having a guest. It was one thing to drag Harper into this, but I had no idea who his companion was. Sure, I could just mesmerize them while we chatted, but it was already risky going to Harper in the first place.

Of course, if I'd had another option, I wouldn't even be here. I sighed, forcing my feet forward. It was dark out, so I could stick to shadows while I entered the building, listening intently for anyone coming to their doors.

It was impossible to avoid everyone, and in times like these, someone was bound to have a guard posted at their peephole. Hopefully, it was enough to hunch my shoulders and walk briskly.

Not like I'd want to be out here long anyway.

Maybe the complex had always been a wreck, but the scratch marks and bullet holes pocking the walls and carpet begged to differ. Even the concrete stairwell was in ruins, with large chunks of concrete tripping me every other step, forcing me to take it slow, as though I were climbing Everest instead of some residential steps.

On the second floor, a new stench began to mix with the lingering mildew and mold. A familiar odor that made my body freeze, if only for a moment. Maybe I'd be lucky and it would be a few floors up. I hadn't smelled it right away, so a girl could hope.

The problem with hopes, they get dashed. I tried really hard not to look as I stepped over the pair of bodies, curled around each other. They were both missing chunks of flesh, and the heel of my shoe stuck to the dried blood at the entrance. One of their arms held the door open as I shoved my way through it.

I forced my eyes forward, deciphering the tiny placard on the wall announcing which room numbers were in which direction. Looked like 307 was to the right. My shoe kept clinging to the carpet, fading a little with every step away from the entrance.

The damage was surprisingly limited at this level. Only a couple bullet holes and the rug was nearly clean, say for the occasional muddy boot print leading in and out. If I didn't know better, I'd say this place was guarded...

The tell-tale click of a gun alerted me seconds before someone hollered "Halt!"

I slowly held up my hands. "Shite."

CHAPTER 21

GABE

"It's a deal, then?" Elias finally sat in the plush chair across from me, his fingers steepled again. I was starting to guess it was a favorite gesture.

"So long as that doesn't count as my question."

He chuckled indulgently and shook his head, holding up his wine glass. "Kindly bring Detective Collins a drink."

I turned to Cillian and gritted out, "No thanks."

"You've been on the run, all over the city since last night," Elias emphasized this point with a long draw from his own glass. "You must be hungry."

At least he wasn't bothering to hide that he was tracking us, somehow.

"We've agreed to be candid in the name of respect?"

Elias arched a brow in a way that reminded me far too much of Lily. My skin tingled and crept along the bone as he nodded.

"Then I'd rather not drink the results of human trafficking." I let the sentence land, waiting for... I don't know what. Would he kill me over such a simple insult?

Elias only grinned and took another long drink of his glass, letting out a satisfied sigh before he set it on the desk. "Surely you've had a steak before your transition. Have you ever looked into the farming practices before it landed on your plate?"

"It feels a little different when I was recently the cow." Guess if I was going to get myself killed, I might as well go down swinging.

The grin exploded; Elias threw his head back and laughed. It took so long I started to wonder if he was intentionally mocking my question. He finally held a finger, begging my indulgence for just a moment longer before flicking a red tear away. "Apologies, you caught me off guard."

Muscles I hadn't realized I was clenching slowly relaxed.

He chuckled again, smiling as though he were about to recount some fond memory. "You know, I'm not sure I could recall my birth name. I vaguely remember my first wife and our son, but I can't remember her whispering my name. Isn't that strange?"

"But you remember being human?" I had a hard time picturing that. He didn't just seem like some cliché English vampire. Something in his mannerisms had me half-expecting a Lovecraftian horror to sprout from that small smile.

"Surely you've realized by now–" another small sip, "there isn't much of a difference."

It was my turn to laugh, though it was cold and short-lived. "You know, a couple months ago I would've said no."

"Yes, I watched your interview with Miss Wright." The smile grew wistful though his eyes became slits. "What I was trying to say, before, was this. When you live off another being, squabbling over how the livestock is treated is rarely productive to your own species."

Was this some kind of argument for veganism? "We both know there's a difference between the cow's sacrifice and the human's."

"Is there really?" His fingers formed that steeple again. "Has this been proven?"

"No, I'm not talking about the intelligence argument." I shook my head. "I mean the human doesn't have to die or feel pain for us to survive. We're not even parasites, our required impact is limited."

"Agreed, one could even argue that humanity is more wasteful, because they kill their livestock, making it critical that more are raised and killed. Even if they're not pumping the animal with chemicals or shoving it in a cage, they raise these animals for slaughter and only get one use out of the meat."

He tut-tutted and my tongue became a rock. That had to be the only reason for my delayed reply.

"We don't use them like you're proposing. And we don't raise all cattle for this purpose."

"I'd rather not squabble over the three percent and bovine ethics." He flicked his wrist, as if deflecting the notion. "I understand your arguments, I simply disagree."

"Fine, are we done?"

Another languid drink before swirling the blood in his glass, watching the light dance off the ruby liquid inside. "You never got your answer."

I had to bite my tongue to avoid clenching my jaw.

"You asked how you're my asset." He finally looked at me. "Simply put, your court case will only bolster my cause."

"That's insane." Either I'd win and Elias' plans would collapse or I'd set vampire rights back... "Oh."

All my indignation drained and my body ran cold.

"I knew she wouldn't suffer a fool." The corner of his mouth ticked up and he emptied his glass before holding it up, nodding to Cillian.

"But... sir..." Cillian's voice shook like he was lifting a heavy weight.

Elias swirled the glass slowly. "I'm sure you'll make it back from the kitchen in time to protect me."

His eyes stayed locked on me, the glass kept swirling and Cillian let out an exasperated sigh of resignation. With that, he took Elias' wine glass and left.

"Always good to have henchmen one can rely on," Elias smirked as though we were old buddies swapping stories over scotch.

I swallowed. "You're hoping that if I lose my case, it'll move more members of the Court to your way of thinking."

"Hope has nothing to do with it." He sat back, that stupid smile still tugging at the corners of his mouth. "That's why you will leave this building unharmed."

"Huh?" I mean, he obviously wanted me back in court, awaiting execution, but I still hadn't expected that.

"Oh yes." He nodded. "Tomorrow, my men will deliver you to your lawyer, which will, no doubt, lead you to another round of solitary confinement while you stand trial."

"Given your certainty, why would I agree to this?"

"It's not a matter of agreement. It's a lack of options." At this Cillian returned, handed Elias a full glass, and retook his post. "Thank you."

He took another long sip and I started to wish I'd taken his offer. Then I'd have something to hurl at him. Now it was all I could do not to tap my fingers on the armrest waiting for his final swallow.

He sighed in pleasure and finally looked at me. "We're both the kind of men that has to see things through."

I was getting pretty tired of him telling me things I couldn't argue against. I was supposed to rail. To fight. To tell this maniac we were nothing alike. And from the outset, that would be true. I was rough where he appeared refined. I'd like to believe that I was an okay guy, that Elias was nothing more than a barbarian.

But Lily had cared for us both. She claimed her husband hadn't started out a monster. And now, sitting here, listening to him, I could almost believe we were two men simply doing what we thought was right.

The thought tied several large knots in my intestines.

Finally, some counter to his bullshit struck me. "If all that's true, then why'd you try to kill me?"

"Yes, I do apologize about your home." Those brown eyes became twin slits, the pupils aimed just beyond my shoulder for the briefest of moments before his features relaxed again. "There was a misunderstanding in my ranks. It will not happen again."

I almost growled, "The house is gone."

"But your life is not. I shall leave that to the humans." He flicked his wrist to dismiss the topic. "Your sense of duty won't be able to resist going back. It's who you are."

Again, I wanted to contradict him.

"I'm not going to let you win."

"I certainly hope not." Elias smiled, the light of the room gleaming off his fangs like sunlight off ice. "You still have to put on a good show, after all."

CHAPTER 22

LILY

"Alright, keep 'em up." The cold barrel of a gun nuzzled the back of my neck like an angry lover. "Don't wanna waste ammo."

"That makes two of us." I waggled my fingers for emphasis.

The stranger patted me down briskly, grunting as he tossed my knives and torch aside. "Where are your friends?"

All my muscles tensed as I resisted the urge to nab the gun from him. "I'm alone."

"Liar." He shoved the barrel deeper into my spine. "Even with weapons, no way a scrawny little thing like you is surviving on her own."

I swallowed. "The only friends I have should be in unit 327."

"Huh?"

"I'm here to see someone. Ya can escort me to the door, he'll vouch for me."

"You're buddies with the captain?"

"If ya don't believe me, let's trot down there." I wave my hand down the mildew-riddled hall. "If he tells ya differently, you can still blow my head off."

My captor hemmed and hawed a few more moments before nudging me with the gun. "March."

I obliged, stepping over my weapons as we went. Luckily, it was only a couple doors before we stopped and a beefy arm covered in hair reached around me to knock. "Hey, Captain, some foreigner here to see you!"

He banged his fist on the wood again just as I heard Harper grumbling, "How many times do I have to tell Josh to stop calling me that?"

"Just go see what he wants, you were kicking my butt anyway."

"Coming!" The response was followed by several heavy thumps, just before the door swung open and Harper beamed at me. "Holy shit, Lily!?"

The dark man pulled me into one of his signature hugs, burying my face in the mess of his beard and barking out a great big laugh. "How'd you even find me?"

I pushed the coarse hair off my face, spitting a few strays out before replying.

"Had the address memorized from the liaison gig." I turned to my escort and beamed. The look of confusion stretched a well-worn set of grizzled features. "I'll take my knives back, thanks."

It took a couple minutes to go back and get my stash. To his credit, Josh helped me pick everything up and shook my hand at the end. "Sorry about the trouble, little lady."

"No worries." I smiled. "We all need to protect ourselves."

He pulled his hand back, shivering. "You better heat up some water for her, Captain. Those hands are freezing."

Thank god it was chilly outside. Being this suspicious, it wouldn't take much for him to side-eye me. Harper and I walked back to his place in silence, waiting until the door was closed.

"Sorry about Josh." Harper rubbed the back of his head. "He's a cranky old coot, but good security."

I shrugged. "Just be happy he didn't recognize me from the news."

Harper barked out a short laugh and shook his head. "It probably would have been in your favor. He's a conspiracy nut."

Harper's home was out of place with the destruction and decay outside. It wasn't Martha Stewart perfect, but it was clean and comfortable. Maybe not warm, but the bite of Oregon winter was diminished by the glow of candles and the merry tune of off-key singing. We left his small entry, coming into a galley kitchen, where a woman danced. The red curls in her big bun bounced while she hummed a hodge podge of mixed songs, wiping down counters and tidying. Like some hippie version of Cinderella.

Harper smiled and shook his head. "Hannah, I want you to meet Lily."

The lady beamed and pranced forward. "Wait, not *the* Lily?"

"Wish I could say the same." I gave a sly grin, side eyeing Harper. "Harper didn't tell me he had a lady friend."

The woman laughed while she explained, "We started dating just before the world blew up."

"Hannah and her dad ran Hammy's Pizza, off Clinton," Harper's dark complexion deepened with blush. "After you went on the lam, I finally got the guts to ask her out. Didn't even have a chance to tell Collins."

I arched a brow at him. "And you're already livin' together?"

"Yeah, what can I say?" Hannah grinned at him, standing on her toes to plant a peck on his cheek. "Courtship is a little faster when the world has gone to hell."

Harper barked out another laugh. "Pretty sure I was just your last resort."

They both grew quiet. Hannah coughed and turned back to me.

"So..." She grasped my hand before I could think to object. "You're the one who pulled the stick out of Collins' butt?"

That was one way to redirect the topic. I chuckled, unable to stop myself. "I think we're good for each other."

It was a little surprising to realize I meant it. Something must have shown on my face because the tone of the room shifted again, becoming incredibly awkward.

"Um.." Harper coughed. "God, I assumed you'd heard. Collins..."

It suddenly occurred to me that Harper didn't know.

"No, no, no!" I warded the ideas away, my hands flailing in every direction.

"Lily, I care about him too–"

"I saw him yesterday!" I shouted, cutting Harper off. His eyes widened and I started to word-vomit everything from my escape to Gabe's capture. "They've got to be usin' him for bait."

They both winced at the eagerness in my tone.

"Damn." Harper blew out a long breath, drawing his hand down his face and over a beard streaked with grey that hadn't been there a couple months ago.

I swallowed. "I need help."

"Ummm." Hannah slouched. "You need a miracle."

"Hannah," Harper groaned, his dark hand still covering his eyes.

"No." I held up a hand against his protest. "She's right. I'm totally fucked. And honestly, I'm risking your whole building by even showing up here. I have no clue how they're tracking me."

Silence swallowed our little space. There wasn't a clock on the wall, yet I swore I could hear each second ticking by.

"No guts, no glory." Harper reached over and squeezed Hannah's hand. They held each other's gaze for a moment before she nodded and he smiled. "You think the phone's got a charge?"

Hannah blew out a long breath and gazed at the ceiling in thought. "I checked in with Mom about two weeks ago. It was around seventy percent, I think."

That made no sense. It wasn't like we had Vampbusters. Who'd they want to call? And why'd they have to check the charge.

"We have to turn it off between uses, just to be safe." Hannah smiled at me. "We've been lucky enough to get cell service, let alone internet so we can pay the bill."

Of course the electricity was out, hence the candles. Half the power lines and cell towers were damaged and it wasn't really top priority for the city to repair them when the next wave of undead was always lurking.

The news had mentioned that those lucky enough to still have electricity experienced brownouts and had to be very particular about device usage. No more doom scrolling or playing video games. I just hadn't realized the true extent before now.

"Why not just charge them at the station?" I didn't know all the details but the government buildings and hospitals got priority. With Harper being a police Captain...

"I doubt they want me in the building since I was sacked." Harper shrugged as he came out of a back bedroom, placing a phone on the table as it powered on. My jaw hung loose before I snapped it shut. Ivan had *promised* me that we would always take care of Harper. It was part of the deal when he agreed to become the new VPB Captain.

"I know what you're thinking." Harper held up a dark digit, telling me to hold on. "I asked them not to intervene with the IA investigation."

The phone hummed some futuristic tone as the screen lit up and I gaped.

Hannah let out a soft snort. "I tried to talk him out of it, but he's a man of very inconvenient convictions."

Harper smiled and placed a big hand over hers.

"I hated that job anyway. It was so... political. And, at the end of the day, I broke the rules." His smile didn't spark the usual twinkle in his eyes. "I'm lucky they didn't have enough evidence to formally charge my ass."

"But..." I swallowed. "I'm the one that put you in that position."

"Nah, I chose to help you." He cut me off as I opened my mouth. "And I would do it all again."

I swallowed my sentence and blinked. It was so much like what Gabe kept saying every time he tried to convince me I wasn't some inconvenience.

Hannah squeezed Harper's hand and leaned on his shoulder. "At least it got you off of Candy Crush."

A small glow lit Harper's eye and he gazed longingly at the ceiling. "I do miss those colorful little dots."

Their interaction was so sweet. So simple. A small pang of jealousy pierced my gut.

"Well—" I swallowed, trying to shove my emotions back. "I hope that's not why ya grabbed that thing."

There wasn't time to wallow about what Gabe and I might have been or how my indecision had screwed it all up. Right now, I needed to save his ass.

Harper shook his head and smiled. "Nah, I want to call Michelle. We didn't talk much before I got canned, couldn't. But I think she'd like to know her client is alive. Who knows, maybe she'll have an idea for rescue. Hopefully, she has her phone on."

He dialed and didn't even have to wait through a single ring before he started talking.

"Hello to you too Mi—" He stopped mid-sentence, his mouth agape. "Is that you, buddy?"

CHAPTER 23

GABE

I almost appreciated the cold, dark cell. It gave me a chance to think. And at least they'd left the bag off my head.

Somehow, I felt like I'd just aced an interview for a job I was horrified to take.

And there wasn't any choice. I reached to rake my fingers through my hair but the chain stopped me short and all I could do was growl into the dark.

Back to square one!

I fell to the ground and slammed my fists on the concrete, yowling in frustration. The whole reason I'd rebelled, sacrificed my life, was because Captain Murphy had wanted to use me to stir panic. My hatred of vampires and the horrific nature of the crime was meant to prime them for slaughter.

Now, Elias had only found a new way to place me squarely back in the same strategy. Worse yet, there was no one to shoot. No boss to take out. The realization of everything riding on the outcome crept through my whole body, colder than the concrete I sat on.

I don't remember falling asleep, only being shaken roughly as Cillian yanked my chains out from the ground and dragged me through the corridor. "Rise and shine, sweetheart."

I stumbled to my feet, tripping to keep up while my mind trudged through the sludge of sleepy adrenaline. It took a minute for my eyes to adjust to the blinding fluorescent bulbs in the halls. And a little bit longer to realize I could see the lights.

Cillian hadn't used the bag. Why? Maybe they just didn't think there was any information to glean from my surroundings. The concrete on my feet wasn't exactly a shock. Neither were the single-stall garage doors, lined up one after another. It was all very familiar but I didn't think I'd been here before. There wasn't much time to dwell on the thought.

The sharp snap of chains was followed by rapid jingling as their captors tried to pull loose. Apparently, one had gotten out, because one cell door was severely warped and dented in several places, a withered finger clawing through a slim opening.

Anyone normal would find the sounds of this prison distracting and unsettling. But for Cillian, all this ruckus was Tuesday.

"Dammit." He glared at the mangled door before giving me a look. "This is what ya get when you work with kids."

"I'd say that's the least of your troubles," I growled.

He rolled his eyes, the pale ruined one barely showing any motion, before turning his back to me and proceeding. "Come on. Boss says ya gotta be back in town before nightfall. I think he's hoping your lawyer has some press parked out front to capture the moment."

"Why bother telling me?"

"Because ya can't do much to stop it." He grinned wickedly over his shoulder.

Cillian did finally remember the bag, just before we left the dungeons. Even so, the ride out was a rather large upgrade from the ride in.

Not being elbowed by a pile of rotting undead in the dark will do that.

The fact that it was only me and Cillian made the ride strangely awkward. Like coming home from a bad fight at a holiday dinner but with an edge of violence. I must have been exhausted to the point of insanity because the idea made me chuckle.

Cillian still seemed a bit glum. "What the hell are you laughin' at?"

This had to be a sign of temporary insanity because I actually answered him. "Just a random picture of you and I having to tolerate each other at Thanksgiving."

The cabin grew silent again and I assumed Cillian had just decided to ignore the lost cause. It was several turns and a couple potholes before he spoke again. "Just be glad Lilé doesn't have to introduce you to our Mum."

The line held humor but his tone did not. There was a wistful note buried in the cold sarcasm that stopped my psychotic chortling the rest of the way. I wasn't sure how much longer we had to go. A ride across town used to only take thirty minutes, maybe forty with bad weather or construction.

Who knew how long we would be stuck like this?

Elias had already confirmed he needed me returned for my court appearance so there wasn't any permanent harm in asking, "What was she like?"

Again, that cold endless silence stretched beyond the bag. My only company was the occasional shift of the vehicle before he grumbled, "She was hard. She had expectations."

I was shocked he'd bothered to answer but something in his tone made it clear that was all I was getting. We fell back into the palpable silence as the car lurched and swerved for several minutes, the motion making me a little dizzy in my blinded state.

We halted with a sudden jerk and Cillian ripped the bag off my head, along with a few hairs. I winced at the brilliant light, closing my eyes and letting them adjust to the warm red glow inside of my eyelids. When I finally blinked, I scowled at Cillian across from my passenger seat in the cargo van.

He didn't wear his usual smirk; all traces of sarcasm were gone. "Now we see what kind of man ya are."

I continued to glare but said nothing. He pointed down the road.

"Your lawyer's house is in that direction, pretty sure ya know the place."

I suppressed the urge to roll my eyes. Of course, Cillian knew about my failed relationship with Michelle. The news had found it two weeks into the trial and turned it into this whole conspiracy theory. Michelle had wanted to play into the forbidden lovers angle, hoping against hope that it would sway the jury to root for us. I had rejected the idea without question.

Cillian reached over slowly, as though he were bored, undid the manacles on my wrists, and let the chains rattle to the floor between our seats before reaching across me and opening my door. "Off ya trot, then."

I looked out the empty door and then back at him. That stony expression never changed. I felt like a stray dog being turned back to the wilds. Finally, I climbed out and slammed the door. As Cillian sped off, I tried to read the van's plates, but there weren't any. Just the shadow of a long removed decal, mostly illegible as the sun reflected on the back doors. I could only make out a few letters.

M... N... T... V... S... How enlightening.

I sighed and shook my head, running my fingers through the greasy grooves of my hair and looking up the street.

I was free. It was unlikely they would follow me but that wasn't a guarantee. And I'd probably notice a tail after a little walking.

I could try to find Lily. She had to be panicking, trying to come up with some crazy rescue maneuver that would only get her hurt or captured. Even without the tracking.

And, really, why should I play their game? I wasn't Elias' pawn.

You don't see me in the mirror.

My last conversation with Olive suddenly came back to me and a chill ran up each vertebrae. Could I leave it like this? The world had always been bleak, but I had a chance to lighten it. It was the only chance any of us had. Even if Elias presumed I would lose.

Even if I agreed with him.

I marched towards Michelle's downtown townhouse. Lily would forgive me, I just had to trust her to stay alive so I could explain it later.

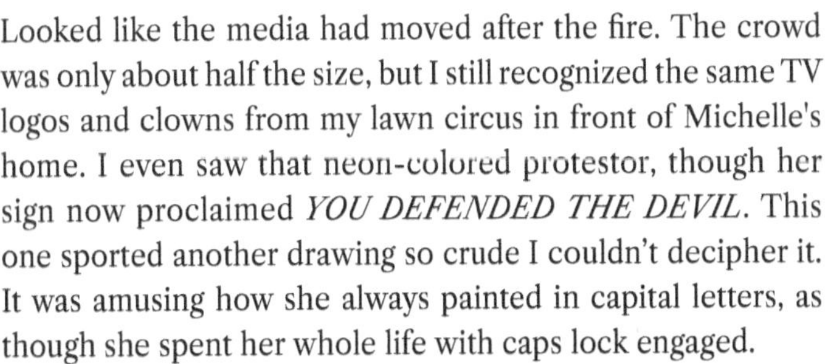

Looked like the media had moved after the fire. The crowd was only about half the size, but I still recognized the same TV logos and clowns from my lawn circus in front of Michelle's home. I even saw that neon-colored protestor, though her sign now proclaimed *YOU DEFENDED THE DEVIL*. This one sported another drawing so crude I couldn't decipher it. It was amusing how she always painted in capital letters, as though she spent her whole life with caps lock engaged.

They didn't notice me as I sat behind one of the many dilapidated cars. The scent of rust and mold wasn't helping me think. I might make it to the sidewalk; a few months ago, a man walking up in singed pants and a ruined button down would have been cause to pay attention. Now it was just a sign that someone else had lost their home.

But as I got closer, they'd be bound to notice. And I would be out of options. I'd only been to Michelle's for a couple dinners. She liked the place to stay pristine and I wasn't always up to the task. Still, I was pretty sure there was a small patio out back with a high wall. She'd once joked it was a shame she didn't smoke.

I waited to be sure the mob in front of her house was occupied before darting behind the nearest row of homes, ducking into their backyards, wondering if this was anything like Lily's passage to my home the other night.

Luckily, there weren't any nosy neighbors I'd had to handle, though I almost got spotted by a kid playing near a second story window.

I finally made it to the right house, recognizing Michelle's lawn chair and the shining glass table she left outside, even though she hated the sound of putting anything on the glass and had to clean it constantly.

The back door had a small, artfully distorted, window. Still, there was someone about the right size in the house. I knocked.

"What the..." Michelle's heels clipped over her floors, rapidly rushing to the door before flinging it open. She gaped but it only lasted a moment before she gripped my collar and yanked me inside.

She slammed the door and glared up at me, turning my head this way and that, her nails digging into my cheek. With each quick jerk, I could see more of her bedraggled state. Her normally perfect curls were frizzy and tangled, her skin was blotchy, and the bags under her eyes would never fit in any overhead compartment.

She finally let go, her hand falling violently to her side. "Where the hell have you been?"

"I'm sorry." It was all I had. There'd been good reason to run after the fire, but I never should have left her worrying like this.

"You bet your ass you're sorry." She punched me like she meant it. Her knuckles cracked against the underside of my chin. "I thought you were dead!"

She punched again, my ribs this time. "I thought Barbara was fucked!"

Apparently, she'd had some mascara on; dark tears streaked in manic directions, like the dead branches of a withered tree. She kept swinging, her movements breaking down into frantic slaps. The carefully cultivated woman I'd never seen with a hair out of place, was in the middle of a breakdown.

I let the assault go on until she tired. Panting and furious, she raised her hand, only to lower it in a limp slap. "We need to clean you up for the press."

"Ah-hem."

The new voice shocked my nerves and I spun. Michelle's home hadn't changed much since we dated. All gray and beige tones, with the occasional pop of purple or teal in a vase or painting. I remember pondering if her house was on the market once. She couldn't fathom why I would ask.

The lack of color made Melody that much easier to spot. She leaned against the wall and slowly examined my state before looking me square in the eye. "Where's Edwards?"

"Nice to see you too." Not original, but the line bought me some time to think.

"Collins, I'm not playing." Melody rolled her eyes with enough exaggeration to twirl the ribbons and dreads of her long ebony hair. "One more time, where is that Irish brat?"

Something in her statement rang a bell but I didn't have time to examine what it was. She stood straight and stalked towards me. "Her stuff was still in your washing machine, so don't bother with the cliché denials."

"Funny enough, I actually don't know." I leaned forward, leveling our eyes. "Or do I?"

Melody's tawny face contorted into a scowl. She opened her mouth but I cut her next sentence short.

"What are you even doing here?"

"They were dropping off blood for Barb." Michelle pointed to a cooler on her glass coffee table.

I thought about it and nodded. "They've been providing it the whole time?"

"We protect our assets." Melody clicked her tongue as though to properly punctuate the sentence.

My smile was cold. "Now that's entertaining."

Melody only replied with a confused tilt to her head.

"I really don't know where Lily is, but you're right I've talked to her." I glared. "So I know exactly what Cyrus was about to do."

"Edwards tried to escape in front of everyone!" Spit flew into my face with Melody's words. "Ritti didn't have a choice!"

Michelle looked at her feet exasperated, pinching the bridge of her nose and shaking her head. "If I wanted yelling, I'd call my boss."

I realized she didn't have the proper context. "You remember the phone call right before the first horde?"

That got her attention. Michelle's frazzled head snapped up, her eyes open and wide. "No..."

I nodded. She knew exactly what I was alluding to.

"But... why?" Michelle stared at Melody. "Lily is one of yours. Why would you torture her?"

Melody's expression scrunched with confusion. "What do you care?"

"I care who I'm doing business with." Michelle's spine turned to steel. "I agreed to keep your secrets in exchange for saving my sister. But if this is the cost..."

Her sentence stopped short. Michelle couldn't bring herself to say it.

"Either way," I interjected, "your business is do–"

Michelle's phone rang and she jumped a mile in the air. "Jesus!"

She flung her body across the shiny glass table and snatched the phone from her brief case, slamming her thumb on the answer icon. "What?!"

Those grey eyes widened in surprise before she snorted, shoving the phone at me. "You've got timing."

I answered tentatively. "Hello?"

There was a gasp. "Is that you, buddy?"

A grin stretched across my features. "How the hell did you know I was here?!"

"I didn't, I was just calling Michelle to ask..." His words trailed off, uncertainty lacing his tone. "Wait, how are you there?"

"Long story. For another time." I hope he'd take the hint.

"Gotcha." There was a strange pause to his words. I can't describe it perfectly. Just something I knew instinctively after working with him in so many intense situations. There was something he was nervous to tell me. Maybe the fact that I was holding back had him hesitating.

"Can we call you back?"

"The phone's only got twenty percent." Harper's voice lost all the prior energy. "I'll try Michelle again this time tomorrow. I'm so glad you're okay."

"Yeah, sorry I couldn't call you after the fire." He had to be freaking out.

"Yeah, if only you'd given me one heart attack this week." There was a hinting quality to his tone. My heart soared when I considered what he was getting at but I kept it off my face.

"I'll talk to you tomorrow." I hung up before he said anything else to give the game away, handing the phone back to Michelle. "His phone battery was getting low."

She nodded and turned back to Melody. "My client will not be answering any of your questions. And if you want his case to proceed, you'll leave my home."

Melody tapped the ground with one of her heavy boots, before snapping her arms down and storming to the back. She turned so fast, a few of her necklaces tangled in her hair, but she didn't stop.

Michelle let out a sarcastic chuckle.

"Might as well call the department." She unlocked her phone and I snatched it away. "Hey!"

I held it out of reach, like some idiotic playground bully. "I can't go back."

CHAPTER 24

LILY

"He's okay?" I was dumbfounded before I could be relieved. "How?"

Had Gabe managed to escape Cillian? If so, why hadn't he come back? Maybe he had and we'd missed each other. A million possibilities raced for my attention. But Gabe was alright, that was the important thing. Even if it left a lot of questions.

Hannah beat me to the punch, placing her palm on Harper's elbow. "Why couldn't you ask?"

Harper's eyes lost their twinkle as he powered the phone down. "I think the Court was there."

"Huh?" That made me reel. "What exactly did he say?"

"Not much." Harper shrugged. "I can't explain it. I just know the guy."

It took a lot of effort to quiet all the questions in my head. My companions waited patiently while I organized my thoughts.

I finally looked up. "What do I do now?"

Ten minutes ago, I'd had a goal. Now it was gone. I was lost in this ruined city. And Gabe would be in police custody soon.

"We still need to figure out where Elias' big evil secret lair is, right?" Harper tried to smile.

"No." I rubbed my temples. "I gotta get out of here before Cillian finds me again."

Hannah hummed with excitement. "Where could you even go?"

"I don't know, but I can't be here." I stood slowly, completely confused, moving for the sake of moving. It was like walking across a ship on choppy waves. The whole world was tilting.

"Lily–" Harper growled, "sit down."

I wavered, confused as much by his unusual tone as my need to protect Harper and his girlfriend.

"Even if I hated you, I couldn't let you leave." Hannah swallowed. "It's dangerous to everyone."

My stomach tumbled over itself.

"Collins has it right, you're important to Elias." Harper nodded. "You said yourself, Cillian tracked you down twice in as many days."

"Yeah, so he'll be here any minute." I didn't want to be alone but I was so tired of getting people hurt.

"There's a flaw in your logic," Harper sighed. "If Cillian was tracking you, why'd he even have to question Collins."

I opened my mouth but only a small, confused squeak came out.

Harper was right, Cillian had considered what Gabe was saying. He wasn't even certain Gabe was lying until he'd emptied Gabe's...

"Shite!" I yanked my jacket off, shaking the pockets out. The mishmash of contents fell to the table, bouncing off one another and flinging themselves all over the floor and towards my companions.

"Hey!" Hannah leaped from the table.

"Whoa, watch it." Harper pushed some loose change and my torch to the side.

I hardly heard them as I sorted through the stash. It all made a skittering, ringing sound as I pushed it over the table, scratching the surface. It was like I was too possessed to consider the damage.

Cillian had been looking in Gabe's pockets for something small. Something specific. Couldn't be the knives or cash, I'd have seen if something was attached.

"Lily?" Harper leaned forward, his hand hovering just over my shoulder.

I snapped my head up. "They've got a tracker on me."

Harper reeled. "What? How?"

"No clue. But it's the only thing that adds up."

Harper nodded slowly, looking down at the small pile. "So what did you already have when you got to Collins' place?"

"The weapons and torch." I pointed to indicate.

"Where'd you get them?"

The idea pinched my guts as I whispered, "Cyrus..."

Harper nodded thoughtfully. "I mean, you two have issues, right?"

"Hey," Hannah waved both hands like she was directing air traffic. "Queue a lady in?"

"Cyrus and I used to date; it ended poorly." I bit my lip. "But that was forever ago. And he doesn't believe in Elias' cause."

Yeah, I'd suspected a rat at Court, only way I could explain how Elias always called at such precise times. But I knew Cyrus; we had our problems but I'd never question his loyalty to Court. And why would he assume I would attack him in the dungeons? Even if this was him, that's the only reason he'd attach a tracker.

"Plus he have to assume you'd escape a fortress."

I nodded. "And if I hadn't managed it, the Queen might have found the tracker."

That'd be one hell of a risk. At the same time, my escape had been too easy. It hadn't occurred to me until after I was out, I'd been too loaded on purpose and adrenaline. But in hindsight...

Hannah's jaw dropped so fast, I was shocked it didn't dislocate. "Vampire's have a queen?"

Harper offered a sympathetic grin. "Sorry for the crash course, hon."

"You kidding, this is better than a daytime soap!" Hannah stepped forward, her eyes keen. "Okay, so if it's nothing from lover boy, what else did you have?"

"Noth..." My voice trailed and my eyes widened.

I lifted my hand and pulled the dead girl's necklace from inside my shirt, letting the abstract jewel dangle.

Hannah sneered then tried to cover it. "How pretty."

"Not mine." I shook my head then looked at Harper. "It was at Stafford's house. But how?"

There was no way Elias could have planned for me to go there. Let alone take this necklace. And I'd stared at this rutty thing for hours while bored or trapped.

"Lemme see." Harper held out a hand in a gimme gesture.

The chain tangled in my hair and I winced, ripping it over my head.

Harper stared intently as the pendant spun back and forth, catching the golden glint of a quickly setting sun. Finally, it stopped spinning, swaying gently as he leaned in and peered at the core. Past the purple and blue swirls to that off-center green dot.

"Couldn't be..." Harper placed another big hand under the pendant.

"What?" Hannah and I asked together.

He turned the piece over in his palm, investigating the back. We all leaned in. It wasn't secured like I'd been expecting. Most necklaces had a near seamless backing, some of them welded. But this was more like a watch. The back could be removed with a tool.

"Screwdriver." Harper requested.

Hannah was already walking, her pace brisk and assured. "Phillips?"

"Flat head, small as you can." Harper looked at me. "You said this was the old bat's?"

"No." I explained how I'd found it, Harper nodding along as Hannah returned and handed him the tool.

Harper slid the screwdriver into a little divot, normally meant for jewelers' tools. It took him a few attempts; his hands kept slipping. Finally, he pried the back off, letting it plunk onto the table, clanging into the coins.

Harper swore. A tiny gasp escaped my lips.

The green speck in the pendant covered a tiny metal sliver. I recognized this from more than a couple cases looking for microchipped mutts.

Harper bolted into his room before we could say anything. For a second I was worried he might bash the pendant with a hammer, but he came back with a basic black pouch, tossing the necklace in and closing it. "Was anyone with you when you found it?"

"What the hell is that?" I pointed at the pouch.

"Lily..."

"Harper..." I mocked.

He gave me a pitying look that made me want to swallow the question. "I bought it because of you."

I flinched but he kept going.

"After you mesmerized me–"

"I did that after I saved Gabe!"

"I know, I know." He held up a dark hand, begging for patience. "But I couldn't be sure of what was in my own skull. For all I knew..."

I couldn't keep his gaze. "I'd never make you do something."

"I know that now. But back then, I didn't want to risk being your fall guy." He held up the little bag. "This blocks towers from finding my phone. Hopefully, it'll be enough."

He held up the pouch for emphasis and the room grew uncomfortably silent. Hannah cleared her throat and danced slowly from one foot to the other.

I finally looked up. "I'm sorry."

"We were all just doing the best with what we had." Harper smiled sadly. "Now, was anyone with you when you found this ugly thing?"

I shook my head in disbelief even as I said, "Cyrus."

CHAPTER 25

GABE

M ichelle jumped on the edge of her toes, stretching to retrieve her phone. Her grey eyes were solid, like the twin barrels of a loaded shotgun. "You have to go back!"

I stepped further out of reach. "Not yet."

She had to understand. This could only work with Michelle on my side.

She shrieked, "If you don't get your ass back in court, I'll lop your head off and mount it on my wall!"

Pointing out that my head would only disintegrate didn't feel like a winning argument. And I started to worry the crowd outside might hear her. Couldn't exactly blame the noise on TV these days. "Would you just listen?"

"Why bother coming back?" Michelle finally rested on her heels, nearly falling backwards when she let herself drop. Then staggering back once and glaring.

It finally struck me. The messy appearance. The out-of-control emotions. Raising her voice without thinking of the consequences. I'd initially blamed it on worry for her sister, but the vampires were dropping off blood.

I pocketed her phone and made a b-line for the kitchen. She stomped after me. "Where are you going?"

I didn't bother answering, just hunted for the coffee grounds. It took a minute; Michelle always got her beans from some woman she'd found at a farmer's market. Instead of the typical brown bag with the home-printed logo, I found a plastic mini-drum filled with something stale and off brand. I guess I should have been surprised to find anything, given the state of things. I prepped the machine.

"We can't waste the electricity," she snarled.

It was getting harder to control my tone. "You're drunk."

She glared. "And you're an asshole."

"Both are true," I glibly replied.

She let out a harsh breath. "I hate when you do that."

"I remember." The coffee machine groaned to life and I absently rubbed at my temples. "How bad has it been?"

Even celebrating, I'd never seen Michelle tipsy, let alone inebriated. She couldn't stand the loss of control.

"The few cases I had left were reassigned." She let out a small, exasperated sigh as I handed her an empty mug. "What, no Splenda?"

I doubted she had it, given the coffee selection. "Don't change the topic."

"Fine." She filled her mug fast, a few drops sloshing on the counter before she quickly wiped them up with the edge of her sleeve. "The only reason I still have a job is because I know far too much about the judges and clerks."

"But with the media coverage..." I let the sentence hang. She could expose whatever dirty laundry she wanted. If the news kept propping her as a race traitor, the public would only discredit her.

She nodded and took a long drink. "At some point, they'll decide it's worth the risk."

"This case isn't just about saving your sister anymore." I nodded to indicate the blood bags. "Without it, your career is over."

"Even with a win, I'm screwed." She slammed the coffee like it was a shot, taking only a couple heavy gulps. I recognized this battle ritual and remained silent. Finally, she gasped and wiped her mouth delicately with the tip of her finger, as though checking for lipstick smudges on her naked skin. "I knew that going in. But now you're backing out."

We sat there in silence, and I let it all sink in. Michelle tapped her foot once before quietly snapping, "Say something. You owe me that."

I huffed and drew a hand through my hair. "I'm not ready to die."

"Oh, don't give me that." Michelle swatted the notion away. "That's been part of the risk since day one."

"Yeah but when we started..." I let the sentence dangle before me. It felt pathetic to even say it.

Michelle's eyes became twin slits. "You thought she was dead."

I nodded.

"So what, you wanted to die too?" She huffed. "Didn't take you for the codependent type."

"No." I shook my head. "My life was in ruins and my job was gone. I was a fugitive for even existing."

Michelle's features softened and she peered toward the front of the house. The protesters' rumblings were barely deafened by the walls and windows. "Yeah, okay, I understand that."

"I needed a purpose," I finally said. "You and Harper handed me one. Then Lily came back and they burned my house down..."

"And you're conflicted on what's more important," she finished. Her tone wasn't exactly sympathetic but there was understanding there.

"Yeah." I sank into one of her kitchen chairs. "Worse yet, I'm realizing how many people are relying on this case. I mean, I understood that intellectually but the past few days have really hammered the idea home."

Michelle sighed and waited. Probably counting to three to steady herself. "You realize that doing nothing is only going to make it worse. Eventually, this will catch up to you and the whole stupid world."

"I know that." God, I wanted to be back out there. Doing something active with Lily, not arguing about my case with Michelle.

"And hiding only makes you look guilty."

"I *know* that," I growled without meaning to.

"So, if you're never going back–"

I tried to interject. "I didn't say–"

"Then *why* bother coming here!?" Michelle shouted.

I stared at her, blinking. I didn't have a good answer. Elias claimed I wouldn't be able to resist doing the right thing, but I sure seemed to be trying. Why was I sitting here, arguing, when the whole world thought I was dead?

"I'll tell you why." She yanked out a chair, scratching her perfect floor, and sat, staring into my eyes. "It's because you know there's only one way through this. Same reason I took your sorry excuse of a case and same reason I'll keep defending you. We have one opportunity to get this right and it's so much bigger than all our bullshit."

Michelle slammed her mug on the table, as though the action would bring the sentiment into reality.

"Here you are, handing me the ultimate comeback-kid story. People need to see the end of this trial, they're hungry for it."

"People will be suspicious. I've been gone for days."

"Some will be," she acknowledged. "But most will be curious. They miss binge-watching their stupid Netflix drama. The city needs this."

"I'm not entertainment."

Michelle twisted her lips in a condescending scowl. "You know better."

Sadly, I did. It had been over 20 years since O.J. Simpson's trial and I still remembered the spectacle it had caused at school.

"Fine." I nodded. "But give me one more call to Harper and a night to sleep before I turn myself in."

Michelle re-screwed her face into an annoyed but thoughtful expression.

"They'll lock me in solitary for sure." Despite my reservations, I dug in my pocket and held the phone out to her. "Give me this one thing."

A sly smile grew from her expression as she gingerly took the phone. "Fine, but you have to do something for me."

I groaned, "What?"

"You've got to give me a better story to sell."

I waited, anxiously tapping my fingers as I watched the seconds tick on Michelle's modern silver clock. Finally, it reached the appointed hour and I dialed. It didn't even finish ringing before she picked up, her voice mildly panicked. "Gabe?"

Cold relief soothed my tired nerves. "I thought that's what Harper was getting at."

"The two of ya must have some psychic bond," Lily chuckled, though the tone was bittersweet. "How'd ya get out?"

"I didn't." I relayed the whole weird experience to her, careful not to use her name. There was so much I wanted to say to her before tomorrow but Melody might be nearby, using that excellent hearing. If she realized where Lily was...

"What's Cillian playin' at?" Her tone was distant, thinking.

"No idea." I blew out a breath. "Elias was straightforward enough."

"And you're still there?" Lily sounded sad but also a little confused, her lilt growing low.

"You have no idea how much I'd rather be there." Just talking to her made me want to drop everything and bolt.

"Then get over here." Lily let out a sniffle so small I almost missed it. "I know I'm a selfish gobshite for even askin' but I don't care."

I leaned forward on the kitchen table, pressing my forehead against the heel of my free hand. It was like the weight of everything was occupying my skull. "You have no idea how much I want to take you up on that."

"I think I'm startin' to." Another sniffle.

My back stiffened. Was she saying what I thought she was saying? Or was I just reading too much into this?

"Just..." She paused, blowing out a long breath. "Promise me you'll be here to talk when it's over, okay?"

I swallowed, trying to force the regret down. Time to change the topic. "What's the plan on your end?"

"Oh... you know." She let out a dark chuckle. "Somethin' stupid."

She relayed everything about the necklace and Harper's foolish idea. It was official. Coming to Michelle was the second worst idea ever. "Put Harper on."

Some of Lily's usual sarcasm slipped back into place. "Ya gonna strangle him through the phone?"

"I'm seriously going to give it a try."

She sighed and I heard the phone exchanging hands. "Is it safe to put this next to my ear, buddy?"

"I can't stop you from doing this."

"Nope."

"You'll stay together?"

"Yep." He let the p pop for emphasis. There was a long pause. "She's not exactly a helpless puppy, pal."

"Life would be easier if she was." I sighed heavily and pinched the bridge of my nose. It wasn't just Lily I was worried about.

"Yeah, because you'd have nothing to do with her." I could just imagine Harper's eyebrows waggling enthusiastically.

I scoffed. "God, I miss the old days."

"Yeah, life was easier when we were hunting for hubbies with deli forks." A woman, not Lily, said something in the background and Harper replied, "I gotcha, hon. Hey, Collins–"

"Hon?" I couldn't help the teasing tone. "Something you want to tell me?"

Harper barked his familiar laugh. "We'll go on a double date soon. But I gotta go, bud."

I nodded my acceptance. "Please be careful."

CHAPTER 26

LILY

"I packed you a little lunch." Hannah zipped up the backpack, handing it to Harper. Her lower lip trembled a little even as she smiled.

"Oooo, did we have grape jelly?" Harper winked as he shouldered the bag and pulled her into his arms. "See you soon."

"Yeah." She nodded and turned to me. "Sorry, I would have made something for you but…"

I chuckled, self-consciously licking my canines. "Nah, I'll be alright."

I was lying. The mug of blood I'd shared with Gabe seemed like forever ago. Experience taught me I'd have to feed soon But Hannah didn't need to hear that right now.

At least three locks engaged with heavy clicks and slaps after Harper and I left the apartment. He stopped at the end of the hall, asking Josh to keep an eye on Hannah.

Finally, we went to the stairwell, stepping over the rotting couple I'd found on my way in.

"I meant to ask…" I flicked my gaze down to them, while Harper helped me step over.

His face seemed to droop. "They tried to break in a couple of times, part of a larger group. We warned them that we protect the space but they kept coming…"

The grief in his voice echoed off the concrete of the moldy old stairwell.

"Okay, but why…" I didn't know how to ask. I hadn't known Gabe or Harper long, especially not by vampire standards, but they were good men. Men who respected the dead.

"Too cold outside to bury them." Harper shrugged sadly. "And they do a better job of warding others off than we ever could."

Hard to argue with that. The rest of our descent was silent but for the soft thumps of our boots padding down the steps, echoing back to us like the march of disorganized soldiers.

We went past the ground level and down another curved flight before finding a heavy metal door. No light shined from the tiny glass window and the letters for GARAGE were faded to a barely legible patina.

Harper yanked on the door and swore. "Locked. Maybe I can smash it with–"

I gently pushed him aside and yanked on the cold door handle. The metal splintered and I dropped the remnants to the ground with a loud, echoing clang.

"Or… that." Harper barked a laugh. "How do I forget you can do things like that?"

"Old habits." I smiled and walked in, clicking the flashlight on. "Where'd you park it?"

"Somewhere over near the back corner." Harper indicated with his big hand. "I think."

I chuckled but let the matter go. "You sure it's got enough gas?"

"Unless someone tried to siphon it." Harper's tone weighed the probability.

I sighed, "Lovely."

Harper was off by a few rows but we eventually found the bike. We rolled it to the entrance, Harper muttering his first bit of gratitude for his building's crappy security. "Thank god they didn't have a fancy security code. We can use the pulley system to open it."

"You sure?" I grinned wickedly. "I could always force it open."

Harper groaned dramatically and drew a hand down his dark face. "Josh would never let me hear the end of it."

The Kawasaki started without incident. It wasn't the same as my bike. For one thing, my Harley was all classic curves in a midnight-blue sheen. Harper's Ninja was sharp like someone had painted a crouching jaguar with nothing but triangles. Second, I'd never ridden in the bitch seat.

Still, it was calming, whipping through the city streets, wind rippling through my ponytail. I hadn't realized how much I needed a ride. Harper was driving a little faster than I liked, with all the junk and debris clogging up the road, but he did it with confidence. He didn't have a guest helmet, so I had to squint against the cold wind. Harper wore his backpack on the front while I kept my arms firmly wrapped around his big back

All I was left to do was think. I was thrilled Gabe was safe, really. But Elias releasing him presented a whole host of gruesome possibilities. Sure, he'd told Gabe he needed him back in court, but that just didn't add up. If Gabe disappeared, the whole world would go back to the status quo. The vampires would be let down, becoming more anxious. Elias had just given them a chance to hope.

Was this some kind of messed up greeting card from my ex? He knew Gabe was important to me. No, Elias had starved me into a monstrous state just to save his cause. He might be hyper-focused on me, but Gabe was right. This wasn't a bloody Valentine situation.

And I couldn't see what Elias was up to. My thoughts scuttled back and forth as I considered everything. Nothing pleasant came to mind.

We finally arrived at a gas station on the nicer side of town. It almost appalled me to look around. While Rockwood and the inner city were left with broken-down cars and debris all over their roads, the Pearl District had maintained its suburban atmosphere. Sure, there was a more solemn attitude than before, fewer people on the streets, and the blinds drawn tightly. A few windows were even boarded up.

But there were people. A gas station was open, and the *bing-bong* chime sounded as the electronic doors swished open and closed. A freaking independent coffee shop had cars in their drive-thru.

I shook my head.

Harper nodded. "We'd better make this fast. Someone might recognize you."

I snorted. "They'd have to care about something other than themselves."

Harper glared at me. "That's not fair."

"Yeah, sure." I shoved my hands deep into my pockets.

Harper grabbed my elbow and whispered in my ear. "You think these people would be here if they didn't need to be?"

I looked away, a little ashamed. Still, a small part of me wanted to argue. "Let's just get this over with."

We strolled over to the gas station, ducking around the corner and nearly running to the pay phone. I couldn't risk calling this number on Harper's phone, even if the charge hadn't been a concern. But going inside to use the business phone was out of the question. There was too great a risk someone would recognize me.

Even now, Harper kept his helmet in place.

I fished in my pockets, pulling out the change and picking out the quarters. Thank god Gabe had insisted on taking it.

The coins clanged inside the machine as I fed the pay-phone, holding my breath. It came out in a heavy, relieved sigh as the dial tone engaged. So many payphones were out of order, unmaintained after cell phones became popular. That was why we'd agreed to go into the nicer side of town, where there was less destruction and the phones were more likely to work.

We couldn't exactly meander from gas station to gas station, hoping to find one that worked and waiting to get spotted. Yeah, no.

The buttons clicked loudly as I dialed the number by heart and waited. One ring... two...

"Come on, come on." I tapped my foot.

Sure, there was a risk they couldn't pick up, but we had protocols for this.

Finally, the line clicked, and a familiar raspy voice growled in my ear. "Just tell me you're okay."

I let out a sad chuckle and thumped my free fist against the wall. "I'm alive and I don't have time. You'll need to yell at me later. Get Darren."

Alex grumbled something I didn't understand before telling Darren to wake up in the background. "Lils needs you."

Darren yawned as he spoke. "Hope you don't need me to hack anything. My computer access has been revoked since you got out."

I swore and shook my head. "I'm sorry."

"You don't have time for the routine," Darren reminded me. "What's up?"

I explained the necklace.

"It's weird they made it so blatant," Darren pondered out loud. "Elias has the funds to make it less obvious."

I shrugged. "They were meant for their... inventory. I doubt they were concerned about someone noticing."

"You sure about that?"

"I'm not sure about anything lately," I admitted. "Can ya give me an idea on range or capabilities?"

"With Bluetooth and cell towers, there's probably not a range." He sounded apologetic as he said it. "You might block the signal in a parking structure, something with a lot of concrete and no windows."

I punched the building, breaking flakes of brick off and bashing my knuckles as I started to softly cry. I was already hungry, and camping out in the garage wasn't an option. I had to take the tracker and get away from Harper and Hannah before Cillian came again.

"What about a–" I tried to remember what Harper had called the thing. "fair a day pack?"

"Faraday?" He snorted

"Yeah, that's what I said."

"Okay..."

I could practically hear Darren pinching the bridge of his nose as the payphone reminded me to pony up. Shit, I only had two quarters left for my next call. Otherwise, it was down to small change. Did payphones even take pennies?

"I mean, yeah, one of those might do the trick. Not sure if any of the stores will still have stock but it wouldn't hurt. And you might get lucky with all the wrecked cell towers but I wouldn't bank on it."

Maybe that was why Elias hadn't been persistently tracking me. More than half the towers near Rockwood and my office were down. The phone chimed again and I shoved in my last dime. "Look, I'm out of time. Can ya tell Alex..."

What? What could I possibly say? I wasn't even fresh out of excuses; they were all rotting in a long-forgotten ditch somewhere.

"I'll tell him, Lils." Darren said something else, but I didn't catch it as the call disconnected.

CHAPTER 27

GABE

The last time I'd turned myself in, I'd simply marched into the police station and put my hands up. It had been risky, but the publicity made it impossible for the department to bury my stunt.

Things were different now. We were at war. The National Guard surrounded the precinct and chances were high that at least one of them would be trigger-happy.

Michelle proposed just calling me in and having an officer come pick me up. I flatly refused. "They'll march me past all the protesters. How will we explain my getting in here without being seen?" It would stir up too much suspicion.

Michelle twisted her lips and combed her curls with a free hand. "Fine, what do you propose?"

"We need someone we can trust." Even if Harper hadn't been sacked, I couldn't ask him. With Stevens gone, my list of close contacts was now non-existent. But I had one idea. Michelle hated it but couldn't offer an alternative.

"Since you don't even have a name, I'll have to look her up in the office." Michelle stretched and grabbed her half-empty coffee mug with a stack of papers as she scanned the living room for more to clean. "Guest room is down the hall on the left."

I nodded. "Thanks."

Despite my exhaustion, I still couldn't sleep. No matter how I tossed or turned, all I could do was lose my mind staring at the ceiling.

Michelle had books, thick heavy legal volumes left over from college. I'd only seen one fictional tome, a romance with a hilarious cover. Michelle hadn't realized I'd seen her squirreling it away at the end of the night.

Everyone deserves a guilty pleasure. And even if I were interested, there was no way I was digging through her room to find the bodice ripper.

That left me popping my lips and thinking. Lily had probably called Darren by now. She and Harper were out there, taking action. And I was stuck here waiting.

I debated heading out, trying to do something until Michelle got home from work but dismissed the idea as quickly as it came. Finally, the garage hummed open. Seconds later her heels click-clacked across the floor before she peeled them off, letting them fall next to her couch.

It took everything in me not to accost her; all I wanted to do was spring across the room and start in with the questions. It was like strolling through mud when I just wanted to bolt. As I leaned against the living room wall, she was placing her briefcase on the table and digging in the back of the cupboards, pulling out a tumbler before fishing out a bottle of vodka from the freezer.

"Isn't it a little early?" I wanted to turn around and plow my head straight into the wall.

"You're right." She glared as she nabbed some kind of cheap neon-colored juice out of the fridge. "It's not like I was busy tiptoeing around my superiors all day."

"I'm sor—"

"You know, the same superiors trying to find any reason to fire me." She added ice to the tumbler, throwing each cube in violently. "And of course, I had a totally reasonable explanation to look up that name."

I swallowed my ridiculous apology and stayed quiet while she mixed everything, cleaning up immediately and letting out a grateful sigh after the first drink. "I couldn't even tell Barb why I couldn't visit tonight. She's finally lucid; she'd hear the BS before I even said it."

I winced. When Michelle only took another drink, I hazarded a question. "Any luck?"

She put the drink down and let out a long breath to steady herself. "Yeah. I even managed to talk to her without being seen. Easier to do when your cases are being yanked away from you."

I couldn't decide if I should feel hope or dread. "And?"

"She says she'll do it. She also said 'He better not make me plug a hole in his six.'" Michelle twisted her brows in confusion. "What the hell is that even supposed to mean?"

"Hard to explain." I shook my head, allowing myself a rueful smile. "So, where are we doing this?"

Michelle asked several times if I was sure. One could almost take her continued questioning for concern.

"It's not as though I need air."

She curled her painted lips in an ugly sneer. "I know, but..."

"We both agreed we can't risk the press seeing me."

"Yeah," she admitted.

"And they are going to see into the car when you pull out?"

Michelle stared at the garage ceiling for a second before nodding. "Alright, get comfy."

I squeezed into the trunk of her Honda. Much easier after she'd removed several reusable shopping bags from the interior, but I still had to bunch my body in several unnatural angles to fit.

Michelle looked uneasy, checking multiple times that the hinges wouldn't slam onto me before easing the trunk lid closed with a heavy clunk. "Don't make a sound."

The eerie green glow of the plastic emergency lever didn't illuminate anything, but it gave my eyes somewhere to focus in the dark.

Michelle's car door thumped shut and the car engine rumbled to life as the garage door groaned open. Despite it all, I could still hear the reporters and protestors through the car. Nothing distinct, just the old familiar buzz of human curiosity cranked far too high.

Michelle slammed on her brakes, knocking me into the back of the trunk while the crowd grew louder. She had to honk several times before they'd let her back out.

Every sound became a muffled mystery as we drove. Was that slosh a snow drift or a pothole-turned puddle? Were the quick thumps kicking up from the road rocks or some of the long-abandoned debris left strewn in our streets?

My legs and neck started to cramp, I tried to stretch which only resulted in bunching my shoulders into a single tight knot.

Still, not the worst ride I've had this week.

Finally, the car slowed and jolted into park. Here, the wind had enough room to howl around us. Michelle got out, slamming her door. Her shoes crunched over gravel and terrain for several minutes while I tried and failed to move my head.

The trunk gave a quick click, hardly any warning before she lifted the lid and light flooded my eyes. I moved to get up, but Michelle placed a hand on my shoulder. "Listen to be safe."

I grumbled but cocked my head to listen all the same. Just wind and the occasional rustle of a dead leaf skittering over the ground. "We're good."

Michelle released my shoulder, and I slowly stretched out, marveling that my neck could pop that many times. Guess even vampire healing can't compete with space confinements. Or maybe my neck popped that quickly because of the supernatural healing. Who knew?

I stretched my back and legs as I looked around.

Road construction in Portland was always slow, so of course, there was a project that had to be cast off after the first wave of Starved. The late afternoon highlighted the forsaken equipment with pavers and rollers covered in weeks of grime and dirt, even on their tires.

The worst was the blood. One big splotch hung from a piece shaped like a giant guillotine. Had there been people at work here during the first or second wave of Starved?

I was liking this new plan less and less. "Where do I go?"

Michelle pointed. "That way. Her patrol takes her past the car lots and shops. She said to be sure you're in plain sight for the dashcam."

I nodded. "You ready for this?"

Michele crossed her arms and sneered. "Stop stalling."

CHAPTER 28

I hung up the phone and collapsed against the wall, rubbing my last two quarters against each other. All the thoughts in my head swarmed, like a bunch of pissed off hornets.

And this next call was going to kick the nest.

Ivan might have someone run this payphone's history and figure out the group's burner, but we couldn't waste gas driving around only to find the next phone busted or disabled. We had to take the risk and hope the Court was too overwhelmed.

Dialing each digit felt like punching in the code to launch a nuke. Part of me really hoped he didn't pick up. It was early by Court standards after all. Most of us kept late hours to keep out of the sun and save energy healing–

"Hello." There was no question in his voice. It was his typical straightforward tone.

I tried to speak but the words were trapped and I ended up swallowing to loosen them.

"I swear, if this is another telemarketer, I'll find you and–"

"It's me!" I gasped out, not wanting to hear Cyrus' next thought. One of his main job duties was designing torture, after all. I'm sure he had some fresh ideas for Scam Likely.

He grunted. "If you're calling to apologize–"

"I'm on a payphone so we don't have time to piss each other off."

"Enlighten me quickly then."

"I found the tracker." I tried to keep the hurt out of my tone. "You can tell your boss I know about it."

"Ivan never placed a device on you."

"I already said I don't have time for games." I deposited my last quarter.

There was only a beat of silence before Cyrus growled, "You cannot seriously be saying I'm in league with him."

"You were there when I found the trinket. You let me out of the dungeon easy enough. Only you and your team knew Ritti had given me my old phone." With each accusation, a cartoonish neon arrow pointed directly at Cyrus. "And lord knows you took forever extracting any real details from Anna. What were you doing? Tickling her?"

Cyrus' voice softened. "This is insane."

Was that melancholy I was hearing?

"Agreed," I spat out. "Ya failed so miserably at covering your tracks, I don't know how I could have missed it all this time. I just want to know why."

"Come in. Show us the device."

I actually laughed at that. "You're fucking jokin', right?"

"I understand your hesitancy–"

"I should hope so," I snapped. "Thanks but I'll take my chances out here. Hope your boss likes his goose wild."

I hung up and walked away, ignoring the tell-tale clink of the payphone returning a dime of my time.

Harper smiled softly. "How'd it go?"

"The hooks baited. We gotta get out of here before they run that number and send a party."

Harper nodded and we headed back toward the bike. I debated bolting for it, then and there. But that bloody tracking charm was at the bottom of his backpack. I had to get it back before I left. Harper and Hannah would object but their building didn't need to be dragged into this mess.

As we made our way back through the streets, I caught sight of something I hadn't noticed before, tapping Harper and pointing. He nodded under his motorcycle helmet as he pulled over and we dismounted.

The signs were old, some faded from exposure, others chewed by the occasional critter. Nothing was complete and barely any of it was truly legible. I knelt low and tried to read.

The power of the peop...

You take our resou... we take your ....

The hands that served you now suffer

Its ur war 2

"Lily?" Harper's big hand landed on my shoulder.

I couldn't answer him even if I wanted to. "When was the last protest?"

Harper took a minute to answer. "They ran out of energy or time just before I got sacked a week ago. Even then, their ranks were thin. It was mostly kids in this neighborhood watching too much national news."

"I sounded just like these eejits on my way in, didn't I?" It was impossible to keep the shame from my voice.

Harper opened his mouth, closed it, then shrugged. "We're all frustrated."

I nodded and kept reading, unable to explain the compulsion. Sure, I'd seen similar slogans during protests over the years. A couple of these could be ripped straight out of the *Occupy Wall Street* movement or marches against Vietnam. But those weren't the chants reverberating in my skull. "'Of no expense and little trouble.'"

"Huh?"

"It's from an old essay about the Irish famines." I stood and dusted my pants sloppily. "Gabe reminded me of it when we first met and I looked it up recently."

"Okay..." Harper looked like he was trying to follow directions to the moon.

"Basically, the writer proposed that the poor eat their young to avoid starvation and reduce the population, solving our country's problem and even reducing the number of abortions."

Harper's face scrunched in horror.

"It was sarcastic. We were all pissed." My tone was almost numb as I still looked at the signs. "Some people say the English were trying to extinguish the Irish through the famines, but I think that gives them far too much credit. You have to care about someone to *want* to kill 'em."

"Wasn't your..." Harper's words trailed with a question he couldn't ask.

I just nodded but I couldn't meet his eyes. "Elias was an outlier at the time. He was a decent landlord."

That simple truth hurt so much. It would be easier if he'd been some mustache-twiddling jackass. But no, the trauma from our village trying to slaughter him was my doing and his undoing.

"The English rule made us plant crops for rent. For years we'd sustained ourselves on potatoes. But a nasty fungus spread through the world and the English refused to change the system. If we didn't give over the crops, we'd lose our homes. People were so desperate, they ate grass."

"Ah." Harper drew out, finally catching on. "The writer wanted to remind everyone of the value in human life."

"Yeah, but the thing we often forgot was that the English were also struggling. It doesn't mean they handled it right, but we were far away and they had their own troubles. It's not like they were bombarded with images of our emaciated bodies during half-time." I shook my head and turned back to the bike. "They were people, just like us."

CHAPTER 29

GABE

The reconstruction had gone on for several months before the first wave of Starved. I almost couldn't remember the last time I'd even used this road. Guess I was making up for it now. The busted concrete was uneven and lumpy under dirty slush, forcing me to take my steps slowly.

Yeah, that's the reason I'm taking my sweet time.

It felt a little like I was crossing a giant desert in a dystopian science fiction. Despite the somewhat familiar surroundings.

Several used car lots and billboards flanked me on both sides. The sight of Memory Lane Motors halted my steps. The fatherly face of the owner peered down from the nearest sign, smiling fondly while sitting in his convertible. I'd seen the sign hundreds of times over the years. It had been comforting and familiar.

Now, the billboard was covered in a mish-mash of graffiti, towering over a parking lot loaded with busted cars. People probably came to steal the vehicles only to realize the staff had taken all the keys.

There was already one legal battle looming over me. I couldn't stop to investigate. My contact would be waiting and I needed to hustle.

I finally made it to the other side of construction, passed a now ruined wrought iron fence, and then walked under the long awning of an auto repair and discount muffler shop. Both were littered in fresh tags. Where the hell were people getting the paint? The answer occurred to me as I passed the hardware store, unable to see my reflection in the busted windows.

A few minutes later, the acrid scent of fresh urine warned me I wasn't alone. A homeless guy dozed softly under a business awning, drool rolling from his chapped lips and pooling below. I step quietly, trying to avoid waking him. A witness might be handy but people were unpredictable in this new landscape. Best not to risk it.

Finally, I could see our rendezvous point. A tattoo school, the letters in the window reminiscent of an old western wanted poster. I sat on the stoop and waited.

I had about another half hour to consider everything. If I wasn't considering Lily and Harper's cockamamie plan, I was mentally rehearsing for my contact's arrival. It was an old habit, born of my time in court, but I hadn't done it in a while. I'd quickly realized that it was a useless exercise. I could never properly predict what I'd be asked or how the defendant's lawyer would reply.

But now it had returned. Probably due to all the practice questioning from Michelle.

It was a little easier to predict this scenario. We had to play it just right for her dashcam and body footage. Everything would be scrutinized and reviewed over and over. Our prior contact wouldn't go unnoticed. The media would have a field day no matter what we did.

But we had to make them dig.

The slow rumble of a car engine roused me from my musings and I looked down the block. A black-and-white rolled down the road, slowly sifting through the lanes to avoid broken bits of debris. I wasn't sure why she'd be patrolling, especially not alone.

But she had a lot worse reasons not to trust me.

I stood slowly, holding my hands like I was going to start the wave at a football game any second, and walked toward the road. She slowed and seemed to talk to herself, before slamming on her brakes and hopping out. "Hands up!"

"Okay, okay." I schooled my expression. Apparently, I wasn't the only one who'd been rehearsing. "I'm not resisting."

The officer reached up to her radio, her service weapon trained on my torso. "This is Officer Delgado. I have a 10-110 in progress. I've found Gabriel Collins"

I wasn't sure if her aim meant she hadn't told anyone about the headshot or if it was just habit. Either way, I appreciated it. Her radio crackled as she barked. "On the ground. Now, Vampboy!"

I nodded and slowly lowered to my knees before placing my belly on the road. I should have spent my rehearsal time choosing where to kneel. My chest sank into slush, the cold seeping through my clothes.

It was going to be a fun ride to the station.

We couldn't talk along the way. There were cameras throughout the cruiser. So I just had to sit there, sopping wet without any heat and my arms stuck behind my back. She'd clasped the cuffs looser than I was expecting. Maybe she figured they were more symbolic. The whole world had seen me shatter a pair just like them during my initial hearing.

Again, I appreciated what little courtesy she could give me. With all these cameras and microphones, it was dangerous for her to so much as wink at me. She was trusting me with her career. Her whole life. Saving her from the Starved and explaining how to kill me had gone a long way.

The broken city rolled by in obscure shadows as I leaned my head against the hard plastic seat. Before, I'd only had to deal with solitary confinement for a few days before being placed under house arrest.

My crappy apartment was gone and now so was my parent's house. There'd be no avoiding prison this time.

CHAPTER 30

LILY

"We don't have time for this." I held out my hand. "Darren says they can still track it through your little sleeve thingy."

"Not a chance." Harper's face scrunched in annoyance. "I've tested it. GPS, Find My Phone, and location sharing. None of them could manage it."

"This isn't a bloody phone," I growled.

Dammit, I was really hoping he'd buy the excuse. If I could just slink off with the necklace, I might get out of here without any drama. I couldn't mesmerize Harper, he'd had vampire blood in his system too recently. And I'd never be able to hurt the big goofball.

"Is it really worth the risk?" I pleaded.

"She has a point..." Hannah gave Harper a sympathetic look. "You didn't even put it in the sleeve until after she got here."

Harper's well-worn laugh lines distorted with despair. "It's been a whole day."

"And every second we wait is another second too long." I shook my head. "Even if that thing is working, they might have seen the last known location."

"The building can't take an assault." Hannah looked at their floor like she was using X-ray vision. "Mr. Lucas is on crutches with an oxygen tank."

Harper sighed and finally handed over the tiny pocket. "Why can't I go with you?"

"I..." I stuttered, looking at Hannah uncertainly. "I need to eat."

Hannah pursed her lips like she could actually button them. Harper eyed me skeptically. "Where will you go?"

"I've got one idea but it's a long shot. Gotta try though." I let out a deep breath. "Everyone in this city is starved or sick. I haven't been this desperate for a healthy meal since I immigrated."

Hannah looked like she was trying to perform a complex calculation, her eyes roaming over my face.

I snorted. "Mid 1800s."

Her face dropped. "Damn, I need your skin routine."

Despite everything, I laughed. By modern standards, I actually looked older than my turned age. Years of starvation and stress will do that to a girl. Hell, I was one of the lucky few in my village who knew their precise age. Tracking such things wasn't a big priority for most mums.

If people had any energy left, it went to food riots or trying to immigrate. Maybe the occasional protest, though they were more rare towards the end...

Something in that thought nagged me. I guess it showed on my face because Harper nudged my shoulder. "Lily?"

I shook my head and tried to smile. "Sorry, just wanderin' down memory lane."

From the shape of his eyebrows, I clearly wasn't convincing anybody that all was well.

"I've got over a century in baggage." I smiled wider and shrugged. "There's a lot of twists and turns in the road. It's easy to get lost."

He looked at Hannah who just nodded, before turning back to me. "Do you know where you're going to lose it?"

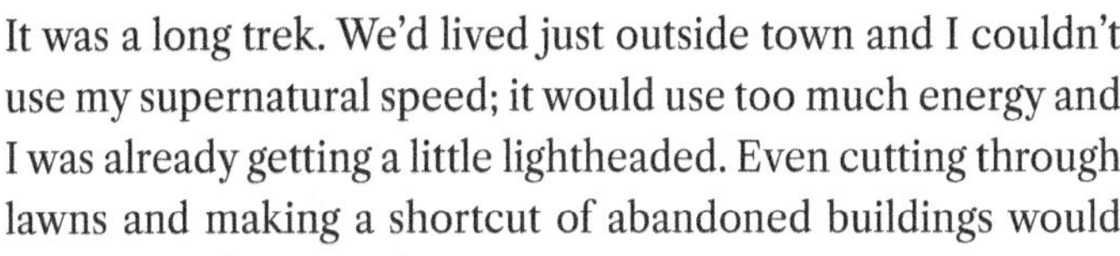

It was a long trek. We'd lived just outside town and I couldn't use my supernatural speed; it would use too much energy and I was already getting a little lightheaded. Even cutting through lawns and making a shortcut of abandoned buildings would take me well over an hour.

Granted, it'd be hard to tell time without a phone or watch. Hard to stay out of my own head too. Even as I occasionally passed someone, the meetings were short and simple. So that left my mind wandering through the comparisons I'd started earlier.

Just as with the famines, the lower class was blaming the upper class. I'd even seen this same principle after immigrating, during the Battle of the Five Points. Violence was becoming an easy outlet during this horrendous time.

Even now, at the edges of town, I was still passing battered poster boards with silly slogans plastered all over them. *OUT OF HERE FANG HEADS* had taken the lead for my favorite. Might have been the doodle that did it.

"Fuck it." I started digging through my pockets. Sure, I'd promised Gabe but that was while we'd worked this together. He was in jail by now.

The kitchen torch took a minute for me to work; I started to worry it was out of fuel. Finally, the ember crept up the cigarette as I sat on a big rock, letting the plume crawl from my lips as I pulled the necklace from Harper's pocket-thingy.

I'd done this every so often, hoping the trail might draw Elias away from Harper's building. It was a risk, any eejit with two brain cells to rub together would figure out where I was headed.

The bloody images of my past still scrolled through my mind while my butt grew sore sitting on the rock. Ivan had always talked about how human history repeated. I hated that I was starting to see his point in real-time. There was an idea there, still nagging at my mind. This instinct had helped me solve more than one case. But I didn't understand how it applied between the famines and this modern insurgent zone.

I shook my head, hating myself the minute I did. My brain felt loose and wobbly inside the skull. It was little wonder I couldn't think straight. I blew out a breath and flicked my half-smoked cigarette into a slushy puddle, placing my head in my hands.

It was a long shot. Court had moved us before the first wave of Starved. Maria and the gang would have packed everything. But I'd still been on the lam, unsure where they'd been moved. So maybe my friends had taken the risk. It was the only way I could avoid going back to Court or feeding directly from someone.

I sighed and stood, placing the necklace back in Harper's contraption and getting back on the road. I only had a little way to go.

Every step became heavier. I couldn't remember the last time I felt so weak. Then I did and I wanted to kick myself for considering it. Just before I'd been Starved, there were snatches of conscious thought, mostly anguish and anger.

If whatever Elias thought I knew lay in that brief delirium, we were all royally fucked. I hardly even remembered coming back to myself with Gabe cradling me while Olive watched me sob. I'd even asked her to tell us where Elias was hiding before going back to Court. But she'd only shaken her head. "That's my only leverage."

I blew out a chilly breath. I couldn't blame Olive for the pragmatic take, but now she was gone and my hope was slowly dwindling.

CHAPTER 31

GABE

The interrogation had been everything I expected. Sanders played it by the book, gritting his teeth when I reminded him of my right to remain silent and requested my lawyer.

Michelle strolled in, her hair frazzled and her make-up missing. I suppressed a snort. Even when she was a mess, it was a show. Made me wonder if the drunken anger had also been an act. Though I wasn't sure what purpose that would serve. Not that I could ask her.

When Michelle kept shutting their nonsense and questions down, they shuffled me directly to prison to await trial, worried I would escape the courthouse holding. We'd anticipated this. The orange jumpsuit, overly tight cuffs, and creative jeers were all on par. What was unexpected were my new accommodations.

It took everything in me not to growl at the guard. "This isn't safe."

"Calm down." My escort was already holding his pepper spray.

Even still it was impossible to relax. Every muscle in my body twitched. "I can't be in gen pop. You have to know that."

I was a cop. That alone would suggest this was a terrible idea. Add my unique dietary needs...

The escorting officer bobbed his head to indicate the cell. "Don't worry, we made sure you wouldn't have a roommate."

"That's not the–" My guard's hardening expression made me realize I was raising my voice. I'd have flexed my hands but they held the only excuse for a blanket I would see outside trial. I forced a slow deep breath.

It wouldn't do to lose my temper. I had to make him listen.

An idea struck me.

I could fix this. I had to fix this. I let that thought guide the intent into my gaze, slowly filling my eyes with a powerful pulse beneath the membrane.

The guard slapped me. "Don't you try that hoodoo shit on me!"

I snarled, "You think I won't report this?"

The guard chuffed. "Go ahead, tell them how you tried to mesmerize me."

I spat out a curse and stared into the cold cell. In the hallway, everything echoed and commingled into nonsense, bouncing through the concrete and around the open walkways. But a large portion of it was the barred entrances to each cell, each one acting as an amplifier back into the cavernous halls.

And every echo was cold.

"I want to talk to my lawyer." My voice still wasn't level.

The intercom crackled overhead, announcing five minutes to lights out.

"I'm sure you do." The guard hooked his thumb into the cell.

I shuffled in, the cardboard-thin soles of my jail-slippers failing to keep the concrete chill from my feet.

"Nighty, night." The guard whistled as he walked away. The ridicule grew as his steps receded.

"Hey Collins, they give you a comfy coffin?"

"Do you think if he bites us, that makes us his bitch?"

"Nah man, it makes you meat."

I sat on the stiff lower cot, dropping the flimsy blanket on the floor and cradling my head in my hands.

I should never have turned myself in. I'd just become a walking time bomb in a house full of fuses and fire.

CHAPTER 32

LILY

After emptying our overflowing mailbox, I checked the fridge, unsurprised by the empty status or spotless shine. For most folks, the fridge was the last thing you packed when moving. Vampires had it as a higher priority, needing extra time to pull out every drawer and shelf for a perfect finish able to fool any CI team. Even now, the bleach still lingered in my nostrils.

The basement was always my best bet but it could be a trap. I'd been a fugitive when my roommates were forced to move, it wouldn't be out of the question that the Court would redo the locks. Or set an alarm.

But I had to risk it; if I didn't eat soon, I would become dangerous. The palm scanner was easy to find in our now-empty pantry. The green light swooped under my hand before a heavy click. The door popped open a mere fraction.

I gulped and practically ran down the concrete steps. My trick with the necklace already limited my time here, but the scanners' easy access meant I had minutes at best.

The first rehab-cell still had a mini fridge, sporting four bags of AB negative, my favorite blood type. It was enough to make me cry.

Even now, months after all the bullshit, my friends were looking out for me. They'd risked leaving these behind in case I was desperate, knowing the Court would leave the electricity running for the scanner.

But here I was, running from them. Again.

I sniffled and flicked the tear away.

It didn't take long to drain the first bag and I let out a breathy, happy sigh before puncturing the second one, coaching myself to drink more slowly. The fuzzy feeling in my mind lifted just enough to leave me lightheaded and euphoric as blood rushed through my weary system. I snatched the remaining bags and started back up the steps.

As my boots pounded back to the main level, it occurred to me that Gabe usually drank the same blood as me. Had my roommates left so much in case we came back together?

Were they hoping for that?

My thoughts were disrupted as a heavy shadow fell on me and a dark voice sadly said, "Hey, kid."

Ivan's heavy mass loomed at the top of the steps, the light behind him obscuring the incongruent features of his face. Somehow, I doubted he was smiling.

"Who else is here?" I chugged the remainder of the blood bag and discarded the plastic on the steps. Littering seemed like a low concern at the moment.

"Just me." Ivan's sad tone was like a cold knife to my gut.

I snorted to cover the emotion in my voice. "Ya gonna take me in on your own?"

He shook his head. "The rest of the team isn't far away."

"Why leave 'em behind?" I stepped back, nearly stumbling as I punctured the third bag with my teeth. Not a chance in hell they'd let me keep them.

"I was waiting upstairs to see what you would do."

I blanched, unable to speak. My adoptive sire had camped out, expecting me. Then he watched to see my suspicious activity.

He came down a single step. "I need to ask you something, kid."

My mind raced as I backed up again, like I could avoid the very echo of his words. He was standing at the only exit and filled the whole door. The team was on the way.

"Do you truly believe Cyrus is the mole?"

I paused, nearly falling again. "What?"

"He told me of your call. And the bauble you found." Ivan held out a large hand. "May I see it?"

Refusing was idiotic and useless. I needed to lose the ruddy thing anyway and they'd only take it once I was in custody. I pulled it from Harper's pouch and reached out to Ivan, the jewel dancing in my shaky hands. I half-expected him to nab my wrist.

Instead, he scooped the necklace up and considered it, taking a step back. My hands still quivered at my sides.

"Where is the device hidden?" He flipped it over in his hand.

"Look at the back. There's a jeweler's catch."

Ivan did so, nodding and considering. "Did anyone besides Cyrus know you found it?"

"Not that I know of." I shook my head.

Ivan nodded and pocketed the necklace. "Let's go."

I swallowed hard. A single tear welled in my eyes. "Please."

Ivan sighed, "I can't let you go, kid."

I nodded slowly, weighing my odds. Ivan had the higher ground, he was huge, and he had far more training than I did. It was useless. I'd only bested Cyrus with a heavy dose of dumb luck and surprise. But Ivan had also taught me something early on. Something I still valued.

I leaped, and Ivan swatted me away like an annoying fly. I slammed into the wall; my whole skeleton cracked and I cried out in pain.

"Don't, kid." Ivan's warning was so low I almost missed it while I flopped to the ground. He started down the stairs, his heavy steps slowly thumping towards me.

"You'll go down one day, kid," I recited between gasps of pain as my bones snapped back in place. "Ya might as well go down swingin'."

His steps faltered as I looked up. Pain slashed those distorted features in a scowl. "I never thought it would be me."

"That makes two of us." I stood slowly, wincing with each pop and crack.

"Wipe your mouth."

I slid the back of my wrist across my lip; the blood was warm on my skin. "That's the last order ya give me, boss."

He nodded and thundered down the steps. I barely had the chance to slide out of his path. He caught the collar of my jacket, and I unzipped it, falling out while he tried to haul me off the ground.

Ivan reached for me again, and I scrambled around his legs. I was two steps up when he grabbed my ankle and yanked me back, smacking my skull on the ground. My world went dark as I kicked blindly, trying to slam the heel of my boot into his hand.

As the darkness lifted, the fuzzy outline of his other hand furiously tried to grab my flailing foot. "Kid, stop!"

His voice cracked, and I almost faltered. I didn't want to kick any more than he wanted to grab. But it was what it was. "Sorry, boss."

I kicked again, sending my foot into his chin this time. His head snapped back and his iron grip finally loosened. I clambered up the steps like a dog. I could see the floor to our old pantry, a can of soup forgotten in the corner. I was almost out.

Then I was hauled into the air by my shoulders and slammed into the wall. I cried and flailed. I couldn't help it. Ivan's big fingers dug into my shoulders. "Please stop."

I went limp and forced myself to look at him. Ivan had done so much for me. What did he see now?

The little urchin who failed to keep Alex sequestered during his transition? The soldier and detective he'd trained when I lacked purpose? The girl who betrayed him the first time I learned about Court policy for children? Or just the pawn Ritti had turned me into?

His jaw was set, and his shoulders were back. I couldn't read his eyes. His words were nothing but a plea. "Please. Stop."

My head became too heavy to hold up and the tears fell, tiny red specks that littered the concrete below. I couldn't fight him anymore. And it wasn't just because I was outclassed.

Just outside, car brakes screeched and car doors *thump-thumped* closed. His team had finally arrived. If it had been useless before, it was hopeless now.

I sagged against the wall, letting the tears fall down my cheeks freely and speckle the floor in awful little polka dots. There was a sad sense of relief in me; I could stop fighting. But I was also terrified. Even if Cyrus wasn't the rat, he'd let me escape. They'd assign someone else to interrogate me, and I was running out of friends at Court.

Friends. The single word hammered through my mind. If I hadn't run from my friends again, I wouldn't be here, cornered and alone. I kept trying to save them by leaving but I fucking needed them. And I'd learned the lesson too late.

"I am sorry, kid." Ivan leaned his forehead against mine.

"I know." I debated flinging my head forward, nailing his skull with mine. But the boots were getting closer, already in the kitchen. Now the pantry.

The voice that echoed down the stairs made Ivan tense and stopped my tears altogether. "Get those nasty mitts off my sister!"

CHAPTER 33

GABE

The odor wafting through the prison cafeteria made me all too glad for my dietary restrictions. It was this confusing stench of dried mashed potatoes and overcooked meat loaf, more bewildering with every tray of grey, sloppy stew that landed on the nearby tables.

That asshole guard had insisted I *mingle*, refusing to let me stay in my cell. I wasn't sure why pretending to read on the top shelf of my bed was a problem but I couldn't afford to argue. The more patient I was, the sooner Michelle could fix this.

The slosh of discolored stew being poured out cobbled with the slap of flimsy trays on the stainless steel tables and the lunch line chatter. It was impossible to drown it out. At least I didn't have to listen to chairs squealing across the concrete; the bolted stools wouldn't so much as budge.

Nobody approached me but they weren't ignoring me either. A few simply squinted from afar, like they were trying to decipher an abstract painting. Others openly pointed with their sporks while making animated conversation.

It was only a matter of time. Even without my police history, looking meek in prison was a bad move.

So I sat, reading every other word of my book from the prison library, just to give my hands and eyes something to do. The librarian didn't have me in the system yet, so the only book he could offer came from the trash. At least, that was his claim.

Even without my trouble focusing, the story would be impossible to follow. Half the pages were torn, the rest had doodles and bits of notes passed between a prior set of inmates. The ink was vivid, seeming fresh.

At least the back and forth gave me something to consider.

Nah man. We'll be out before the month is done.

I can't believe ya trust them.

They ain't all bad, just like you and me.

I was still piecing their conversation together when I felt it. Like an ant crawling on the back of my neck. Somebody was staring at me.

A second later, a man sat at my table, abruptly ending the mystery but adding a whole new type of tension.

He was a round man. His male pattern-baldness had advanced over the last few months, those ugly sideburns growing bushy and long. Something about it made him look like an angry little troll as he started tapping the tip of his spork against the shiny top of the table.

"Why the hell are you here?" I wanted to slam my head through the table the minute I asked.

"Shouldn't that be my line?" Contempt dripped from each word. Jack O'Neil had been sentenced to life in prison right when I'd met Lily. It seemed like a lifetime ago. Either way, he should have been transferred by now. And reminding him of that was not my brightest move. At my silence, he stopped the incessant tapping. "They were getting ready to move me, but I guess you unleashed a bunch of zombies on the city."

Great... Not only had an inmate recognized me, it was the jackass who killed his wife with a meat fork and tried to pass it as a vampire attack. Not someone I could realistically reason with.

I forced my posture to relax. "Should I keep one eye open at night?"

His heavy brows fell with his scowl as he hissed, "You best watch it, *Detective.*"

"You can't blackmail me." I tried to sound nonchalant. "Everyone recognizes me."

Jack's mouth curled in an ugly sneer as he looked away.

"Oh..." I scoffed. "You want something."

Well at least this broke the tedium of my day. Though I couldn't imagine what he thought I could do for him. We were both in prison. His jaw tightened and his fists shook when he couldn't clench his hands any tighter.

"Look, if it hurts to even ask me..." I placed my hands on the table and started to rise.

"My roommate is an asshole." Jack glared at me. "Somehow you got a cell to yourself."

I blinked. Trying to absorb it. "You want to stay with me?"

"No. But I can't stay with him." He pulled the collar of his neon jump suit aside. A big bruise was turning yellow at the base of his neck, fading to a dark purple that stretched out of sight. He let the shirt fall back in place and glared. "I figure if you're in here, your pompous ass probably broke a few rules. Maybe you can get off that high horse and help me."

"High horse?" I shook my head and leaned in close. "You murdered your wife."

"I had my reasons. You probably had reasons for whatever landed you in here."

My laugh was low and mirthless. "That has to be the most cliché argument you could have made."

"It's not like you were fair to me."

There was no stopping the snort that escaped my lips. "Still the victim, I see."

Jack ground his teeth and glared across the table. "You insulted me every minute of that interrogation."

"You. Murdered. Your. Wife." I knew he was dense but, come on.

"Oh sure that was the reason." Jack shook his head. "You think I don't remember the sympathy?"

"Huh?" We hadn't pulled any good-cop-bad-cop routine with Jack. Really, the interview had been a formality with the evidence we had.

"In the beginning, when you started investigating Carla's death." His smile was like ice. "You were kind. I almost felt bad for what I did when you were talking to me."

"Yeah, well, lying doesn't tend to—"

"It wasn't the lie." Jack leaned in close. "I saw it in your eyes. You were angry that I wasn't a vampire. You were mad you missed your big break."

I slammed my hand into the table without thinking. The metal dented under my fist, the thump echoing around us. Across the prison cafeteria, plastic cutlery clattered into styrofoam trays. I closed my eyes in resignation as all the clatter died.

I'd spent all day winding myself up for the inevitable conflict, letting the energy build until I couldn't contain it. Nobody stood. Nobody loomed. But they all stared. Those too far away to see the table murmured questions, trying to understand what was going on.

Jack grinned. "I guess the rumors were true."

I didn't have the energy to reply. Or the time. The guards marched, their movements simultaneously jerky and formulated, like soldiers on an unfamiliar drill.

I laid my hands on the table, palms up, and waited.

"Collins!" A guard I vaguely recognized from court stood before me. His stance reminded me of an old wind up toy with the key stuck, ready to spring into action the second he was released. "On the ground."

Jack O'Neal snickered but I ignored him, nodding and slowly raising my palms as I stood and lowered myself to the ground, lacing my fingers behind my head and laying my cheek on the concrete. "No problem."

My voice sounded foreign, distant in my own ears. I had no idea what might provoke these officers. They shouldn't have even been dealing with me. In their eyes, I was little more than a coherent lion someone sent here instead of the zoo.

And I was hungry. I prayed it didn't show on my face. I'd been so preoccupied with getting into solitary, I hadn't given the specific reason much thought. Trying to ignore the beast in my belly. But now, after that last burst of energy, under the tension of these guards, it was all I could think about.

They pulled my arms up to cuff me, the metal digging into my wrists and the hinge pinching my skin as soon as they clicked shut. Pretty sure the regulation was to leave enough space for one finger, but I kept my thoughts to myself.

It wasn't like circulation was an issue and the damage would heal soon enough. Finally, they lifted me to my feet and escorted me out.

The silence of the cafeteria was concerning. This had to be the best change to the daily humdrum for most inmates. While I wouldn't expect the clichéd jeering from a movie, the slow whispers were not a good sign. Only one idiot hollered something about piggies but he was quickly hushed by the surrounding inmates.

The guards said nothing as they escorted me through new halls. Colder, lonelier ones. My hopes rose.

My stupidity might have also been a solution. As we passed the heavy door, I heard the muffled voices of inmates echoing inside their single cells. Some singing, some yelling, one acting out a Shakespear monologue I vaguely remembered from high-school.

All of them locked up tight. Alone.

I'd still need to talk to someone about blood bags, but it was a start.

Suddenly, behind me a new noise arose. The *thwap thwap thwap* of shoes running quickly behind us.

"Wait!"

I recognized that voice and groaned.

"Whoa, Chuck," the officer holding me chuckled. "Where's the fire?"

"Yeah, that's original." My favorite security panted heavily. "You can't put him in solitary."

CHAPTER 34

LILY

Seeing my brother always sent my emotions to war.

The first time had been shock, a little hope, and a wash of horror. Now, with his scarred face scowling from the top step, it was hard to decide if he would be my savior or my inevitable oppressor. Maybe the two roles were more intertwined than I'd like to think.

"That's rich, coming from the likes of you," Ivan growled as he shoved me behind him, becoming a brick barrier between us. "You think I don't know the hell you put her through?"

It was tough to decide who I was rooting for. Neither outcome ended with my freedom.

Cillian snorted rudely and began descending the steps, his hands in his pockets like he was getting ready to whistle a merry tune. "At least I don't *pretend* to help her."

Before I could ask what the hell Cillian meant, Ivan threw his giant fist directly into my brother.

Cillian ducked and winked at me. "Too bad ya didn't check the garage first."

"You leave her out of this!" Ivan grabbed Cillian's collar, tossing him into the wall. My brother's body snapped against the bricks and I shrieked, despite myself.

I clamped down on Ivan's arm with all my weight. "Leave him be!"

Ivan's face fell in absolute shock. "So it was you?"

It took me a minute to realize what Ivan was getting at. And yeah, this didn't look good. My brother didn't deserve the help, but he was my responsibility.

"It's not her, old boy." Cillian laughed in a pained little wheeze; his whole body cracked as the joints popped back in place. Deep crimson smeared across his scars as he wiped his mouth. "And I think you know who it is."

Ivan's jaw set as he flung me to the floor. My head slammed against concrete and I gasped in pain before his boot landed on my throat. "Stay down, kid."

The anguish in his voice caught me off guard. Not that I could move the big man. And he couldn't risk letting me up, not after the stunt I'd just pulled. So I was trapped watching my adoptive sire and my demented brother fight.

Every punch or block ground his boot further on my neck. It was a miracle he didn't crush my throat. He was huge with both height and muscle, but Cillian had all the mobility.

And he used it.

My brother pulled a big knife from a sheath I hadn't noticed before, tossing the handle between his palms just out of Ivan's reach. A cat playing with a mouse.

"Ya gonna take the risk, big fella?" There was a wicked glint in his good eye. Something I recognized from when we were kids. The last time I saw that look, Cillian broke my pinky.

Ivan's foot blocked my windpipe; all I could do was croak and claw at his leg, trying to warn him. Ivan ignored me, rolling his shoulders. "You gonna stop running your mouth? Or does that run in the family?"

Cillian lunged high and Ivan went to block the blade, giving my brother a perfect opportunity to barrel into Ivan's stomach with both feet. His stance wasn't strong, between pinning me and trying to block high, there was nothing supporting his core. All I could do was watch as Ivan flew backwards, off my throat and into the wall, before Cillian slammed the blade into his eye.

Ivan's face slacked. His body stilled. My vocal cords were still healing, so I couldn't even scream as Ivan's disproportionate face turned gray, then crumbled into dust.

Cillian stood and wiped the blade, turning back to me. "You are a troublesome one, aren't ya?"

I lurched, crawling backwards on my legs. Cillian snorted and reached down but I swatted him away, finally able to scream, "You've taken everythin'!"

"I didn't take your pretty boy. Had a wide open chance with you two all cozy on the couch, didn't I?"

His words froze every nerve in my body. Even my brain had to thaw before I could process it. It still came out in a stammer, "You set the fire?"

Cillian knelt before me, shaking his head and tsking. "I've done what I can, Lilé. But I can only tug on the leash so mu–"

There was noise outside. The crunching of several trucks pulling up the gravel road before several more doors slam with their *thud-thuds*. From Cillian's expression, he wasn't expecting more backup.

The gunfire was immediate, screaming and yelling to duck or fire growing fast.

"What the–" Cillian didn't have the chance to finish. I shot my boot straight into his chin and ran for it. His skull cracked against the wall and he slumped into Ivan's still-smoldering ashes. I swallowed a scream in my throat, taking the stairs three at a time. My brother swayed towards the steps, recovering fast as I turned to shut the door. He saw me, shook his head, and started climbing as I pushed the reinforced metal.

His steps grew louder and closer. Just as I was about to shut the door, his broken gaze found mine and he reached out. I slammed the heavy door on his hand.

The reinforced steel barely muffled his screams as I kicked the severed digit away and punched the palm-scanner. It wouldn't last forever but it should slow my brother down. If I was very lucky, it might get him into Court custody, but I had no idea who I could trust.

The gunfire was still raging outside as I peaked through the edge of a curtain.

"Shite..." I groaned.

The battle was all over my front and side lawns. A stupid part of me was pissed they had stomped in the flower beds Maria had worked on for years.

Aside from the front door, the only other exits from our home were in the garage. The overhead doors were out of the question and the side door led right into the mayhem outside. No matter how I left, someone would see me.

Maybe I could sneak through on foot, but if even one person saw me, I'd be overwhelmed by either side.

"Double shite." I sank to the floor, resting my head in my hands. My brother kept pummeling the pantry door. That steel was made to withstand a new vampire in a blood craze; it could take his tantrum. But his raving was making it hard to think amongst all the other racket.

A bullet whizzed through my front window, glass sprinkling me as it snapped into our old fridge, emphasizing my thoughts.

Should I hide upstairs, maybe wait it out and hope both sides killed each other? A grim thought, I didn't want people from Court to die, I just didn't care to be their captive.

Cillian kept raving and I stuffed a fist into my mouth just to muffle my own frustrated scream. God, could he just shut up? Even before he killed Ivan, he insisted on giving me a hard time...

Too bad ya didn't check the garage first.

My hand slipped from my mouth as the idea whirled in my head. What had Cillian meant by that? It couldn't be...

My friends had promised they'd moved it but then Court had confiscated it. And no one had seen it since. Was it possible?

Another bullet whistled overhead, taking out a cupboard door this time and I swore. There was no use waiting here if there was even a chance. I quickly crawled across the floor, my hands ripping over the occasional shard.

Finally, I reached the steps and gazed over the edge of the window frame. Nobody was close and everyone was occupied. Someone might still see me; the door to the garage was in plain view of the front lawn.

I ran in an awkward crouch, snatching the handle and flinging the door open without bothering to close it. The light in the garage was dim, but I could still see her. Glimmering blue under my shadow.

My baby.

I ran forward and nearly cried, checking the saddlebags to find my stupid kitty helmet and keys. She was here and I had a chance. I quickly tucked my hair into my hoodie to keep it out of my face and walked the bike over to the side door. The overhead garage would open too slowly and loudly, giving them every chance to swarm me. I had to be quick.

I cracked the door and peaked out. The fighting was a few feet away. Not ideal but better than right on top of me. I flung the door open, started the engine and rolled out.

Someone tried to grab me but their hand slipped and I left them tumbling into the side of a big blue moving van.

"See ya, sucker!" My big belly laugh quickly strangled itself into tears as the adrenaline faded.

CHAPTER 35

GABE

The security guard's words echoed ceaselessly as I stared blankly at the cold, grey wall of my cell.

You're not getting out of this that easy, you traitor. He'd said it low, no one else would've heard.

They'd marched me back here, talking the whole way about some break-in at holding. How lucky I'd been transferred out of the courts when I was. As though none of them knew I'd turned myself in a second time

Not that it mattered.

My stomach growled and my fangs poked the inside of my lips. Lunch would be over soon. Already, inmates shuffled down the halls, towards rec time or the pathetic excuse this prison offered as a library. I didn't dare leave my cell. Just sat, staring at the blank canvas of a wall and waiting.

They had to let me call Michelle. And even if they didn't, Michelle knew better than to assume I was taken care of. I just had to wait.

But how long could I last?

Shoe slaps echoed just outside my cell, flap-flap-flapping over each other quickly. Under the noise was a distant clink-clink-clink. It was out of sync, inconsistent. And growing closer.

Or was it? That could just be my supernatural hearing, dialing in on the one sound that stood out in this dank cave. Anytime I rolled, the metal bedframe echoed my sentiments in its creeks and groans. The ceiling was about as mesmerizing as the wall.

The whole experience reminded me of vampire rehab. Or more precisely when I woke up, trying to puke but unable. Pain had sliced through every nerve in my body and my vision had swam in a noxious cloud. I'd been certain my life was over. In a sense, I'd been right.

Even now, my skin prickled at the memory of my second day.

Cold water gushed over me as Alex called out, in an over-cheerily tone, "Up and adam, newbie!"

I rolled out of bed to avoid another frigid spray and landed hard on the concrete, breathing angrily. "I'm not in the mood."

"Yeah, well I don't want to help the asshole who threatened Lily last week." Alex chuckled darkly as he tossed the hose back into the concrete hall. The metal tip clanked against the floor and the tap squealed as he turned the faucet off.

I clapped my hands over my ears. "How the hell do you deal with this?"

"You'll get used to it," Alex snorted as he kneeled in the puddle next to me. I guess, given his work, he'd dealt with worse messes. He held out a blood bag, the red liquid glinting in the low light of the cell. "Time to get to work."

Even as I looked away, those fucking fangs poked my bottom lip.

Alex sighed and stood, leaving the bag on my now-sopping mattress. "Pouting isn't going to undo this."

I still didn't look at him. "I want to speak to her."

"You and me both." Alex's shoes splashed out of my room and the door squealed shut.

"You gonna stay in bed?"

My trip through memory lane was abruptly halted and I glared at the opening of my current cell. "Get out."

Jack O'Neal shook his nearly bald head. "We didn't finish our conversation."

I looked back at the ceiling. "Both parties need to be listening for it to be a conversation."

"Fine, you listen and I'll talk." Jack entered and only now did I notice the blanket and pillow in his arms. "You can keep the top bunk, I'm used to bot–"

I rolled off the bed, landing on my feet and stopping him just before he could put the ratty old blanket down. Jack hunched but he didn't back away. Even as I kept staring.

"You won't even know I'm here." His voice was meek. Pathetic. It reminded me of his confession. My fists started to shake.

"Please." Jack's lip quivered. "You can... feed off me."

My blood boiled and I pointed to the door.

"Oh, come on!" Jack dropped the blanket and clasped his hands. "I know they aren't feeding you here. They can't."

One of the inmates outside whistled. "Jackie boy wants to be a whole new kind of bitch."

Another one chided, "You made that joke earlier, dumb ass."

Jack flinched at my expression. "You know I'm desperate if I'm asking you."

"That's your own fault." I felt the words reverberating in my throat, but I didn't recognize my voice. "You think I'm only angry because you lied and led me and my partner on a wild goose chase?"

Jack backed up before I even noticed I was stepping forward. "I mean..."

"You didn't just kill your wife, you pathetic troll." We were in the hall now, Jack slowly backing towards the wall.

"That bitch was going to take my son. I mean she said he was..." His voice trembled and I almost hesitated. I remembered when we delivered the news, DNA results confirming the boy in Jack's care had not been his own. The results had come from her divorce attorney. Jack had known about the divorce, that's what had started this whole mess. But he'd thought Jimmy was his right up to that point.

And then he'd cracked. Just like now. "She had me convinced that was my son! Thirteen years and she played me like a fiddle."

"Oh yeah, and that excuses stabbing her with a meat fork and then leaving her to bleed out!"

Inmates murmured around us and someone made a bet about the outcome. But I kept my eyes on the little gremlin in front of me, not even bothering to blink. I was too worried about my control.

Raw sewage was more appealing than his blood, but that didn't stop every word from scratching my barren throat. Or my fangs from stabbing the inside of my lips. If this rat kept offering his vein, I didn't know what I might do. What I might become.

I hadn't been this close to eating someone since vampire rehab. Maria's lecture started to hum through my mind.

"You left Jimmy without any family, you snake." I growled the next part low before returning to my cell and kicking his blanket into the hall. "I wouldn't touch you to beat you."

I didn't yell, but everything I said echoed clearly through the cells and catacombs, around everyone in multiple waves. One big swell, followed by the briefest of undertows, just to make sure the inmates remembered every word.

CHAPTER 36

LILY

The rumble of my engine must've alerted Harper that I'd made it back. No sooner had I parked my bike before I was crushed in a giant hug. The big guy didn't even let me dismount.

"We didn't think you were coming back." Harper held me at arm's length, taking everything in. The familiarity of the scene shattered my already fragile control.

"Neither did I," I choked out in a sob and looked at the stained garage floor. No matter how glad I was to see him, I couldn't meet that earnest gaze.

Harper had to lead me back to his place, all I could do now was shamble along. I didn't even remember stepping over the bodies in the hall, but I must've. There wasn't any blood on my boots when I kicked them off.

Hannah ran to greet us but stopped short, the grin melting from her face. "What happened?"

Harper gave a helpless shrug as I sank into the kitchen chair. I hadn't been able to process anything while riding back. There was too much debris in the road to consume my attention. Now, there was nothing to distract me.

My brother had killed the one man that vouched for me and Alex all those years ago. The man who'd given us a home and helped us find purpose. We'd never be able to resolve this disagreement. And maybe that wouldn't have happened anyway, but now I'd never know. Ivan was gone.

After two centuries, death wasn't exactly new. But there was nothing in my long experience that could have prepared me for the acute pang of losing so much so quickly.

And it didn't help that I'd contributed to the very war causing all this fucking chaos. Gabe might have been right about me taking too much responsibility for Elias, but that didn't absolve me entirely.

When I finally stopped staring at the wall, Harper and Hannah were seated at the couch, the sun was setting outside. I could barely croak, "Why does everyone around me have to die?"

Hannah took a cautious step towards me, like I was a wounded tiger ready to pounce. As she reached for my shoulder, I flinched away. Epiphany or not, I was still terrified of damning my friends to Ivan and Olive's fate.

Harper shook his head but stayed on the couch. "We're soldiers."

Harper had never used such a flat, emotionless tone. My heart turned hollow with his words.

"We don't have the luxury of forsaking human connection, and that's the very thing that wounds us the deepest."

I swallowed, forcing myself to look at him. I'd never considered who Harper was before I met him. What this loveable goofball had endured. I'd just taken his happy nature for granted.

Harper finally looked up from the carpet, and his dark eyes were bottomless. I decided I was better off not asking. But I still nodded.

Ivan always thought wisdom came with age. Here was the very proof of how bullshit that really was. Wisdom came with experience, but only if you got out of your own stubborn way.

I took a deep breath to steady myself. "So what do we do now?"

"You're going to start by telling us everything." Harper leaned forward; a new expression crossed his features. One I'd seen on Gabe a couple times. "And I mean everything."

CHAPTER 37

GABE

Investigations always uncovered the muddiest, deepest secrets. As a consequence, I knew first hand how very few people in this world were actually innocent.

Most of Nora O'Neal's employees had become suspects after their first interview. Words like Karen and wicked witch had been common in the recordings. The affair hadn't been hard to discover.

Even so, that crime scene was stacked in my nightmares. Her body had been twisted, with long, ragged gouges in her neck. And I couldn't forgive her husband. Scaring Jack O'Neal had been a guilty dream of mine, making him piss his pants and terrifying him as badly as he must have scared his wife. And not just for the murder.

Jack hadn't been any kind of angel before marrying Nora. For every awful trait we unearthed about his wife, Jack had matched her perfectly. All the stereotypes of a toxic dynamic were present.

Yet, guilt and satisfaction coiled through my body. How different was I? Jack had killed his wife because she'd angered him. Did I have much better cause to terrify Jack?

As I mentally traced the outline of each brick in the wall, my mind wandered through its own maze. Back to one of my first conversations with Maria.

"Heard you're having a hard time adjusting."

My head snapped up, shock freezing every nerve in my body. It was only my fourth day in rehab. *"You can't be here."*

She leaned casually against the concrete frame of the door, a sardonic smile crossing her brightly painted lips. *"It's my house."*

"Get out!" I backed up, tumbling over the now-empty cooler and scrambling away.

My incisors extended, stabbing my lower lip. The taste of my own blood only taunted me. She shook her head, the beads in her long braids slowly snapping against the wall.

My back slammed against the other side of the holding cell; every muscle in my body grew taut.

Her throat seemed to twitch. Maybe it was my imagination. No, there it was again, a vein pulsing slowly.

I licked my lips before I could stop myself. My eyes were fixed on her neck, the delicious vein throbbing with blood. The pulse started to echo around me. Thump thump. Thump thump

Slow. Melodic. Enticing.

"So what you gonna do?" Maria smirked and something in that simple gesture snapped all my self control.

I lunged, squishing my still-soppy mattress and stretching my arms out to capture her. My fingers almost grazed that chocolate skin. Then, suddenly, Alex was in front of me and the weight of a semi truck slammed into my guts.

I coughed and spat, landing on the floor in a heapless mess.

"Thanks, Maria." Alex's voice was a low murmur.

"I knew you had him." Maria knelt before me, still behind her friend. Her smile was sympathetic and I couldn't meet her eyes.

"I..." What could I even say? Was I going to apologize? Maybe acknowledge what I was about to do? Or was I going to make some lousy excuse? It didn't matter. Words were useless. I just stared at the floor.

"You didn't choose this life." Maria moved back into my line of sight. "But you can't stay here forever."

Alex and Maria had risked everything just to make their point. And here I was again, trapped in a cell. What the hell was I doing?

"Good news, traitor." My favorite guard's smile looked small under his oversized mustache. "Judge says you get a juice box."

I was about to ask for my lawyer but the last word made me do a double take. He was dangling a blood bag from his pinched fingers, the light dancing playfully off the plastic as his stupid grin grew.

I rolled off my bunk and landed on my feet, holding my hand out. The sudden motion made him back up a fraction of a step, the smile faltered, and I suppressed a wild chuckle.

He regained his composure quickly enough, handing the bag over as though he expected me to grab him.

"I have a question for you." I took it slowly and something in his posture made me think that unnerved him more than if I'd snatched it.

"We've already notified your lawyer that you want to talk. She's on her way." The guard watched intently as I popped my fangs through the plastic and quickly drained the bag.

Well that saved me some time but that wasn't what I was getting at. "Great. Now why are you keeping me with gen-pop?"

He blinked, uncertain. "Judge's ord–"

"Bullshit." I held out the now-saliva covered plastic. "I'm a walking lawsuit and we both know it. What are you playing at?"

The guard chuckled and pulled on a glove before retrieving the blood bag.

"I didn't meet you on the beat." I hadn't been the most so-ciable person back then but I remembered faces well enough. Habit from hunting for suspects. "So what? Did I pick a fight with you in court?"

Something twinkled in the guy's beady little eyes and his belly rumbled with suppressed laughter. "Do I need a reason?"

My brows rushed to meet in the middle.

The guard smirked and nodded toward the hall. "Your trai-tor lawyer will be here in half an hour."

CHAPTER 38

LILY

Harper scratched his beard in thought. "You said the minion who tried to grab you hit a moving truck?"

What the hell? I'd just lost my adoptive sire and he was worried about body damage to a bloody moving van? "Um... yeah."

Hannah gave Harper a quizzical look but he just kept staring at the table in thought. "Babe?"

She placed a hand over Harper's. He patted it but got up without a word and went into the bedroom. Hannah and I looked at each other but didn't have a chance to say much before he came back with an old fashioned file box.

"I printed these when the brownouts started." He plopped the box down and threw the lid to the side, rifling through a set of manila folders. "Let me see..."

Hannah and I exchanged another glance but something in Harper's hurried hunch kept us quiet. He slapped a couple folders on the table, discarding them in a quickly growing pile before opening one and going. "Ha!"

The sudden shout startled us both, and we jumped.

"Sorry." He smiled sheepishly as he laid out the file slowly, pointing at a particular page. "Right there."

My blood chilled. It was an account of the first wave of Starved. Part of me wanted to slap the folder away. Though Gabe and Olive had assured me repeatedly they hadn't let me off my... leash, I still didn't want to imagine what I could have done in that state.

"Lily?" Hannah's hand hovered over my shoulder.

I shook my head, trying to clear whatever expression had worried her from my face. "I'm alright."

Harper and Hannah wore the same disbelief in their features, but said nothing. I tried to smile before turning back to the page and skimming the paragraph Harper had indicated.

Mass casualties, lots of injuries. Nothing terribly shocking there. There were a few reports from people burning the beasts or chopping them to bits. The gruesome visuals made me squirm.

Finally, I found what Harper *had* to be indicating. My eyes snapped to his, my mouth agape. Harper just shrugged. Hannah looked like she was about to start tapping on the table, her elbows shaking as she tried to wait.

I read it again. And again. "The news mentioned semi trucks..."

"Yeah, that was due to a lot of eyewitness accounts. There was too much chaos to get a news helicopter out, so all they had was a bunch of panicked people." Harper shrugged again as he finally sat, scooching the box over so he could see me. "But before the hoard was released, we had reports of moving vans being parked all over the city, blocking the road. It almost got lost coming in on the non-emergency line right before..."

He let the sentence trail and I nodded.

Hannah finally caught up. "The moving van today... you think it's related."

And just like that, I got it. "I never lost the bloody van."

They both looked at me, confused and a little worried. I started laughing and that obviously didn't help.

"I never lost the bloody van!" I smacked the table and stood, elated and out of my mind.

"Um... Lily..." Hannah approached me slowly and Harper looked ready to grab her shoulders.

I beat him to it, shaking her a little and too excited to realize how much I had to be scaring the poor woman. "Where did I lose the tracks for Cillian after he took Gabe?"

Harper barked out his big laugh, stretching an old set of laugh lines I hadn't seen in days. "Next to a moving company!"

"Right, and the cells in my prison–" my mind was racing now, "they rolled down from the ceiling!"

"Like a self storage unit!" Harper slapped my back so hard it hurt, but not nearly as much as the wild grin stretching my face.

Hannah's eyes lit up as she pieced it together. "Did we just find your big bad ex?"

***

Part of me wanted to just storm the gate, knock down the door on my motorcycle and ask for a divorce. But I'd just gotten my bike back and I was holding out hope I'd be able to ride her again.

Hannah was hardly a soldier, leaving Harper and I against a fortress. That left us with few options.

"We can't risk going out to a payphone." I shook my head slowly. "We don't have time."

"They'll know you're here." Harper didn't sound accusatory. More resigned. And that honestly made it worse.

I stared at the table, unable to meet his gaze. "I can't promise what they'll do. Ivan..."

I couldn't even finish the sentence. Ivan had given everyone the benefit of every doubt, sometimes turning all the way around just to look the other way. It made me miss him all the more. My voice was barely a croak. "They'll likely give you the same consequences as me."

Hannah and Harper's shared expression more or less said *duh* as the big guy spoke. "We're soldiers."

I nodded and picked the phone up off the table. It had powered up by the time I started to dial. The first ring was cut short by a familiar but unexpected voice. "We don't have time right now, Captain."

I checked the number I'd dialed before asking, "Melody?"

There was a sharp intake on the other end of the line before she growled, "Edwards. Do you have any idea—"

"Yeah, yeah, I'm a horrible wretch blah blah freakin' blah." I flapped my hand in a too-much-talking gesture and rolled my eyes. "Trust me, I already feel like shit. What are ya doin' answering Cyrus' line?"

"Let's see, a traitor called Cyrus and now Ivan is dead. What do you think?"

Shit.

Well, at least if Cyrus really was the rat, he was already in custody. Though the way he handled my last call had doubt twisting through my intestines. "Hopefully this lead goes better."

"What are you doing with Captain Harper's phone?"

"I was in the neighborhood, but I won't be for long so ya better stop arguin' with me."

I explained where Elias was and my plan. "I'll be there providing a distraction in thirty minutes. Maybe a little more."

"Wait, Edwards—"

"Save your warnings. Ya've never cared about me anyway." I hung up and tossed the phone to Harper. "That oughta do the trick."

Harper nodded and hugged Hannah tight. "We gotta start walking, hon."

CHAPTER 39

GABE

"Oh, just wait 'till I bring this to Judge Taffet." Michelle flung her briefcase on the table, with a heavy thump against the metal surface. "She can't stand violations to prisoner rights."

"Great. In the meantime, how do we get me in solitary?"

"Normally, I would just request protective custody but..." She snapped the case open.

"I'm the one the prisoners need protecting from." I looked glumly at the cold table. The steel didn't reflect anything; I could only see the haziest outline of myself.

"Yeah, so unless you want to start eating people." She gave me a look and I scoffed half heartedly. "Yeah, that's what I figured."

"But I'm a prior officer."

"I know, I know." Michelle blew out a long breath. "But we have to think about optics here."

"Screw your optics!" I slammed my fist down, denting the table. She flinched, staring at the new cavity as I bit out a curse. "It's not going to look too great when I do this to someone's skull."

She heaved a breath and slowly brought those grey eyes to mine. Her voice was shaky. "You won't–"

"I don't even know that." I pushed my hands through my hair.

Maybe I should have been more guarded in my language but the interview room was one of the few places I didn't have to worry about recording devices. Yay attorney client privileges.

"You're a pain in the ass."

I glared and she sneered in response.

"You stayed up every night, ignoring dates, sleep, and everything else because of whatever case you had." She rolled her eyes and shook her head ruefully. "You won't screw this up."

I was too exhausted to argue. The blood bag from earlier had taken the edge off, but I still couldn't rest. Every clank and bump became an alarm, getting worse with each repetition.

"The guard assigned to my block is doing this on purpose." I rubbed my temples.

Michelle's eyes sharpened. "Explain."

I relayed everything.

She blew out a breath and pinched the bridge of her nose. "I can't decide if I'm happy or infuriated you weren't in the courthouse lock up."

My brows surge to meet in the middle. "Huh?"

Michelle looked stunned. "You didn't hear?"

"Hear about what?" I realized it was clichéd before asking but originality wasn't the top of my priority list.

"The vampires–" Michelle gulped before clarifying, "Elias' goons broke into the court and stormed the holding cells."

My blood chilled. "When?"

"This morning." Michelle shook her head, a sarcastic noise trilling her lips. "News is all over it, claiming they were trying to rescue you."

I groaned and ran my fingers through the greasy groves in my hair. "So much for optics."

"No shit." She leaned her head on the heel of her hand, letting out a small yawn. "I've been up since four running damage control and requesting body cam footage from your arrest. Maybe I'll add it to YouTube."

"Is that really a good idea?"

"Do you have a better one?" Even her sarcasm was exasperated. "Then, right when I was napping, I got the call about you."

Guilt stabbed me in the belly. "Go home."

She shook her head. "I can't leave my client like this."

"Do the paperwork you need, appeal it or whatever." I crossed my arms, nodding to the door. "But you're no good to me, or Barbara, exhausted."

Something flickered in the stone of her eyes and Michelle growled, "That's low."

"Am I wrong?" I shrugged, though it felt like I was lifting the whole prison instead of my shoulders.

She glanced away, then glared at me. "Fine. I'll go get everything prepped. Can you hang in there for another two days?"

My stomach dropped through the floor. The lie was dry on my tongue. "I'll be fine."

CHAPTER 40

LILY

The anxiety built with every step.

We had to do this. Someone needed to distract Elias and for whatever bloody reason, I was the perfect bait.

Of course, Elias might see right through it, but it was the only card I could play. One way or another, this had to end.

Harper's boots splashed in the slush next to mine. "How do you feel about Collins?"

My head snapped up and I laughed in a suppressed kind of shock. "Where the fuck did that come from?"

The big guy shrugged a beefy shoulder. "You've had an effect on him."

My cheeks tingled with the urge to blush. "I think I love him but..."

"Your crazy ex complicates things?" Harper smiled sadly.

I nodded.

"Why?"

The question rocked me and I almost tripped over some moldy junk in the road. "I mean, because..."

My thoughts trailed off along with every coherent reply.

Harper smiled. "It took years before I realized Hannah always remembered my favorite order at Hammy's. Then

Collins had to leave before I noticed her dancing on my regular days..."

A pang of guilt stabbed me. Maybe I should ask him to hang back, but I couldn't face this alone.

"Collins is my buddy." Harper's grin widened, the contrast of his teeth and his dark skin making his whole face seem even brighter. "I'll always be there for him, but I'm not that kind of partner."

The question was implied, but I couldn't answer him. The rest of our walk should have been awkward, but instead we fell into a comfortable silence. The calm before the storm.

The building finally came into view. Before I'd dismissed it without much thought. Now I was analyzing every brick and window.

Or the lack there of.

Most self storage facilities had their units, whether internal or external, on prominent display. Yet this place was one big grey tower of nothing. Nondescript and easy to ignore.

This also made the cameras odd. It might make sense to have a few covering their exits or gates. But, with no outside storage, I still counted ten on the front gate alone. Some PI I was.

"Heavy security," Harper noted. "But no guard station."

"It would disturb the facade. Probably a security office inside, with a couple people stationed at the doors."

"Are you sure you wanna go in by yourself?"

I offered a smile I didn't feel. "Someone has to let the Court know what's going on."

I stepped up before I could lose my nerve, leaving Harper around the corner, and hopefully out of sight behind the buildings and trees. I shoved my hands into my pockets and tried to whistle. If these were my final moments, I didn't want to crouch or cower.

Sadly, my lips were too dry and I had to settle for humming. As I reached the gate, I looked directly into the nearest camera, smiled, and shouted, "Honey, I'm home!"

The reaction was immediate. The metal gate buzzed and something heavy clicked before the gate slid open. I arched a brow and stepped forward, forcing myself to keep my eyes straight ahead. The last thing Harper needed was for me to give away his position.

Just as I stepped in the gate, it slid shut again with a heavy rumble and a clang that made my guts fall into my shoes. Planning for this didn't mean I was ready for any of it. The metal handle of the front door was cold under my shaking finger tips.

I barely had one boot in the building when a rifle was leveled at my head. "Weapons."

I held up my hands and nodded. "Ya know who I am?"

"Weapons," the soldier repeated, though there was a note of confusion behind the command.

"I'm not tryin' to be a Karen." I flicked my gaze to my boots. "If you know who I am, you know where I stash 'em."

The guard followed my gaze and nodded as heavy steps thumped behind me. "Keep 'em up."

My spine stiffened as a gun prodded the back of my neck. I just nodded.

As the first guard pulled the knives from my boots, the one behind me checked the sleeves of my shirt. I let out a dark chuckle despite myself. "You've done your homework."

I'd stashed a blade up my sleeve before, it was the only reason I was able to surprise Mrs. Stafford at the beginning of this nightmare.

"You can talk to the boss when he gets back." The guard gruffly checked the other sleeve. "We've got nothing to say."

"We best take her jacket." The other guard was patting my legs, using the back of his hands. The one at my back gruffly removed my jacket one sleeve at a time and tossed it to the side.

Their examination was my only chance to check my surroundings, though I was becoming a bit doubtful of my conclusions. For one thing, these guys weren't exactly dressed in tactical gear. More to the point, this hallway was nothing like the lair I'd briefly rushed through during my imprisonment.

Instead of the heavy woods and lush tapestries that painted my nightmares, the cold grey of the exterior echoed inside. Every breath and tap came back to me, haunting the halls. These guys obviously worked for Elias but maybe this wasn't his main stay. Maybe it was just an operation.

Had I led the Court astray? They would be here any minute. And my arrival had to set off all the alarm bells. Elias knew I wasn't looking to rekindle a damn thing. And yet... I was only met with two guards.

"She's clear," the first guard stood. "Let's get her inside."

"Move." The gun on my neck drove deeper into my spine.

My grin was like a shark. "Now, I know hubby dear demands manners."

The second guard rolled his eyes. "Please move."

"There we go." I strolled in the direction they indicated, keeping my hands visible. No need to make them any jumpier. They had to be assuming I was some kind of Trojan horse.

Our footfalls echoed quietly and nothing in the surroundings seemed substantial for several seconds. Lots of storage units, no noise. They lead me to a large set of metal double doors. As they opened them my skin tried to scuttle off my bones.

The concrete and metal exterior camouflaged the extravagant prison in my nightmares.

It was empty of people, so I could see everything. The tapestries and paintings. The thick carpets I tripped over when I tried to escape.

"Please move," the guard growled again and I realized I'd stopped at the doors. My feet struggled to go backwards while my mind forced them forwards, making me tremble.

Not even a week ago, I'd told Cyrus I'd never come back here. Now I was back with the flimsiest of plans. Sure, it could create an opportunity. But... there was nobody here.

"Where is everyone?"

The guards didn't answer. The silence of the ornate cavern became oppressive. Finally something they said clicked in my skull.

"You can talk to the boss when he gets back."

I stopped walking. "Where the hell is Elias?"

"He'll be back soon, ma'am." The first guard reached for my elbow. I wrenched it away.

"With everyone else, I assume?"

They didn't respond. My skin chilled.

There was no army to conquer. Where the fuck were they?

I didn't have long to ponder the question. We turned another corner of the big hallway and walked straight through a heavy wood door. And my stomach sank.

This library was the last place I'd seen before Elias tossed me in the dungeons. Back then I'd wondered at the lack of windows, but now it all made sense. And I hated the newest feature.

Melody sat on the big desk, cleaning her nails with a knife.

CHAPTER 41

GABE

The banging started low. At first, I ignored it, trying to focus on the final chapter of *Odd Thomas*. It was probably just another riot; I was already growing used to them. Dust peppered my face and I spat wildly, shaking my head to keep it out of my eyes.

"What the..." Riots didn't shake cinderblock. I sat up straight on the bunk. Another loud boom reverberated through the building. The prison alarms and city siren now sang in chorus.

Just as I ran out of my cell, the doors all slammed shut with a repetitive *clang clang clang* that echoed through the cavern-like halls. The racket almost drowned the overhead speakers, garbling out orders for a lock down.

Prisoners started to hoot and holler from their cells. A few shouted to each other, asking who was starting shit. God, they needed to shut up so I could focus.

The thought had barely grazed my mind when something slammed on the entrance door and Cillian stepped into the hall. "Gooooood mornin' prison birds."

What the hell?

What was Elias playing at? Had this been his plan all along, luring me to go back. Just how would that even help him?

Some of the inmates started whistling, cat-calling Cillian's *pretty smile*. The wicked grin grew, intertwining with his scars. "My, my. If I'd known I'd have this many admirers, I'd have done *somethin'* with my hair."

Laughter grew in the peanut gallery and I ducked down, barely able to see Cillian through the banister bars but hopefully less conspicuous. If any other prisoner caught sight of me I had little doubt they'd point me out. I'd already walked right into their trap once, I couldn't risk it a second time.

"I'll keep this short, ladies," Cillian chuckled as he spoke. "Our home was compromised earlier today and we're in the market for new real estate. Like all you lovely folks–" he took a minute to twirl with his arms out, "society has found us wanting. So all of ya have an opportunity. If you'd like to be food, insult us or cause some trouble. And if you'd like a chance at immortality... Well, let's just say there's an interview process."

I couldn't tell if the hoots or boos were winning, they all swirled together as my guts twisted into one another.

"Is that why you sent that pretty boy cop?" Someone from the floor above me hollered down, turning the open portion of the hall into Cillian's amphitheater.

Cillian stopped mid-twirl and looked up to the man. "I beg your pardon?"

"That vampire cop, he came in yesterday. Was he here to scope the place?" Another voice, sharper than the first and coming from below.

"Well isn't that interstin'?" Cillian looked between the two speakers, his brows curling with confusion. "Hey, kids."

There was a chill under the relaxed tone of his words as children filed from the open door. Cillian didn't even look at them as he spoke. "Go check solitary for my sister's toy."

"He ain't in there, man." The first voice was starting to remind me of an ass-kisser in my high school English class. "He tried to start a fight, but they still left him out."

"Must've used that vampire mojo he showed off with the judge." This one sounded excited to offer an answer.

Cillian was already ignoring them, his good eye scanning the crowd. Every muscle in my body tensed and I tried to sink into the ground, looking to each side. I couldn't stay here forever and I certainly couldn't count on the good nature of my fellow inmates.

Cillian spoke over his shoulder while still looking for me, almost inaudible under the growing cacophony. "Find him."

I bolted to the end of the hall as the riot ignited. Screams rose when one of the kid-soldiers took down some tough guy who wanted to prove themselves. It was worse when prisoners stood up to the other vampires and called them monsters.

It didn't matter how big they were, everyone bawled like a child with enough pain. The echoes rang through cinder block halls and back to me, somehow louder and more terrible with each repetition.

I didn't know where the guards were, but without them, this place already made hell look like a tea party. I'd only made it about halfway down the steps before someone called out. "There he is!"

"Shit!" I ran faster, tripping over a body and sliding in a puddle of blood on the bottom step. Cillian's soldiers thundered towards me as they caught up. It wouldn't take them long. I rounded the corner and almost made it into another hall before a big hand snatched my collar and yanked. "Got you!"

I punched my attacker. It wasn't until he looked up that I recognized Jack O'Neal. He smiled viciously as he whistled through a now-missing tooth. "Over here! Come and get–"

"Oh, shut up." I kicked his stomach and ran.

CHAPTER 42

LILY

"Thanks for escorting the brat." Melody nodded to the library entrance. "I can handle her from here."

The guards nodded and slammed the heavy door, making me jump. Melody was already pulling out her phone, her thumb rapidly clicking out something without looking at me.

My mind raced as I checked my surroundings. Even the tiniest sounds in the library felt different and it took a moment to see why. The shelves were empty, letting the tiny *plip plop* of her fingers echo softly in their bookless catacombs.

I swallowed, unable to look at her. "Why?"

"Does it really matter?" Her tawny skin held an eerie yellow tone from the light of her phone, her eyes almost black in contrast.

"Does it really matter if ya tell me?"

She let out a short sarcastic sound before looking at me. "I'm tired of watching Ritti suffer."

There was too much to unpack from her answer. I couldn't narrow my follow up down to anything more specific than, "Huh?"

"Maybe that's why I'm not mad at Elias for not killing you." Melody put her phone down. The screen stayed illuminated as she mulled her reply over. "Just because you're getting in the way of the mission, doesn't mean he stopped caring."

I blinked stupidly, my mind trying to catch up. "Wait so, you and the queen–"

There hadn't even been a rumor. Was Melody just infatuated or was I being dense. Maybe she just really admired the queen. Neither would really shock me but it was a lot to process at the moment.

"She puts everything at Court ahead of herself." Melody shook her head sadly. "It's killing her. It's killing... us."

Welp, there went any misconceptions. Hopefully I made it out of here to tell Darren. His conspiracy-riddled brain would go ape-shit for this.

"And here I thought the old biddy was nuts." I shook my head at Melody's insanity. "You do realize Elias will lock Ritti up the minute this ends. If she's lucky."

"He agreed to let us take Canada so long as we leave him alone after this. Ritti can take the subjects who prefer her way of doing things."

My jaw dropped and the words tumbled out before my brain caught up. "She'll never agree to that."

I might want to smack Ritti for half her rules and laws but she had principles. No way in fuck would she just let Elias murder and enslave thousands. That bitch would fight and claw her way back out. Or die trying.

"Then she'll be all mine, unable to rule anything."

My spine chilled as I tried to imagine caging Gabe just to protect him. It would be like chopping the legs from a tiger. Yet Melody was ready to do just that. She had no problem keeping her lover like an animal at the zoo.

"So callin' your ass only tipped Elias off, huh?"

"Yeah." She rolled her eyes. "Leave it to you to bump up our moving date."

"Looking for a better view?" I arched a brow at the lack of windows.

"Nah, better fortification. And I guess your honey bunny was feeling nostalgic for something a bit more gothic." Melody smiled sadly at me and crossed her arms. "Any chance you'll save me trouble hunting for Captain Harper? For old times sake?"

"Considering how old times were." My voice quivered as I tapped my chin in mock thought.

"Let's get this over with then." Melody sighed, finally stood from the desk, and cracked her neck.

I snorted. "You always did want an excuse to kick my ass."

This would be tough. Melody had lived as a modern street rat before the Court found her. Her vampire body was scrappy, covered in lean muscle. Cyrus had trained us both and Melody's days in the dungeons gave her far more knowledge of anatomy.

"Oh you have *no* clue." She shook her head. "Listening to everything you've put her through—"

I lunged, shooting my fist at her throat. Melody didn't waste any time, crouching low and sweeping my leg. My head cracked on the corner of an end table.

Pain blinded me as she hauled me up by my hair. I clawed her arm before grabbing and twisting, hard. She howled in pain and her grip loosened. I flung my head forward, yanking several strands out while kicking backwards. Something snapped and she crumpled next to me. I punched her throat and she coughed out a hideous sound, glaring at me.

At least I wouldn't have to listen to her yapping while that healed. I punched again but she tackled me and we rolled across the floor, slamming into an empty shelf that creaked and groaned. I grabbed her face and smashed her head into the floor, she clawed at me until she latched a hand over my ear and yanked.

I yowled as she shifted her grip and slammed my skull into the hardwood floor and climbed on top of me. She sat on my stomach and all the air in my lungs expelled in a pained gasp as Melody smiled down, coldly.

A thin trail of blood seeped from her nose, painting her lips and teeth as she croaked, "Honestly. I'd kill you now. But I doubt Elias will keep his word about Ritti–"

I bucked my hips up and to the side, slamming her face into the nearest shelf. I bucked again and she had to choose between holding on or steadying herself. She grabbed the shelves and I slithered backwards and clutched a big metal stand of some sort before scrambling up.

Turned out to be an honest to god candelabra. Thank god my ex was a walking cliché. Melody stood just as I swung the ugly piece of metal. It collided with her head. She staggered back and I pinned her to the wall, shoving the base into her neck.

Hot wax dripped on my arm as we held each other's gazes. Sure Melody could knock the candelabra away, but I could easily swing it into her skull.

"Ya got one chance." I pushed the base deeper into her neck.

Those dark eyes were steaming beneath the surface, the calculation clear. "What, talk or I die?"

"Fuck that." I shook my head. "I'm gonna bash your skull in with this thing and call the Court no matter what."

Her eyes flashed. "Then what's there to decide?"

"What I tell Ritti." I flicked my eyes to the phone, still open with her unfinished text.

Her eyes widened and I smiled ruthlessly. "The only chance she has to survive, without you, is me."

Melody's whole body shook, her eyes still as stone with her mind whirling behind them.

I sighed and tightened my shoulders, like I was getting ready to swing. "That's alright. I'm not exactly her fangirl anyw–"

"The prison. Elias wants a *proper fortress.*" Melody spat the last words in a pathetic imitation of an English accent. "He meant to wait until after Collins' court case, but you figuring out the lair made that unrealistic."

I cocked a brow. "Couldn't you have just kept that to yourself and stuck to the plan?"

The shake of her head was barely perceivable. "What if you told someone else. Especially once I knew you were with Harper."

"How many people are still here?"

She paused to answer but I leaned on the stand and gave her a look. She growled before spitting out, "Not many, maybe twenty to run basic security and load boxes in the moving vans. You'll have an easy time getting back out with the Court's help."

"What's he done with the Starved?"

"He has them all loaded up with him at the prison, said something about using them after initiation."

My stomach crawled inside itself as my brain fought the images. "And why the hell does he keep bugging me?"

Melody's face contorted in confusion. "Seriously, that wasn't an act?"

I hefted an exasperated sigh, "What are ya on about?"

"I thought your ignorance was a front, just something to keep you alive. But you really didn't get it. Did you?"

"Get what?"

"This." Melody glanced around the library. "He wasn't sure what you'd read last time he caught you in here."

"Seriously? I hardly read anything before he found me." I laughed like a lunatic. "I'd barely learned about the Starved."

Here, I'd been digging through all my memories of the famines. Over a hundred years and it all came down to Elias being paranoid about the thirty seconds I'd spent reading his notes.

The only reason I could take Elias down was because he bestowed power on me that I'd never had. It was just that simple

"Jesus, you really didn't know anything." Melody looked like she almost wanted to laugh. I snickered, a little let down by the answer.

"Anythin' else?" I had no illusions what would happen once the conversation ended. We were both hedging our bets.

She stopped and considered something. Maybe she was debating how much to tell me or considering if she'd left anything out. Every second of thought, I had to fight my shaking muscles. Vampire strength or no, this fucking thing was heavy and my mind was racing. If Melody lied to me, I was royally fucked.

Even if the relationship with Ritti was just a wild crush, Melody was a well known pet. If I called the queen from Melody's phone without something useful, I'd probably be starved and murdered on live TV. And I rather doubted Melody would regret that.

Melody finally shook her head. "Just promise me you'll keep her safe."

I nodded. "I'll help her win."

Ritti and I had our issues; we were nowhere near done with each other, but I could recognize her better intentions. Besides, it was either her or Elias.

"Good enough." All civility left Melody's tone and her arms shot up. I pulled the stand from her neck and swung the bar. Her hand flashed up as the heavy base smashed into her mouth and chin. She spat teeth and coughed while trying to punch me. I jabbed, shoving her already damaged head into the heavy shelf behind her and she stilled. The golden skin paled with an ugly grey undertone and crumbled around the large dent I'd left in her face.

My stomach convulsed and I dropped the candelabra while dry heaving. Melody and I could never have been friends but we'd worked together. We'd had conversations and fought side by side. I'd once trusted her with my life.

And now I'd killed her.

My stomach rolled on itself again and I collapsed to the floor, gagging on nothing and forcing useless breaths to calm myself. Bad idea, the bitter odor of her ashes flooded my nose and I was crying while heaving again, the adrenaline depleting and my body shaking.

There wasn't time for this. Elias was out there, storming a fortress. My blunder had been bad and it was about to cost more lives. But it also gave us one shot.

I gritted my teeth and forced my body up, refusing to look at the ashes and ribbons piling up in Melody's clothes. I staggered over to the desk, fumbling for the phone. The text still sat on the screen, Melody's reply typed but unsent.

I love you, too.

A pathetic little whimper escaped me as I debated what to do. How much worse would it be to read something like that right before you found out. And why hadn't Melody sent this before we started talking?

I shook the ideas free, leaving the text as a draft and hitting the green phone icon.

CHAPTER 43

GABE

Footsteps, hoots, and hollers rapidly grew behind me. They seemed to come from all sides, only amplified as I ran into the cafeteria. And now I knew where the guards had gone.

Several prisoners were tossing one back and forth like a toy, while others corralled the remaining guards between tables. Their manic chortles stopped short when I slid into the room. One of the prisoners caught a guard in his grip and all their eyes grew wide with delight.

Just as the steps behind me stopped, something rumbled low outside the prison. The snickers and jeers leveled as we all listened intently.

Once we all identified the *thwup, thwap, thwap* of a helicopter, one of the prisoners laughed. "Think that's the National Guard?"

"Maybe." Another smirked at him before turning his miserable gaze on me. "Either way, it means we're almost out of time."

I lunged, grabbing the nearest object as they swarmed. The stool squealed as I wrenched it from the bolts. It barely gave an inch.

"Guess pretty boy didn't make himself a shank." Prisoners chuckled and sneered, a few even stopping to take in the spectacle.

Somewhere in the distance, shots rang out, someone bellowed orders and the sharp crack of gunfire cut through the ongoing racket. Just then I yanked the stool free and climbed up on a table, sliding into the ring of prisoners still tormenting the guards.

The metal rang as I swung the stool into a prisoner. He flopped to the ground and a guard staggered away from him. A quick glance over my shoulder showed my original attackers would close the gap quickly.

I didn't have any friends here, but I needed allies.

I whirled, flinging prisoners from my path until I could grab the first guard's arm and draw him back to me. We looked at each other and a little of my hope fell.

My least favorite guard glared back at me, then looked at our assailants, then me again before nodding sharply. "Enemy of my enemy."

I placed my back to his, praying I wasn't misinterpreting who the enemy in that scenario was. "Do you have any weapons?"

"My fists."

I suppressed the urge to growl. I knew guards couldn't carry weapons around the prisoners, but I'd been hoping he'd come running from the guard station armed with some rubber bullets or a baton. Instead we had a prison stool and his flabby arms against a bunch of pissed off inmates.

Guess today was the day I'd punch my ticket. I clenched the base of the stool harder in my sweaty palms and got ready to go down swinging. "How far is it to the supplies?'

There'd never been cause to learn where the guard station was, but somewhere was a room full of riot gear and rubber bullets. It wasn't perfect but it was something. Better than the makeshift weapon I cracked across an inmate's face before shoving another one back. Still there were more coming.

Behind me, flesh slapped against flesh and the guard grunted, "Too far, we're better off grouping here and waiting for the National Guard. They've handled a few riots since the first wave."

It hit me, then, as I turned the stool and slashed wildly at another inmate with a shank fashioned from a dirty toothbrush. While I doubt he knew a good place to stick that, the last thing I needed was for the crowd to start playing *pin the death on the vampire*.

"You realize the other vampires are here, right?" I grunted through slashes, gouging the man's arm and splitting open his neighbor's side with the shredded metal of my weapon. Swinging it was awkward and cumbersome, even with my strength, but I didn't have another choice.

"What?" The guard stuttered and I heard a loud whoop. I couldn't even spare a glance but it felt like a fist fight behind me. "You mean besides you?"

I explained as best I could between jabs and slashes, blood spirting all over me. "Pretty soon, Elias' goons will find us. We need something to work with."

He didn't reply right away, unless I counted the howl of pain just before he yelled, "Yeah, that's fucking right! Take that!"

"Are we seriously working with *him?*" A new voice shouted as two more guards flanked me, one with a night stick he used more adeptly than I'd imagined.

"Eric, if you want to die on principle, be my guest." My guard squared up next to us. "We might be able to use some of the equipment in the yard."

"It was already overrun when I ran through there. Radio said the machine shop is a nightmare, I think it's how those things got in." Nightstick growled as he snapped the weapon over an inmate's knuckles. "I vote we head to the library."

"The library?" Several of them chorused before one of them was dragged away. I tried to grab him but only caught his fingers, the wedding ring slipping off when I wrenched my hand back and swung the stool again.

"Shit, Tony!" Eric lunged but my guard pulled him back and kicked an inmate in the gut.

"Why the library?"

"Single entrance to the prison, shelves are bolted to the floor and very few windows." Nightstick yelled then screamed as he dropped the weapons and gripped his arm, trying to stem the blood flow.

Figures, even now literature would become my only escape. I nodded, flipped the stool and swung wide, giving us a half circle to step forward. "Stay behind me and get the sides. Grab anything you can use."

We marched. It was slow and I almost lost my battering ram from the slick coat of sweat on my palms. Blood sprayed and bones crunched with every swing. So far, no ash. No vampires. But that wouldn't last long.

CHAPTER 44

LILY

It was difficult to talk in the helicopter, even with the microphones and ear protection. At least that was the excuse I gave myself. I wasn't in a chatty mood. It had only been while I waited for Ritti to fetch me that everything in my mind settled and clicked.

Gabe had just turned himself over to authorities. His house and apartment were both gone, so he had to be in solitary, which gave him little recourse to defend himself or move about. Elias might have let him go once, but something in my gut said he wouldn't bother doing it again.

Luckily, Melody hadn't been lying and I hadn't had to marinate on those thoughts for too long. Once Ritti's team stormed the old fortress, they made quick work of the soldiers left behind. It had taken them mere minutes to verify the self-storage dungeons were empty.

My mind reeled as I considered what Elias might use those poor beasts for. Maybe he'd clean up the current population, but by his fucked up logic, that would be a waste of perfectly good food. The idea made me gag as Cyrus droned on about the plan. "We'll have to enter through the yard. Hopefully the towers will assume we're back-up or be too swamped to shoot at us."

"Well, that's not cynical," Harper grumbled.

"You're welcome to stay behind," Cyrus glared from his seat across from us. The expression was almost swallowed by the large helmet and big goggles.

"I think everyone's in, providing they don't shoot us down." My leg tapped incessantly. I just hoped we'd get there in time.

Cyrus turned his glare on me. "How'd you even get her to let you come?"

I snorted sadly. "I threatened to call the local police if she didn't give me her word."

Ritti probably figured I'd either be locked up or dead by the end of this. So long as I saw this through, I didn't much care. Not just because of Gabe.

A big hand squeezed my arm. "We'll find him."

I couldn't even hold the soft attempt at a smile for Harper. If Gabe was gone, we'd have nothing. His ashes would be mixed among the rest. Sure I might find some prison footage to figure out what happened but...

"Hey." Harper shook me, hard. "I don't know what you're thinking, but stop it."

I swallowed and nodded. We'd be there any minute. My worry would have to wait. I turned to Cyrus. "Why not just land near the office space, if that's where Elias'll be?"

"We assume he took the warden's office for security but we can't know. And we know there are vampires in the main building that need to be contained as well as a riot. No matter what, we'll need to deal with them."

"Seems like a waste of upfront energy, if ya ask me."

"Good thing I'm not," Cyrus growled.

"Oh, fuck off Cyrus." I gave him a single fingered salute as the pilot announced our descent and instructed us to grab the *oh shit bars*. "You've called me the enemy and threatened to torture me. Ya can take all those hurt feelings and stuff 'em."

"I had orders," Cyrus spat.

Harper's face contorted into an angry scowl so foreign I think his face had to learn the expression just for this occasion. I just rolled my eyes, too tired for this shit.

"And I had evidence. So I guess we're square." I nodded at the prison now visible from my window. "But we've got a job to do, so let's get on with it."

Cyrus and Harper checked their weapons again. I groaned and reluctantly checked the guns they'd hoisted on me were still in my pockets, making sure the one in my hand had a round in the chamber. My skin scuttled at the idea of using the thing but leaving it behind was just foolish.

This close, I could finally see the bullet-riddled moving vans rammed through the prison gates and slammed into the main entrance. The watch towers weren't in much better condition, smoke rising from the windows and large chunks of cinderblock missing, as though one of those giant movie monsters had stopped in for a snack.

The vans rocked ominously and I swallowed.

Harper scowled over my shoulder. "Shouldn't we blow that thing up?"

"Can't risk it." Cyrus shook his head. "Right now, they are contained. If we blow a hole in that thing, it might release them."

Those things were awful in the open space of the city, where they could fan out and people could run. In a prison, it'd be like tossing a bunch of piranha in a barrel with a few goldfish.

Sure, these prisoners weren't exactly girl scouts, but some of the men in here had committed embezzlement or burglary. Nothing friendly, but not everyone here deserved to be shredded like coleslaw.

Besides, the chaos would only delay our progress. We had two objectives, rescue Gabe and capture Elias. We couldn't even just kill him, the legend would live on if he didn't die publically.

Yep, this was going to be a picnic. No problem.

A cold shiver ran through every nerve and I hugged myself. One thing at a time.

The chopper hovered over the courtyard and Cyrus tossed a weighted rope out of the now open door. He gestured to his back. "Climb on."

I'd never trained for a fast descent, and there wasn't exactly a safety line so my options were limited to snuggling the asshole or jumping onto the concrete of the yard. I slapped a helmet on and hooked my arms around his neck before we propelled down. Our helmets banged against one another as we whipped towards the ground. Harper's boots were just above my head, and another just above him.

A couple prisoners ran to us, grasping desperately at the rope before Cyrus pulled it away.

"Please, you don't get it!" One screamed.

"It's not a normal riot!" Another pleaded.

"Oh no, we get it." Cyrus hissed, baring his fangs. The prisoners scrambled away. I wanted to lecture Cyrus about image but we didn't have time. Luckily, the yard only had a couple prisoners, all running away from us as the first few shouted about more of those *things* attacking.

We ran in, our helicopter zooming away to make room for the second team. I almost slipped in blood as we entered the cafeteria.

"Holy shit." Harper scanned the room quickly, taking in the chaos. "What'd they do, feast during the battle?"

"There aren't any punctures." I shook my head as I looked around, confused by the mayhem. The bodies were knocked over in a strange arc I didn't understand. This wasn't natural to any weapon I'd expect in a prison. Even riot gear wouldn't leave this many bodies behind; the prisoners would have started to run.

So what had caused this?

"No ash either." All the emotion had left Cyrus' tone. "This wasn't a feeding."

"So, what then?" Harper looked around and his eyes found me standing next to a table. "Lily?"

I stared at the torn stump of a stool, remembering a similar stunt when Gabe and I had battled those blood thirsty little nose pickers in a broken café. My guts twisted in on themselves. "Cyrus, how certain are you that Gabe was in solitary?"

CHAPTER 45

GABE

We'd already lost two guards. We couldn't afford to hesitate.

"Keep going!" I bellowed.

"But they're–" Nightstick fell back with a boy latched on his neck. I cursed, tossed my club-stool down, and wrenched the deadly little urchin off him.

Blood gushed from his throat as I slammed the kid against the nearest wall, stuffing my guilt into the darkest part of my skull. *Live now, regret later.*

I dragged the man into an alcove and slapped a hand over his wound to stem the bleeding. He was already choking on his own blood. Another guard bent low and tore the sleeve off his uniform. "Here."

"Won't work." It was impossible to think as Nightstick's blood oozed through my fingers. He needed medical attention but there wasn't any...

The idea wasn't fully formed: I just brought my wrist to my mouth and bit, before shoving the open wound into the guard's mouth. "Drink this, right now."

His eyes flew wide and I shoved my wrist in further. "Do it or die."

Nightstick's buddy tried to pull my arm away, screaming something about a plot to make more, but I held my ground. Our eyes locked and something in my face must have reassured him. Or maybe he was just that desperate. Either way, he took a long swallow. Then another.

His face scrunched in distaste before he coughed and blinked. The blood slowed to a trickle between my fingers. When it stopped I nodded and took my wrist away.

His neck wound closed a millimeter at a time and his buddy stopped squawking as I looked up. "None of these kids will hesitate. You can't give them the benefit of the doubt."

I stood, grimacing at the blood now covering me. Not entirely in disgust. As my stomach growled I turned to find the other three guards covering the opening, my asshole guard using the stool to bat our assailants away. I squeezed between them and kicked a kid away, sending them into the hallway railing with a sick crunch that made me want to vomit.

We punched and kicked our way down the hall until we found the library and I had to pin one of the inmates to the wall. He tried to stab me with something I couldn't identify before I twisted his wrist and tossed it aside.

He held his injured hand and whimpered, "Find your own place, man."

I glanced around him at the nearly empty library, the metal shelves bolted to the floor with a few mousy men hiding among the old paperbacks. "I think we can all fit."

A little of the adrenaline rushed from my body as I sat between shelves and took stock. The librarian's office door was closed. Hard to blame him. The chairs and tables weren't bolted down like the cafeteria, but they were pretty flimsy. A busted one sat in the corner and I suspected the weapon I'd tossed away had once been part of it

My head felt light, swaying on my shoulder while I tried to think. "We need weapons."

"We gathered these as we went." Nightstick pulled a small stash from his pocket. Old combs, toothbrushes.... was that a piece of glass wrapped in some kind of cable?

At my questioning look, the guard only shrugged. "Not the most creative shivs I've seen but they'll do damage."

I gingerly sorted through the rusty pile. I wasn't sure if I still could get tetanus but now seemed like a bad time to test it. Lots of hilts were composed of electrical tape with points made by filing everyday objects against the prison walls or floor. The most unique was a crude mace, made with a hairbrush handle and torn bed sheet, the end tied into a thick knot with something sharp inside.

"To a human, sure." I shook my head, and hated the way that woozy feeling grew. My brain was floating off in space somewhere. "If you poke a vampire with any of these you'll only piss it off."

"You okay?" To my surprise, the asshole guard was kneeling by my side. He actually looked worried.

I used my limited energy reserves to shrug. "Hungry, nothing to be done about it."

He blanched. "You're not going to become one of those..."

I scoffed. "Now we care about the danger of leaving a hungry vampire out?"

He scowled but had the good grace to keep his twisted mouth shut. I leaned against the metal bookshelf and sighed, shoving a hand through my hair. "It is what it is."

His beady eyes scanned my face then looked at Nightstick, focusing on the dried blood still crusting the man's throat. Without so much as glancing at me, the asshole yanked up his sleeve and shoved his forearm at my face. "Take what you need."

It was tempting to tell him to piss off, I almost did, but something in his expression stopped me. His eyes scanned the hall feverishly, waiting to see if anyone had followed us.

He spared me a glance and nudged his arm closer to my lips. "We need you."

I took his arm, nodded, and sank my fangs in before I could think too much about this.

CHAPTER 46

LILY

C redit where it's due: the prisoner didn't come with any cliché line. He'd simply slammed me against the wall, and realized he wasn't holding a man. His whole demeanor changed as he ripped my belt.

Giving me the perfect opportunity to slam my knee into his groin.

"You bitch!" He dropped me, cradling his privates, and I threw the same knee into his gut.

"So sad." I plunged a knife into his side. "Looks like you're out of order."

"Come on!" Cyrus grabbed my elbow and hissed. "This is precisely why I didn't want you here."

"Yep, ya totally predicted that." I rolled my eyes. True, that idiot prisoner's reaction wasn't exactly unexpected. A bunch of sex deprived inmates, some who probably hadn't seen a woman in years... Still I was pretty confident that Cyrus was just having trouble trusting me.

Gun fire cut any retort short, echoing wildly through the halls.

We had to get to the offices, find Elias, and end this; we couldn't spend our time hunting all over the prison for Gabe. I just had to hope he was alright.

We turned the corner, running smack into another group of short soldiers. A small girl with bouncy curls barrelled into Harper, knocking him over and punching on the way down. Cyrus lunged like he meant to help when another lept, kicking him in the stomach.

Before I could do anything to help, four knocked me to the ground. I managed to grab one by the feet, tossing them against the wall and smashing their skull. I refused to look, to see if they disintegrated. I just grabbed the next two kids and knocked their heads together and hauled the last one up by their throat.

Their wet gurgling had fuck all to do with breathing as the scrawny boy clawed at my hand.

"Ronald?"

Something knocked me over and I dropped the wayward orphan. My attacker clamored on my back, grabbing my hair and yanking it backwards. Even with the helmet, pain exploded in every nerve.

They stabbed me in the side and I howled. I rolled, blindly plunging my knife into something solid; the kid on my back let out a yowl and the pain lessened. I forced myself up, slamming us both into the nearest wall. It took about five more slams before the hold on my hair slackened and the pain at my side stopped.

As I braced myself against the wall, I almost lost it at the sight that greeted me. The kid on my back had been using stirrups to needle my sides. The ash in those tiny boots would fucking haunt me.

Harper growled obscenities into the hall and I looked up just in time to see Ronald stabbing and slashing at the kids covering him. I scrambled over, grabbing the first kid I could find and plunging my knife into their head before nabbing the next.

Already the air was filled with blood and ash. Everyone was coated in the stuff. When we fished Harper out, his skin was littered in punctures. The little terrors had even taken his helmet and bit his face, giving him macabre freckles. I slashed my wrist with a blade and held it out to him.

Harper sneered but drank quickly before I hoisted the big guy up.

"Any chance we can keep that between us?" Harper wheezed out a chuckle as the holes in his face quickly closed.

The conversation fell as Cyrus urged us forward. The prisoners were a lot easier than the kids. They were bigger, sure, but most of them weren't trained as effectively and didn't understand our supernatural strength.

Unfortunately, they hid the adult vampire soldiers, which occasionally caught us off guard in all the commotion. The battle to the door was slow and ragged. We set off the metal detectors as we ran through the inmate entrance, hanging a left into the administrative building. I'd never really given much thought into the office workings of a prison before but it felt like traveling into an alternate dimension.

The cracks of gunfire mingled with the howls of battle, distant but not gone. Still, it was the closest thing to a break we'd had. We all ducked into an empty office, Cyrus glaring at Ronald. "What's that doing here?"

I growled. "Did you miss the part where he saved Harper's ass back there?"

"Is that supposed to erase everything else?" Cyrus spat, pointing at the boy.

Harper stepped between them. "Haven't you been down this route before?"

The two men glared at each other. Something flickered between their gazes, as though they shared the spark of an idea, back and forth.

"Let it be on your head." Cyrus pulled his phone from his pocket. "We have to get to the next level up and the opposite corner of the building."

"Oh, just that?" Harper sighed heavily, popped the magazine from his gun, and checked his rounds.

"Maybe we can stop for ice cream." I investigated my own weapons. "Shit."

Harper popped the magazine back in as his dark eyes snapped to me. "What is it?"

"Gettin' low over here." I showed him the lining of my boots, pointing at the multiple empty loops. "I lost a good chunk with the inmates."

Harper's face grew grave. "You haven't used the gun once."

It wasn't a question and I didn't bother answering. Not that I had the time.

"There they are!" Was all the warning we got before the office windows above our heads shattered. Glass crunched under foot, quickly drowned by the rapid pops of gunfire.

"Luck's run out." Harper and Cyrus fired back in a near synchronized gesture. The rest of us ducked behind office furniture between rounds.

"Lovely." Cyrus growled, flanked by Ronald.

Cillian burst into the room, smashing me into the wall. I howled in pain and Harper spun to shoot, stopping short when he found my brother using me as a shield. Cillian held me by the throat, squeezing hard while he glared at Ronald. "You little traitor..."

Ronald spat on the ground and shot at his mentor.

Cillian ran out of the office, dragging me with him. He didn't even flinch as I scratched and clawed his flesh.

"Time we finish this."

CHAPTER 47

GABE

Every muscle in my body tensed. The asshole guard winced in pain, his other hand squeezing my shoulder harder with each pull. I'd only ever taken blood from the palm, limiting the flow and preventing me from overdoing it. And never in such a high stress situation.

The beast in my belly growled louder in my ears as the guard squeezed harder and harder. My shoulder popped and I swatted his hand away like a gnat with my last swallow, wiping my lips with the back of my hand.

He stared at the long red smears on my skin as I pricked a thumb on a fang and closed the holes with a couple drops of blood. "Where's the entrance to the offices?"

He stared at his arm a moment longer before visibly shivering and nodding to the closed librarian office.

"Fantastic," I groaned as I rose. We didn't have a lot of time. The chaos in the hall was getting louder, the crack of rapid gunfire echoing in and out between screams and the sharp slap of flesh on flesh as people pummeled each other.

A quick inspection of the door showed it was heavy duty, thick steel with a matching knob. But no electronic access, just an old fashioned lock. I turned back to Asshole. "You got a key?"

He shook his head. "Couldn't let you and the other inmates through, even if I did."

I glared. "Seriously?"

He shrugged but his eyes grew wide as the battle in the hall reached a crescendo.

I grabbed his collar and drew us eye to eye. "You have a duty to protect us as much as keep us in line. Or have you forgotten that?"

His expression grew stricken, with his lips quivering under that broom handle mustache.

I shook his collar to drive my point home but he only shook his head. "I still don't have a key."

I sighed and dropped his collar, turning back to the door. Even my new strength couldn't bust it. Then I eyed the knob again, remembering Lily's ginger touch when she checked the locks at her office. As though she'd been worried about overdoing it.

Could I? If I did, any of them could follow us. Inmates might escape. Then again, Cillian's grand entrance showed he already had access to the rest of the building. And some of those inmates needed to flee for good reason.

"They're he–" One of the prisoners let out a wet gurgling. I turned to find a kid latched to his throat, drinking fast while stabbing and slashing at anyone who came near.

No time to reconsider. I grabbed the handle and twisted. The lock popped under my grip and the door swung open as I shouted. "Go!"

Asshole shouldered past me, to the next door, flinging it open and holding it as everyone filed through. Another prisoner came through, looking ready to grab one of the guards for security.

I slammed the door shut, just as a batch of prisoners and vampires alike grabbed another man near the entrance. I tried to relock it, buy us some time, but I'd shattered the mechanism.

Something slammed against the door and I flew back, scrambling towards the office. Asshole yanked me up by an elbow and we ran.

Even with the door open, the battle noises grew distant and out of sync as we passed cubicles and water coolers. Suddenly the gunfire doubled, sharp and chaotic as we rounded a corner. We stopped, backed up, and slammed our backs against the wall. A quick glance back showed me all the guards had made it out of the library along with a few scrawny inmates. Asshole and I spared one look at each other, nodded, and I slowly looked back around the corner, expecting to find guards locked in combat with Elias' men.

Instead I was greeted by tactical gear and voices that were all too familiar to me now. A tiny boy whirled in the chaos grunting and huffing next to a large man in kevlar. Cyrus's low growl barely made it through the gunfire. "Keep it up! We're pushing them back."

Under the barrage, I could just barely make out my partner's shout. "But where'd they take her?"

"We'll figure that out later." Cyrus grunted, pulling a machete free and slicing an opponents helmet and head clean from their body. With every step, the two sides stirred ash and dust on the ground.

Asshole peered over my shoulder, raised his makeshift weapon. "The vampires!"

I shoved his hand down. "Some of those are on our side."

He looked confused and angry and I shoved his hand harder. "You've let me bring you this far, and time's running out.'

The group that infiltrated the library would catch up soon. I wasn't sure what was holding them up but we were on borrowed time. Asshole huffed out a breath and nodded. "Don't prove me right, Collins."

I returned the nod and considered our next move. Cyrus and Harper were making good progress. Going in front might only distract them.

I gestured to the wall of cubicles leading behind Elias's group. "We need to get back there."

"Either you're trying to feed them or you're an idiot." Nightstick scowled. "They have guns and fangs. I have a shitty shiv crafted from fence wire."

I swore and pushed a hand through my hair. He was right, we didn't stand a chance. But I couldn't just stand here waiting for the other group to catch up. I pointed to the nearest empty cubicle. "You guys duck in there and keep an eye out."

One of the guards looked back and forth between me and the battle. "What about you?"

"I don't have a gun." I shrugged and rounded the corner. *But I have fangs.*

I ran into the battle, slamming a shoulder against a cubicle wall and smashing it into the nearest vampire. He lost his target, gunfire spraying the wall near Harper's head as he shouted. "What the–"

I punched the man and kicked his gut, just as another man body checked me into a fax machine, hard enough to break the trays and crack my spine.

My body went limp in a messy heap, numb and cold. My attacker pointed his gun straight at my head. His own skull exploded and Cyrus stepped in. "There you are."

He grabbed both my arms and dragged me away, not caring for the pain his movements caused or any of the debris he pulled me over. He tossed me into an office and pointed at my head while looking away. "Be useful and watch him."

Cyrus left without a backwards glance and Ronald appeared in front of me. If I wasn't paralyzed, I might have asked what the hell he was doing there. Then my back snapped and I screamed. One after another, I lost count as my spine repaired itself. My throat hurt from screaming by the time it was all done and I barely gasped out. "Where'd you come from?"

The skinny boy rolled his eyes and gave me a look. Of course he couldn't answer but I didn't have time to feel foolish. The battle still raged. "I have guards with me. We need weapons."

Ronald shook his head. Sure, he had plenty of reasons not to arm the guards, but we didn't have time for debates.

"You'll have to trust me on this one." I was finally able to stand but Ronald grabbed my sleeve and pulled, pointing down a hall before miming an L on his forehead. I shook him off. "There's no time for charades."

I ran into the fray just in time to throw a vamp off Harper. The big guy clutched his arm, stemming a thick blood flow. "Cutting it close there, buddy."

I pulled him up from the ground by an elbow. "We need to stop the bleeding."

I moved to score my wrist on my fangs, a little disconcerted by how easily I'd come to accept this new reality.

"Someone already topped me off." The wound stitched together as he spoke.

"I have a group of unarmed guards, sitting useless." I bobbed my head to their cubicle.

"We can fix that." Harper started fishing in his pockets for magazines and grabbing a spare glock from his left holster.

Before I could ask who was here, someone socked me in the ear and kicked my groin. Harper shouted something but it was cut off by a heavy slam. I doubled over on instinct, throwing my shoulder into their gut

My assailant stumbled over me and we tumbled in a heap on the ground, punching and kicking. I grabbed his helmet and twisted. Nothing snapped but it dislodged him from my body, so I could push him away and stand, kicking until the helmet shattered. He tried to get up but I didn't give him the chance, pushing us into one of the cubicles with every kick. My flimsy prison slippers ripped under the fiber glass shards, my foot came away bloody, the skin shredding.

Some part of me knew adrenaline was playing its role. Another, far darker portion of my brain, didn't care. If I survived, I would heal.

It's strange how fast the mind adapts to the sickest of changes.

And so, I hobbled away from one fight, looking for the next. Two close calls with death and a broken arm later, Asshole and Harper found me. My relief at seeing them whole was short lived when I saw Harper's expression.

"Who died?"

It wasn't glib, just a point blank question after years of working side by side with Harper. He swallowed, looked around, as though making note of the calming battle. "We can't find Lily."

My internal organs seized. "You brought her?"

God, with the prisoners and all this chaos... and that might be the luckier outcome.

"Do you really think she gave us a choice?" The gravel tone told me exactly who was behind the fiber glass shield. I whirled, snatching Cyrus' collar and pulling him close. "Who saw her last?"

Ronald appeared at my elbow, pointing down the same hall as earlier and miming the L again.

I dropped Cyrus, finally getting it, and ran.

CHAPTER 48

LILY

It was just like when we fought as kids. No matter how I tried to kick or scratch Cillian, it was useless. He just kept dragging me backwards, one arm locked around my throat.

He wasn't even phased when I buried my fangs in his hand, just kept his quick march past the higher end offices. My wild kicks knocked over a janitor's cart and smashed the window on a door.

"Knock it off before I make ya." My brother grabbed my ponytail and shook my head.

"If ya could've, ya would've." I spat in his face, disappointed when I missed his good eye.

He wiped it away and pulled me up by my hair. "You brought this on yourself."

"Yep, this is what I get for tryin' to save your sorry ass." My scalp roared in pain.

Cillian's face scrunched in confusion, his scars deforming with angry swirls. "What are ya talking about?"

"I brought all this shit on me when I betrayed Isaac." It was impossible to get my feet under myself and stop the pain. Cillian kept moving me, probably trying to keep me from getting a stable base to kick him. "If I haven't thought that—

"I mean me!" He shook my head again. "How do you think you've stayed off his radar this long?"

I stopped scrambling and stared, confused.

"He ordered me to find you." My brother rolled his mismatched eyes. "Ya didn't exactly get creative with your name changes. Lily, Lillian, fucking Lilia. Do you really think I missed you all this time?"

I gawked. Those were indeed my last three names when Court made me re-register. It was why Alex called me Lils. *Because of all the Lils*. "But then–"

"I pretended you couldn't possibly be that dumb, that it had to be someone else." Cillian pulled me up and grabbed my shoulders to shake me, my feet dangling from the ground. "I convinced myself for years that it was all a coincidence so I wouldn't have to tell him."

I blinked stupidly. Elias had programmed my brother before turning him, conditioning Cillian to obey his orders. And my brother had been gaslighting himself just to keep me alive. Freeing Gabe. The motorcycle hint back at the house. He'd been looking out for me the whole time. It would have required exhaustive mental gymnastics on a daily basis.

"If I could, I'd kill myself now." Cillian growled, spit flying with every word. "But there's no getting around that order. So instead I have to hand you over or kill you myself."

Without another word, Cillian tossed me over his shoulder, latching his arms around my leg to prevent any kicking. I pounded my fist and tried to grab a door frame but it was pointless. So I reached around, grabbed his ear and pulled.

He yowled and I threw my elbow into the back of his neck over and over, until he dropped me. Cillian tried to stomp on me but I kicked just above the knee before scrambling backwards. I slammed into someone else's legs and started to crawl away but they caught me, lifting me by the arm pits.

"Let go of me, ya son of–"

"Vulgar as always." Gabe's familiar laugh was a balm on my rattled nerves.

"Just how we like her." Harper flanked me on the other side with Ronald by him.

Cillian looked up, realized I wasn't alone anymore and sprinted down the hall. Probably gathering reinforcements. We didn't have long.

"He was taking me to Elias."

"Good." Gabe dug in his pockets and shoved a pistol into my hands, his expression leaving little room to argue. "I'm sick of this cat-and-mouse game."

The weapon felt like acid in my hands but I just nodded. "Thanks."

"Always." He squeezed my hands once more, those green eyes locked with mine.

I grabbed his shirt collar and dragged his face to mine, kissing him fast. "You American eejit."

"You two have the weirdest timing." Harper barked a laugh as he checked his weapons.

Gabe ignored him, kissing back like it might be our last before grabbing my hand and dragging me through the corridor.

"Where's everyone else?"

"Still hunting for Elias in the warden's office." Harper motioned to Gabe, pointing at his eyes then the left side of the hall. Gabe nodded and went right.

"They tried to make us go with them but I had a bad feeling once Ronald relayed they'd taken you." Gabe slowed as we passed more office doors, turning to check around corners and through windows, Ronald double-checking behind him. They grimaced at whatever they found but made no move otherwise.

"And it wasn't like we were going to leave you two to have all the fun." Harper smirked as I followed close behind listening for any clues he might miss. When he opened the door and the big man's face fell, a large part of me wanted to run. I had no desire to see whatever he found, but you never knew what he'd miss.

I forced my feet forward and peered into the office, a tiny squeak escaping my lips before I could stop it. A woman sat in the chair, her body slumped and her neck at an unnatural angle. The puncture on her throat and beneath her rolled up sleeves left little to the imagination. But she wasn't the worst.

A man was sprawled over the desk, office supplies scattered every direction on the floor beneath him with his remaining arm and legs spread eagle. His shirt had been ripped open, the buttons laying in the haphazard spray of paperclips and pens on the floor. His torso was riddled with fang marks and gouges. He'd obviously screamed and someone had decided to bite his face.

I gulped and looked away. The lack of chaos in the hall meant these two had been brought here for this expressed purpose. "If everyone else went one direction, and Cillian was taking me to Elias—"

"I know." Gabe grimaced as he backed out of an office, his eyes lingering on me just a moment longer before he went back to clearing the way.

One of the two parties was almost certainly walking into a trap. Cillian's kidnapping might have been bait, but to what end?

If we were headed into the lion's den we had two vampires, a traumatized kid, and a fired police captain to take on a whole army. But, what could we do?

We couldn't just turn around. That would only let them come up on us while we floundered to catch up to Cyrus and the others. I stared at my shoes and ordered them down the hall. There weren't a lot of turns or intersections. Finally, some of the walls flattened to regular windows, showing a grim scene outside.

Some time after we arrived, the truck outside had been bombed. Starved crawled and clawed all over the front of the prison, some still burning. Prisoners and guards ran for their lives while men in camouflage kevlar tried to clean the mess. But the Starved moved with a dogged purpose and the National Guard didn't know where to aim.

"Jesus." Gabe's voice made me jump.

"We should get down there." Harper's voice dropped, as though he already knew the answer but couldn't bring himself to accept it.

I shook my head. "We have to end this."

Ronald made a rude noise that matched my mood.

CHAPTER 49

GABE

None of us spoke after we walked past the windows, just nodded or shook our heads as we marched on. The gruesome nature of each office only intensified as we walked along, yet the hallway stayed pristine. A scratch here or a discarded paper there, but nothing to even hint at the grizzly scene behind each door as we walked.

It was quickly becoming a gruesome countdown. Because Lily was right, this had to end. I just didn't see how we could do it.

That resolve was finally tested when a group stormed down the hall. My least favorite Irishman at their helm. Cillian raised his hand in a closed fist and the march stopped. Some tall, some short. Many more than us.

"Well... well. What have we here?" Cillian smiled but it felt off somehow. The expression didn't even seem to curl the jagged scars of his face. "All of Ritti's big talk and this is all we get?"

"It's all your sorry ass is worth." Lily's voice quivered as she spread her legs into a fighting stance, palming a few knives. I internally groaned at her refusal to use the gun I'd loaned her. Even with her piss poor aim it was an asset with this many combatants. But we didn't have time to debate it. I took aim and fired at Cillian but he was already in motion. My bullet didn't even graze him.

Lily tossed her knives into one hand, grabbed my elbow, and pulled us side by side. A quick glance showed Ronald next to Lily and Harper next to me. We'd all quickly realized our only advantage was the narrow hall, constricting the combat. But if they got behind us at any point we'd be doomed.

I took aim again, shooting for their legs. Harper let out a dark chuckle before copying me. "That's just mean, pal."

"I like it." Lily flung a knife. Soldiers yowled in pain, flopping to the ground and tripping their comrades.

"Cowards." Cillian glowered, stomping right over his squad without so much as a glance down.

"Don't be jealous just 'cause we're pretty." Lily flung another knife then yelped as a bullet sliced her shoulder. Then again when a shot blew out her knee. I stepped to the side, hoping to block any more rounds when pain raced through my side and my arm exploded above the elbow. Despite our best efforts, they surrounded us, guns leveled at everyone's heads while Cillian continued to climb over his men to stand before us.

He snorted and glared at his sister. "Did ya really think you could win with this little rag tag team?"

I edged nearer to her, cursing under my breath as my arm slowly regrew and putting my gun down to take her hand. We didn't look at each other, just squeezed. I wanted to keep firing, but it wasn't going to help.

Now that they'd surrounded us, I easily saw at least forty soldiers. We never stood a chance.

Clap. Clap. Clap.

Lily's whole body tensed; her grip turned sweaty in my hand. The soldiers parted, as though being slowly split by a knife.

Elias carefully stepped around his still healing soldiers and glared at Cillian. "Walking on your own men?"

Cillian ground his teeth and looked away.

"This conversation isn't over." Elias tsked and looked down at his men, shaking his head before turning his cold gaze to Ronald. "Though at least I know where your loyalties lie."

Ronald hissed at Elias and the man laughed indulgingly before finally turning to Lily and me.

"I'm sorry, Detective. I meant everything I said but I'm afraid she forced my hand." He reached out with his knuckles, like he planned to run them over her cheek. "Always impatient."

Lily recoiled as I growled, "Don't you touch her."

Elias stopped an inch from her face, seeming to absorb the wide blue eyes and pinched lips.

"I wish you hadn't come." Elias sighed and held his hands up, as though surrendering.

"I told ya before—" Her voice shook and she squeezed my hand. All the while keeping her eyes locked with his, "I would do it again."

I closed my eyes for a moment, accepting it all. Even if we fought back now, we'd last seconds. "I'm sorry."

Harper's bark of laughter was too quiet. As though he only let it out because it was his last. "You heard the lady."

Elias's eyes flicked to Harper and he nodded, as though acknowledging some unspoken contract, before standing and backing up. "Take aim."

Several rifles and guns clicked or snapped around us and my internal organs sank, leaving an empty pit. Everywhere I looked, the dark, cold tunnel of a gun met my stare. If I looked long enough, I was convinced I'd see the round intended for my skull.

Lily lifted her chin though her lip shook, closing her eyes and loosening her grip to interlace her fingers with mine. Then the firing began.

I'd expected searing pain or immediate black. When my ears found surprised shouts and a volley of gunfire from far away I realized the problem.

The firing was behind us while soldiers shouted about re-inforcements. Elias' head snapped up and he growled, "How did they survive?"

"You'll have to ask the kiddies." Cillian flicked his hand at us. "I've been a bit busy with these clowns."

Any further argument was swallowed in gunfire and Elias barking orders. "Keep the prisoners–"

Lily chose that moment to prove how horrible her aim was. She pulled out the gun I'd loaned her and fired wildly, getting Elias in the shoulder and stomach before scrambling into the chaos with me in tow.

Harper shouted something but I didn't have the chance to see what happened as I grabbed the first soldier I could find and slammed his skull into the wall over and over until he stilled. As his body fell apart, I quickly confiscated his gun and knives.

Lily yowled and I looked up to find her wrestling on the floor, trying to pull a weapon from her combatant. I chambered a round and shot the man. Lily huffed out a breath. "Thanks, he snuck up on me."

I pulled her up and we stood back to back, slashing and firing. I lost count of the number of fights, and how many close calls we saved each other from. I shot one in the back; he fell apart to reveal Cyrus mid-machete swing.

"How are you two still alive?"

"We're stubborn," Lily grunted between punches and slash-es. "What's your excuse?"

I finished reloading and blasted her opponent in the neck. "Can we swap stories another time?"

Cyrus laughed mirthlessly and slashed through one of the enemy, spraying blood and ash all over us. Without another word, we swung and shot. I lost my hand at one point and had to take one of their guns after it grew back. Lily got sick of people grabbing her hair, and kept chopping the ponytail to a jagged stump.

And so it went. I couldn't tell how long it lasted or how many we killed. It only got worse when the child soldiers joined in the fight. We couldn't avoid them, no matter how we tried. And now wasn't the time for pretty speeches.

Somewhere in this fray, Elias was waiting. We might not get another chance. Maybe that focus is why I lost her.

One second we were fighting back to back. Then I heard her shout and my back went cold. I turned but she was already lost in the battle, a quick dash of blonde curls my only clue. I didn't have time to look. Elias flew at me, swinging for my face.

CHAPTER 50

LILY

The asshole had grabbed my arm and threw me into the wall like it was nothing. All the air left my lungs in a pained gasp. So I didn't even have the breath to scream when he slammed his gun into my spine. I flailed, kicking blindly. It must have made him back up, because I suddenly fell. He raised his boot to stomp on my head and I punched his other knee. He toppled and I rolled away, bumping into someone else's feet before I stood.

A little boy grabbed my leg and started crawling up my body like a damn jungle gym. I tried to fling him off but the hallway was packed and there wasn't any wiggle room. He clung to my back and dug something hard into my neck. I threw myself backwards, hoping to smash the kid into something. I stumbled through an office door and tripped onto a desk, landing on the boy.

The kid bit my shoulder and I screamed, lifting myself to slam back down on the desk. His fangs dug into bone and I growled, "Let go ya little shit!"

I lifted myself again and slammed back down. My head hit something hard, maybe the side of the computer and I saw stars. But at least the kid stopped biting. It took several more slams before his body stilled.

Stumbling away, I leaned on the doorframe and surveyed the area. Even now, ash stirred through the hall, growing thicker and making it hard to see. A few bodies littered the floor, most of them wearing the uniforms of prison guards or office attire. They were lumpy and disfigured, and it didn't take long to see why as I watched people trip or step all over the corpses.

Enough was enough. We all needed to stop dying and there was only one way that was going to happen. I scanned trying to see through the sea of helmets and kevlar. The ash made it impossible to spot the grey suit I was hunting.

But Gabe's tattered, orange, prison jump suit stood out like a beacon. He grappled with my shithead of an ex, but he was alive.

I didn't have time to let the relief in, watching them push each other back and fourth, shouting wildly. Somehow, despite the cramped quarters and complete havoc, a flash of movement caught my eye.

My brother, rushing toward Gabe and Elias, cocking his gun.

"No!" I ran out, grabbing the last few knives from my boot. We both had to make it through a crowd. But Cillian didn't even glance my way, hadn't seen me yet. I had to get there first. Someone tried to grab me and I slashed their arm, slicing a tendon and running on. Another stepped in my path and I drove a knife up, into the soft part of his chin. If they followed me, I'd deal with it, but I didn't have time to stop. Cillian was closer and stronger, it wouldn't take him long to get there. I lost three more knives in the guts of my next opponent, looking down in horror at the only one I had left.

There wasn't time to think. A child raced towards me and I slashed out, suppressing all the guilt when a red strip tore her cheek. I kicked her away and chucked the knife at my brother. It flew right past his face. Cillian looked at me, his eyes widening as he sped up.

"Shit!" I ran forward, using nothing but instinct as I reached into my waistband and retrieved the gun, cocking it and raising it just as I met my brother. Even I couldn't miss this close.

But god, how I wanted to.

Our eyes met, and I pleaded. "Please..."

The scars in his face seemed to droop with the expression. "Fight me."

I pulled the trigger. His head snapped back and his face finally relaxed as it turned grey and fell apart. I wanted to fall to the ground and cry. I'm not sure how the hell I stayed up right.

But one look at Gabe and Elias showed they were still fighting with Elias's back to me. This close I could see they were both tugging at a gun. I couldn't shoot, not with my aim and them wiggling like that. But I could make things bloody hard for Elias. I ran, grateful no one got in my way as I threw myself on Elias' back. Gabe's eyes widened and Elias grumbled something about poor manners.

I growled in his ear, "Ya didn't marry me for my classy upbr–"

It was all I could say before he tossed me over his head, right into Gabe. We toppled to the floor. Elias stalked toward us just as Gabe raised his gun and fired.

"No!" I lunged for the gun but couldn't reach it in time. Elias halted in his steps, his expression confused. His neck and face started to match the filthy grey suit he wore and his body swayed.

Someone next to Elias gasped and backed up. Then another. His men, the few close by. Our only witnesses to his death.

The hallway slowly grew quieter and quieter, as though the decaying body before us were an auditory bomb killing all the sound. Gabe looked at me, slowly placing a palm on my cheek. "Why'd you try to stop me?"

There wasn't time to answer, as the alarms finally went silent and Ritti's voice boomed through the overhead speakers. "Because we needed proof. Without that, their leader could be lurking in the shadows."

My spine became steel as I glared at the intercom overhead.

"Luckily–" Darren came on and I swear I could hear his devilish grin. "–prisons have excellent security cameras."

<hr>

Even after Elias died they put up a fight, but it was less enthusiastic. Many ran, mostly the kids. The National Guard didn't help matters; the fighting almost started again until the prison security stood between us and them.

We did what we could, digging dead inmates and guards from the ash, lining the halls with their bodies. We found Harper and Ronald later. Both had holes in their clothes and expressions on their faces I didn't much care for, but they were whole.

Gabe and I were silent most of the time, working side by side. Every so often he'd touch my back or I'd take his hand, just to verify the other was there. When we looked up and realized there were no more bodies to move and no more enemies to slay, I collapsed into a seat, not even sure of where I was. Turned out to be a bench in the cafeteria.

Gabe plunked down next to me and ran a hand through his hair, smearing the ash and blood on his face into an even more hideous pattern.

I sighed, "What now?"

"I go back to court."

"Shit." It came out in a cry. I couldn't help it. After everything else, the idea of one more battle, one more time I might lose someone I cared about was too damn much.

"Hey, hey." Gabe pulled me into his arms. "It's almost over."

Over wasn't necessarily favorable for us here.

"Don't go." I clung to him grabbing the collar of his tattered prison pajamas so tight they ripped.

He leaned his forehead against mine and let out a long, slow breath. "I need to finish this."

I hated this. He'd broken the city to save me. It was his duty to fix it. I understood all of that but I didn't care.

"We need to get out of here." Cyrus' gravel tone interrupted the conversation. We looked up to find him escorted by the National Guard. "They said we should leave now before they change their minds."

"But—"

"Lily." Gabe nuzzled my neck. It had to smell disgusting; I was just as coated in grime and gore as he was. But he acted like it was nothing, just squeezed me tighter and whispered in my ear. "I can't lose you again."

My sob turned into a pathetic squeak and I held on tighter.

"Edwards." Cyrus prodded my shoulder.

"Go." Gabe nudged my nose with his. Those green eyes were bottomless, sad. He wasn't sure he would see me again. If he would ever walk free again. But he still had to see this bloody case through to the end.

The guards came up behind him, and a pudgy one with a big mustache nodded to me. "We'll see to him, ma'am."

I swallowed and looked back at those eyes. I couldn't stay and he wouldn't go. I hated it. I grabbed his face and kissed him hard, whispering against his lips. "Fuckin' eejit."

My whole body grew colder with each step as I forced myself up and away. Cyrus came to one side and Ronald the other. I eyed the boy and the vikinger in turn.

Cyrus saw my expression and shook his head. "He can stay."

The ride back to Court was grim. Nobody spoke. Even Harper didn't try to comfort me. He just sat quiet after he called Hannah and let her know he was coming home.

Someone in the back started prattling about Elias' death being broadcast on every news outlet while Ritti did a quick interview with Amber Wright about the next steps in human vampire relations. Someone started watching the video. I heard my brother's voice and snapped, "Turn that shit off, or I'll break ya!"

The whole van of men just stared at me, one of them muting his phone before they all looked down at their screen.

I knew what they were seeing. But I doubted they truly understood it. Sure, I'd killed my brother, the monster. I'd even helped to take out Elias in the end. I might have even cleared the doubts about my loyalty. But they didn't see the absolute peace taking over Cillian's face as it fell apart.

My brother had wanted that bullet. And who could blame him, after everything. I just wondered if that peaceful expression would ever leave my nightmares.

It was impossible to stop the tears. Harper quietly patted my shoulder and I was too choked up to say anything.

I fucking hate guns.

Apparently, killing the big bad didn't take me off Ritti's shit list. Here I was again, back in the damn dungeons. But at least nobody was coming to poke or prod me for information.

I sat on the cold bunk, waiting. I hadn't fought when Cyrus brought me down. Only asked to see my friends, give them a quick hug. That favor hadn't shocked him but the second one sure had.

So I sat on the hard-as-nails cot and stared at the door. It felt like a day but it was probably only hours. The lady was busy after all. I almost doubted she'd show.

Finally the door squealed open and Ritti glided in. Her sleek, amber suit was at odds with the dank surroundings. With me sitting there in dirty tatters, still covered in crap from the battle, we were a vision of good and evil itself.

She sneered but made no comment. "Cyrus says you have a single request."

"More of an idea how to save your sorry public image." I stood, swaying on my feet. Cyrus had given me a couple blood bags, but I was still exhausted. If it weren't for the idea rattling in my skull, I'd have passed out long ago. "Or at the very least, finally be rid of me."

CHAPTER 51

Had it really been a week? That couldn't be right. Not that I had a good way of tracking time.

Asshole Guard, or Chuck, had helped me move into solitary. They turned the light off for bed, and they brought me books, but it all just blurred together.

Chuck sat outside my cell when he dropped off bags, making awkward small talk about all the things we didn't have in common. Sports, kids, a house.

Still, it was a nice gesture, and the distraction was welcome. My dreams were always dark. More than once I'd punched the cinderblock hard enough to break my hand and leave a dent. When I was awake, my thoughts bounced between two things. My impending case and Lily.

You American eejit.

When I'd first told Lily how I felt, I'd called her an Irish idiot. That line couldn't be a coincidence. Even in the heat of battle, she'd taken time to say it in a way only I would understand. Imagining the relationship we might have was a pleasant distraction from the grey walls around me.

It was also easy to lose myself in the daydream. My career as a detective was nuked and her business was up in smoke. It was hard to think of what we'd actually do with Elias gone.

But the idea of struggling through something as mundane as paying bills or finding a house was oddly calming.

The door to my cell clanked and squealed as someone unlocked it, startling me. I blinked at the shaft of natural light as Chuck beamed down at me, cuffs jangling from his arm. "Ready to clean up for court?"

The war room hadn't changed since I was last there with Olive and Michelle. I didn't even bother looking at lady liberty.

"What are you so excited about?" I tried not to grumble.

"Can't tell you." Michelle was practically bouncing around me, triple checking for stray hairs and loose threads in my new suit. "I need you to be surprised and you can't fake that for shit."

I tried to glare but it took too much out of me. In all this chaos, I'd honestly forgotten her courtroom theatrics, if only for a moment. I have no idea how she figured out my measurements, but I was grateful to not be going to court wearing a prison suit after my entire closet burned down.

Michelle backed up and nodded sharply, looking more and more pleased. "Alright, let's go."

Her upbeat attitude and bouncy demeanor was trampling my already damper mood. I just nodded.

The courtroom hushed as we entered, our steps mingling with the soft murmurs of the audience. I realized I was staring at my shoes, already resembling a dead man walking, and forced my head up.

My feet halted while my brain had to recoordinate with what I was seeing.

The guards, every one of them from my team, all sat on my side of the court, directly behind my table. Harper was grinning broadly next to Chuck and offered a stupid little wink.

"Move it," Michelle grabbed my sleeve and pulled, but I could hear the humor. "The court officer is giving you a look."

I staggered forward, still confused as I whispered, "Are they here to show support?"

The idea had merit. I doubted it would make or break my case, but it was a start.

"They want to testify about the prison battle. And they called in a few favors." Even Michelle couldn't hide her smile.

Favors? I looked down to ask Michelle what she meant when another face caught my eye. Officer Delgado kept her hand low and waggled her fingers beside Harper. And next to her, a woman Olive and I had rescued in the first wave bounced a toddler on her knee. Then was a man I vaguely remembered pulling a vampire off of, right before I'd lost Olive.

I finally got it. The guards had found the people I had saved since turning. I had no idea what Michelle intended to do with it. None of it didn't technically change whether or not I'd been turned intentionally or against my will. But, still...

It was daunting, seeing them all here, in one place. Something about it eased a weight in my soul I hadn't realized I was carrying. It wasn't gone, but it was lighter. I sat, feeling strange with the wall of human support behind me.

"Ooooo." Michelle shivered with excitement. "Gordon looks pissed."

I glanced at the opposing council and sure enough. While Michelle was brimming with energy, Gordon was stewing. Maybe this could help. A small gleam of hope lit in me and I tried to sit up straighter. It was time to earn the support these people had shown, despite the risk to their careers and reputations.

The bailiff stood and bellowed. "All rise for the Honorable Judge Taf–"

The doors boomed open just as the audience stood and Judge Taffet stopped in her tracks staring at something I couldn't see over everyone's head.

"Ma'am, ma'am!"

"Oh, don't ya ma'am me, ya freakin' cabbage. Ya know damn well who I am."

My gut sank. *I'm hallucinating. No one is here to support me. This is a stretch too far. No way she'd—*

Lily stepped into the front of the aisle and shrugged off the guard from outside, verbally ripping him a new asshole with words no courtroom should ever contain but often did. I couldn't be imagining this. If I were, she'd be in her tattered tank top and jeans. Instead she was wearing a blouse and slacks, her hair plated in one long, neat braid. She still wore her motorcycle jacket but somehow, that only convinced me it was really her.

Judge Taffet had apparently gathered herself and marched up to her bench, banging the gavel immediately, and shouting for order.

Lily smiled at me then the judge. "Thanks, your honor. That was gettin' annoyin'."

Michelle grumbled something and I elbowed her. I had no idea what Lily was up to but that smile... this wasn't a rash display. She had a purpose.

"What is it with vampires and public demonstrations?" Judge Taffet growled as she sat. "Miss Edwards, may I assume you're barging in here for a reason?"

"Yes, your honor." Lily dug in her pocket and held up a crumpled envelope. "I was summoned as a witness to these proceedings. Sorry about the delay, I haven't been home to check the mail in a bit, city gone to shit and all."

The jury let out a surprised chuckle and Michelle huffed, "She's got guts, I'll give her that."

My mind raced. Coming here meant turning herself over to the court. Lily didn't have the same argument as me. Was she simply trying to save my ass in exchange for hers or was she trying to set another precedent?

There was no time to come up with the answer. Gasps rose from the crowd, murmurs and the tell-tale click of the press gathering new photos behind me. It was impossible to see through the on lookers. I only caught a glimpse of Cyrus' mohawk and tattoos, walking along the back wall. Then Alex, Darren, and Maria. A bunch of people I'd never met, but could easily tell were vampires by their pallor alone.

And finally, Ritti herself, walking regally. The news went mad and the courtroom erupted in a torrent of questions. The vampire queen held up a hand and waited for the courtroom to hush as Judge Taffet banged her gavel again. "I will happily answer any and all questions at the end of the day. However, I am here to observe this case, and wish to respect the court's authority in these proceedings."

Ritti waved an imperial hand to Judge Taffet who grumbled about vampiric dramatics again. She stared at the crowd, mixed as it was. I gave Lily another look and she mouthed, *If you go down, I'm goin' with you.*

The judge's eyes scanned every vampire in the back, to Lily still standing in the aisle, and then landing on me before slamming her gavel once. "Be seated. Court is now in session."

CHAPTER 52

LILY, FIVE YEARS LATER

"Mr. Anderson, last time you thought your daughter was on drugs or somethin'," I sighed indulgently as I filed the unsigned contract back in my desk drawer. "Turned out she was working as a lounge singer to afford music lessons."

"Yes, but I knew she was up to something. And you helped me prove that!"

I suppressed a laugh. On one hand, it was nice some of my older clients weren't deterred by our public vampire status. But I would still love nothing more than to never see Mr. Anderson again. We weren't that strapped for cash.

I rolled my eyes. "Before I take a chunk of your wallet, how about you *talk* to your wife about her nights out."

We argued a bit more, Harper suppressing a bark of laughter several times before Mr. Anderson finally stormed out, grumbling under his breath.

"I heard that!" I shouted after him.

Mr. Anderson's back stiffened and Harper finally lost it, bellowing gleefully. Gabe walked through the waiting room, eyeing the now red-faced Mr. Anderson before leaning against the office door. "Cabbage?"

I snorted and shook my head, but I was grinning. "Ya still don't say it right"

Harper flicked a tear from his eye. "You missed the battle of a century, buddy."

Gabe scoffed and shoved his hands in his pockets, "Tell me about it over lunch?"

"Deal." I stood and walked to him. "You comin', Harper?"

Harper hunched like I'd caught him elbow deep in a cookie jar. "Uh no, thanks. You guys have more options without me."

I blinked confused. Harper never seemed worried about going to a bar before, and a good chunk had blood on tap.

"Let us know if we can bring something back." Gabe took my elbow and rushed me to the elevator.

I shook my head and waited until we were out of earshot. "Does he not like us drinking in front of him?"

"Don't worry about it." Gabe rolled his eyes. "So what's up with the client?"

I side eyed his change of topic but decided to drop it. "Just an eejit from my old business. Gets suspicious of every family member every so often. Kind of a regular, and it's always fun to prove him wrong."

"So why not take his contract?" Gabe stopped and checked the office window for any new tags. We still got the occasional graffiti on the door, or a protester chucking a brick in the building after hours. But that was becoming more rare and the guys didn't seem fussed over it.

Honestly, our public outing showed how well we all worked together and made us hard to forget.

Some of the very people holding up picket signs would schedule virtual consultations later. And really, the occasional ugly vampire doodle over the sign for *Strictly Paranormal Investigations* only acted as solid advertising.

"It was tempting," I admitted as we strolled down the sidewalk. People stopped glancing at us or staring after a couple blocks. "But you can't really investigate one family member without digging some dirt on the rest."

"Worried about what you'll find about the rest of his family?" Gabe's eyebrows scrunched together in confusion. "That's not like you."

"Nah, I already know what's up from last time." I shook my head. "His wife's a worse chef than Alex and her husband loves fancy Italian. She's been taking cooking lessons on the weekends. I can't take that from her."

Gabe chuckled ruefully.

I glared. He was up to something, I just knew it. "What?"

He looked down at me, those green eyes swimming with something I couldn't name. After five years, most of it living together in one cramped space or another while we built the business, you'd think I'd read Gabe like a book.

We knew each other's worst moods, fought our demons almost every night, and dealt with the occasional backlash hand-in-hand. Yet, he still managed to surprise me everyday.

He let out a slow breath, like he was steadying his nerves, but his smile only grew. "Do you remember the first time I said 'I love you?'"

"Ya called me an Irish idiot," I snorted. "What's your point?"

"I had this whole speech in my head, but you threw me off balance and I just shouted it in the moment."

"Okay..." I stopped walking and tilted my head. "What about it?"

"I didn't even bother preparing a speech this time and now I can't think of the right words." He pulled his hand from his pocket and held something out. "So how about you be my idiot, and I'll be your eejit?"

My jaw fell and I kept staring at his face. No way. No fucking way.

"Lily?" Gabe's earnest expression started to lose its certainty.

I looked down and was met with a tiny ring, a simple band with a ruby set deep in the middle. Something that wouldn't snag or catch when we were working. It wasn't flashy so it wouldn't get me noticed unintentionally during stake outs. Damn, he'd thought about this.

"Lily?" His voice snapped me back into reality and I launched myself into his arms, locking my lips with his.

"Dammit!" He laughed and wrapped his arms around me, stumbling back a step. "I think I dropped it!"

I smiled wider and kissed him again. We'd find it. We always figured shit out.

WHAT'S NEXT?

SUPERHEROES AREN'T NAMED MOLLY

The first time it happened was also the last time she hit me. She didn't even have a good reason.

We'd just moved, again. Mom tried to make it out to be an adventure. Again. Really, we'd been evicted and stuck in some nasty hole of a hotel for the last couple weeks while she scrounged enough money together for a deposit. Again.

Sure, I'd expected a smack or two in the hotel. She was stressed and overworked. But then she had the deposit and found a single-bedroom apartment. My futon was set up in the living room, available when one of her friends didn't crash on it.

Usually, she was happy for at least a month in new apartments. We might even go buy some new clothes to celebrate.

Well, thrift store clothes, but they'd be new to me and they'd actually fit. But this time, we didn't celebrate. Not even a trip to Dairy Queen. Maybe it was the apartment.

They were always hell-holes but this was a special kind of gross. My hand stuck to the walls and God help the poor soul that took their shoes off. Every inch of the carpet was stained, turning it into a disgusting patchwork quilt. Some places crunched under my feet, like walking in beer-soaked sand. The cabinets were older than me, some of the drawers hanging crooked, and the shelves sagged under a single can of chicken noodle soup.

The linoleum in the bathroom was cracked and peeling, showing speckled concrete below. All of this made the already cramped kitchen into a foreboding cave. We could only co-exist there together because we were so skinny.

My mom tried to make eggs while I put Eggos in the busted toaster, debating if we needed the last tablespoon of margarine to make dinner. Would Mac 'n' Cheese work without it?

We still had some sandwich meat, maybe we could do that instead. But if I chopped up some hot dogs and put them in the Mac, we might be able to stretch that two more nights.

We'd used every penny on the deposit, and food stamps wouldn't come for a couple weeks.

So there I was, contemplating snatching butter packets from the Waffle House down the street, when she started.

Whack!

The back of my skull exploded with a familiar pain. No warning, as per usual.

The ritual was oddly comforting, but she'd caught me off guard.

"Ouch!" I turned, rubbing the back of my head. "What'd I do?"

It's so weird being beaten by someone who looks like you. Brown eyes just like mine stared back at me, squinting in anger. The same frizzy red hair sprouted from her skull like it had caught fire with her mood. She glared down the same upturn of her nose.

All my features, stretched with age and molted by rage, turned blotchy and red.

Maybe the beatings would be easier if I looked like my dad. Then again, she might just hit me more. I'd certainly like to smack that weasel around.

"Where does this belong?" My mother shoved a wooden spoon in my face, still glowering.

"Ummm..." I backed up, letting my eyes focus and unblur the offending object. "In the drawer?"

Whack! Pain exploded over my cheek. I tasted blood from a bite in my lip.

"Don't get smart with me." She raised her arm, ready to bring it down again.

"Ow!" I rubbed my cheek and hated myself for showing any weakness. I always promised that next time I wouldn't flinch. I always failed.

My reactions only fueled her. If I could only shut my emotions off, she would have stopped. No wood for the fire.

"*Ow!*" She sneered at me, her tone like a big bully in the playground.

My mother wasn't particularly tall but she'd started the beatings when I was little. Muscle memory made me cower in a tight little ball.

My Eggo was burning in our crappy toaster, acrid smoke clogging my flaring nostrils as I backed away. The sharp corner of the counter struck my spine, pinning me between the counter and a tiny window.

The window was too small to escape through. Plus it led to an alley where people found their vices, my mother's services included. Even if someone saw this, they wouldn't help.

Nobody ever asked about the bruises, not even when we were moving in. Nobody cared.

My mother ran at me, raising the spoon like a warrior charging into a battle. "I should have gotten rid of you!"

This wasn't a new statement. Every time I failed as a daughter, she'd wished me gone in some fashion. I kind of agreed with her. "I wish you had!"

The spoon came down on my shoulder, the momentum coming together in a perfect slice of pain.

Whack! This one burned the top of my hand, making me shrink even further. Trying to become a smaller target.

Each blow set my skin on fire. Large welts grew, obscuring every freckle underneath. And the last ones had just healed.

That should have been my first warning. Beat. Heal. Repeat.

"Where does this go?" My mother paused to push the spoon in front of my face.

"I don't know, so hit me."

I'd heard a guy in a movie say that. He made it sound cool. Like he was stronger for taking a beating. Be careful what you wish for.

My mother's face deepened in its red. "What did you say, you wretched brat!?"

I was so stunned I couldn't respond. I could only gape like a dead fish.

"What. Did. You. Say." The spoon came down with each word. Then again. And again. I lost track of where she was hitting.

Across my arms, over my head, on my shoulders.

Everything hurt.

"Put your arms down!" My mother grabbed my wrist.

"No!" It wasn't a strong command like her voice. More like a pathetic plea before the barrage began again. My mother yanked my arm to one side and I couldn't protect myself with the other.

I needed two arms to protect myself. I needed a shield.

I wrenched my arm back, pulling from her grip like it was wet paper.

For a moment, the kitchen was silent. It was only then that I realized I was crying. Not just from the pain but from the still burning Eggos, their smoke leaking slowly into the air. It didn't even surprise me our smoke detectors weren't working. The dark cloud gave my mother a terrible aura as we stared.

I'd never pulled away. Never even tried. I think we were both stunned by the action more than anything.

"You little brat!" My mother ran in for another assault. "Put your arms down!"

"No!" This time, it was a command. I don't know where it came from. Maybe the same place as the strength. I just knew I could do it. So I pushed.

She fell backward in a clumsy heap, the spoon clattering from her hand against the cabinet. Her head slammed against the wall after she slid across the floor.

I stood slowly and we stared. For the first time, my mother was scared of me. Even as I gawked, horrified, at my own trembling fists.

Maybe the beatings would be easier if I looked like my dad. Then again, she might just hit me more. I'd certainly like to smack that weasel around.

"Where does this belong?" My mother shoved the wooden spoon into my face, still glowering.

"Ummm..." I backed up, letting my eye focus and unblur the offending object. "In the drawer?"

Whack! Pain exploded over my cheek. I tasted blood from a bite in my lip.

"Don't get smart with me." She raised her arm, ready to bring it down again.

"Ow!" I rubbed my cheek and hated myself for showing any weakness. I always promised that next time I wouldn't flinch. I always failed.

My reactions only fueled her. If I could only shut my emotions off, she would have stopped. No wood for the fire.

"*Ow!*" She sneered at me, her tone like a big bully in the playground.

My mother wasn't particularly tall but she'd started the beatings when I was little. Muscle memory had me cowering into a tight little ball.

My Eggo was burning in our crappy toaster, acrid smoke clogging my flaring nostrils as I backed away. The sharp corner of the counter struck my spine, pinning me between the counter and a tiny window.

The window was too small to escape through. Plus it led to an alley where people found their vices, my mother's services included. Even if someone saw this, they wouldn't help.

Nobody ever asked about the bruises, not even when we were moving in. Nobody cared.

My mother ran at me, raising the spoon like a warrior charging into a battle. "I should have gotten rid of you!"

This wasn't a new statement. Every time I failed as a daughter, she'd wished me gone in some fashion. I kind of agreed with her. "I wish you had!"

The spoon came down on my shoulder, the momentum coming together in a perfect slice of pain.

Whack! This one burned the top of my hand, making me shrink even further. Trying to become a smaller target.

With each blow, my skin was on fire. Large welts grew immediately, obscuring every freckle underneath. And the last ones had just healed.

That should have been my first warning. Beat. Heal. Repeat.

"Where does this go?" My mother paused to push the spoon in front of my face.

"I don't know, so hit me."

I'd heard a guy in a movie say that. He made it sound cool. Like he was stronger for taking a beating. Be careful what you wish for.

My mother's face deepened in its red. "What did you say, you wretched brat!?"

I was so stunned I couldn't respond. I could only gape like a dead fish.

"What. Did. You. Say." The spoon came down with each word. Then again. And again. I lost track of where she was hitting.

Across my arms, over my head, on my shoulders.

Everything hurt.

"Put your arms down!" My mother grabbed my wrist.

"No!" It wasn't a strong command like her voice. More like a pathetic plea before the barrage began again. My mother yanked my arm to one side and I couldn't protect myself with the other.

I needed two arms to protect myself. I needed a shield.

I wrenched my arm back, pulling from her grip like it was wet paper.

For a moment, the kitchen was silent. It was only then that I realized I was crying. Not just from the pain but from the still burning Eggos, their smoke still leaking slowly into the air. It didn't even surprise me that our smoke detectors weren't even going off. The dark cloud gave my mother a terrible aura as we stared.

I'd never pulled away. Never even tried. I think we were both stunned by the action more than anything.

"You little brat!" My mother ran in for another assault. "Put your arms down!"

"No!" This time, it was a command. I don't know where it came from. Maybe the same place as the strength. I just knew I could do it. So I pushed.

She fell backward in a clumsy heap, the spoon clattering from her hand against the cabinet. Her head slammed against the wall after she slid across the floor.

I stood slowly and we stared. For the first time, my mother was scared of me. Even as I gawked, horrified, at my own trembling fists.

ACKNOWLEDGEMENTS

I once said acknowledgements are a pain. I stand by that. If the first book had a village behind it, this last one has a whole city. Let's give it a go anyway.

To you, the reader. Pushing through to the end of this series has been a challenge unlike any other. But knowing we had a loyal fanbase who cared about these characters made it impossible to ignore the goal.

To my critique partners, Aisling Wilder, Ellie Maureen, & Song Eretson, thank you for the encouragement and criticism, especially the harsh ones. It all made me a better writer.

And finally to my family. You help me be okay being weird. We all need this from time to time.

While I have many ideas in the *Blood Herring* universe, I think Lily and Gabe deserve some peace after everything they've been through. Hopefully, you'll be just as engaged with my upcoming zombie western and young adult super hero novels. The sneak peek of *Super Heroes Aren't Named Molly* will likely change a little by the time you get the whole book, but I wanted to give everyone an idea what to expect.

Like all my characters, Molly is deeply personal to me. Her story is inspired by many things, some real and some heavily exaggerated. We artists must use our lies to discover the truth, after all.

About the Author

Visit our publishing website at ehdrake.com by scanning the code below for signed copies and free samples of other books. You also can join our Discord or search for the E.H. Drake Podcast on Youtube & Spotify for author interviews, free audiobook samples, and more.